THE
Legacy
OF
Tatterhood

RACHEL BALES

TWICE TOLD PUBLISHING

*To my parents,
for being my greatest supporters
and my first readers.*

TABLE OF CONTENTS

I

Det finnes ikke dårlig vær, bare dårlige klær

There is no bad weather, just bad clothes

The darkness was closer today.

At least, everyone said it was so it must be true. It was said in lieu of good morning. On good days, the baker would tip his hat and say the darkness remained. Not gone, but not growing. On bad days, the darkness was growing, encroaching on what little land remained in the humble kingdom of Ayworn. On bad days, everyone huddled a little closer and petty thieves took advantage.

Brenna had never been close enough to the borders to see the darkness up close but if she climbed the highest tower, she could see a hazy black line on the horizon, cutting through forest and mountain. Soldiers that returned from the border didn't talk about a wall, but a shadow. A shadow that encroached so slowly that by the time it surrounded them, the monsters were too close to escape.

The darkness appeared before she was born. Before her parents were born. In fact, Brenna had never met someone who lived before the black shadows stretched through the land, cutting them off from their neighbors. The darkness was a curse, staining the land with monsters and death, a physical manifestation of magic gone wrong. The only land unmarred by the darkness was the Lost Isle, an island that belonged to the fae.

She shook her head, focusing on the task at hand; navigating the winding paths of the capital. Stone walls and thatched roofs stood at attention at her sides and the whisper of her cloak nipped at her heels. Behind her, the castle stood just barely visible over the low roofs. The Sticks, the poorer region of the city, stretched out beyond the fortified circle of city protections.

"Tatterhood! Tatterhood!"

Jerking up at the call, Brenna checked the hood over her face, ensuring it cast plenty of shadow to hide the distinguishing mark on her cheek, and turned to the little girl yelling her name. Her hood wasn't actually that tattered. Ragged and patched maybe, but she kept it in the best condition she could.

A girl, no more than nine, ran up to her, messy hair stuffed in a braid, tears creating clear paths on her cheeks. Brenna knelt to her level, careful to keep her face in shadow. "What's wrong?"

"Draug! In the woods." And then the girl was off, running the way she came, confident Brenna would follow.

Not that Brenna considered for one moment not following. This was why she was out here on a bad day, on a day that was gray despite the sun. Because darkness bred desperation and discontent. When the darkness was closer, so were the monsters.

So she raced after the girl, following her to the outskirts of the city where stone walls shifted to clay and wood, and cobblestone gave way to packed dirt. The wind shifted from the forest, bringing the sharp tang of decay and rot that emanated from the black borders with a hint of pine from the trees.

The young girl ran to a farm that had deep gouges in the dirt and a broken fence line. A cluster of sheep shifted uneasily in a crowded pen, away from the destroyed fence. The young girl raced to her family, who were gathered under a large pine tree near the farmhouse. The father spoke of lost sheep and lost causes, urging Brenna to return to the safety of the city. She set her shoulders and headed for the woods, where a wide swath of destruction trailed from the farm. Birds trilled high in their branches, beckoning her with the song of her childhood.

The trees stretched to the sky, tall and regal as anyone from her mother's court, and twice as kind and welcoming. These trees urged the lost and lonely to find comfort in their shade. Their soft pine laden branches reached for her skin and caressed her. The wind shuffled the leaves and enticed fae-born children to dance for lost knowledge in the dappled light.

Brenna knew these trees. She knew them as surely as she knew the fading corridors of her home. Whispering leaves and secretive paths replaced crumbling walls and faded tapestries. How many years had she spent fleeing the cruel words of her mother and taunting rumors of court? She knew these trees. These trees were home.

And something invaded her home. Tainted it. Left a large swathe of destruction and decay in its wake.

Draug.

The draug appeared with the darkness. While her people always had stories of the sailors lost at sea returning to land to terrorize, the draug that now threatened them lived in the shadows of the borders, venturing out to feast on whatever flesh they could find: sheep, goats, children. Brenna had never encountered one. The capital had been a safe haven against the black stain, too far from the borders to deal with the vile creatures.

The monsters of her people come to life, born from the black borders that plagued them for generations. Soldiers that protected the border towns always returned with reports of another farm lost, another city devoured, returned with haunted eyes and new reasons to flinch. The darkness always seemed a nebulous threat, far off and ever present, but now it had reached her home. Now she had to face the reality of her world succumbing to death.

Letting her sword be a familiar weight in her hand, Brenna recalled her training. While her father had been initially reluctant to let her 'play soldier', he eventually acquiesced to her request with the command that her training be used for the kingdom. Masquerading as Tatterhood wasn't what he had in mind. She knew the king would have her as a spy, something to continue her life in the shadows, but Brenna wanted more.

She shook her head. Focus. Go for the head. Strike swift and sure. Don't take unnecessary risks. If there were more than two, she would turn and flee.

It was easy to track the draug into the woods as they left a wide path of gray matter across the forest floor. And if that failed, the stench of rotting flesh could guide a blind goat. Her stomach rolled at the scent as she drew closer. Birdsong faded and colors dulled the further she went. Branches pulled at her clothes, begging her to turn back. Thick black and white mold scarred the trees, making them sickly. Her stomach churned once again. Pulling a handkerchief from her pocket, she quickly tied it around her face to stem the reeking scent of death.

When she finally found them her eyes were watering and her breathing shallow. With skin mottled black and blue and gaping holes for eyes, the draug were the embodiment of decay. Vaguely humanoid in shape and size, but only enough to make her shudder. She wasn't sure which was worse: that these creatures were once human or that they never were. Only two showed themselves in the woods, grunting and shrieking as they pulled at sheep they stole from the farm.

Her knuckles grew white as she tightened her hand around her sword. Swift. Sure. Deadly. This was just like her training. She could do this. The sheep were beyond saving, but these creatures attacked her people, her home. She would gladly let them take her before she let such a slight pass. Before children were their next victim.

The first disintegrated to ashes the moment her sword removed its head and she was eternally grateful she had something covering her mouth as the resulting ash sought to cling to her. Even so, she coughed and jumped back.

The remaining draug turned like a puppet without strings, dark and sightless eyes somehow piercing into her soul. She lifted her sword, eyes narrowed.

"Just try it."

It rushed at her.

The draug did not move like a human. It stuttered and jerked and bent in ways that were unnatural and unpredictable. She backed up, raising her sword and bending her knees to swerve. The draug fell towards her, quicker than she expected. Jagged imitations of nails grabbed at her and she swiped on instinct, cleaving the arm off.

The draug shrieked and lunged at her with unholy speed. It slammed into her. Her sword wrenched from her hand.

They both tumbled to the forest floor in a heap.

Brenna gasped, fighting off clawing hands and gnashing teeth. She rolled in an attempt to break the hold it had on her, kicking at the creature, but it held on like a leech.

Another roll and the knife at her waist came loose.

Brenna rolled back, momentarily stopping her desperate defense, grabbing the knife that had fallen. Weapon in hand, Brenna raised her arm. Blade out, aim true.

With a shick, ash coated her once more.

"Ugh, so gross."

She rolled to a stand, doing her best to wipe off the worst of it. Her body ached where bruises were forming. Her leather armor protected her from scratches, but her back screamed at her and her arms drooped as if her bones were jelly.

Brenna went back to the farmer to deliver the news of the draugs' demise before turning back to town. The runes around the farm glowed a faint blue as she passed. Runes that did not stop the draug. She paused and stared at the symbol for protection, at the meager magic running through the faint glow, and prayed it would be enough. Only farmers and border cities were permitted these types of runes, ones that the court magician bathed in power to serve as an alarm and protection. That didn't stop everyone else from drawing the familiar shapes on doorways, stitching it in clothing, crafting the runes in jewelry. Even without power, the runes acted as a silent hope and prayer for safety.

The sun was already making its descent, so she would have to hurry to get back home before the dance tonight. Or maybe she could fight another draug to put her out of her misery. Her steps slowed in weariness and pain as she approached the castle. No other child called out her name.

She kicked a stone down the street, following as it clattered down the road, tumbling into a twisting alley. No use prolonging the inevitable. Brenna slipped into the side doors of the castle.

'Castle' was perhaps stretching it. It was the tallest building of the capital and was made of weathered stone and thick oak, but like everything else, it had deteriorated with the darkness and age and lack of resources. Passages collapsed, tapestries ripped, doors cracked. It remained a stronghold, littered with reminders that it was all temporary. One strategic attack would leave the castle a pile of rubble. There weren't enough resources and people for the upkeep.

Brenna slipped in the servant's entrance, knowing the guards routes well enough to avoid attentive eyes.

Stopping in the kitchens, Brenna pretended to not notice as Hilde glared at her. Hilde, a formidable woman with dark hair going gray and strong shoulders, wiped flour off her hands and huffed. "You rolling in the mud now?"

Like a naughty child caught stealing sweets, Brenna's shoulders tensed. "I'll clean it later. Promise."

"Good, I ain't your nanny." While that was true, Hilde practically raised her and her siblings, transitioning from governess to cook to seamstress as the needs demanded.

Brenna pulled off the cloak, her hands tracing various patches and meticulous mending. It survived the fight with the draug without sustaining too many tears. She carefully folded it and stored it in a chest for safekeeping. Unfortunately, her dress suffered worse, with rips and tears from the draug and the sooty ash of its remains staining the brown dress into a murky gray. She would have to be careful being caught with another ruined dress.

"Hilde, have you seen— Bri!"

Brenna turned and grinned at her sister. They were twins, which was meant to be lucky, a blessing from the Norns. And Freja was a blessing: regal and beautiful and everything a princess was meant to be, everything their mother wanted. Brenna was….not. It went beyond the mark on her face, a red stain that bloomed across her cheek, around her eye, back to her ear. The mark immediately separated the twins from being identical. No, it wasn't enough that she was ugly; she was too curt, too sharp, unrefined, uncivilized.

"Come. We'll sneak you in and get you ready." Freja eyed the state of her dress with a quizzical frown.

Brenna groaned but let her drag her through the lesser used halls to their rooms. "I could just not go. I think everyone would prefer my absence."

Freja raised a perfectly sculpted brow. "You are not leaving me alone tonight."

"Fine." Brenna pouted.

"Girls."

Their mother's voice made Brenna's blood grow cold and her shoulders tense. The bruise forming along her back creamed in protest and she resisted the urge to wince. Freja squeezed her hand in support as they turned.

Queen Beret was once the star of the court, the epitome of refined tastes and graceful beauty. The girls inherited their blue eyes and red hair from her, though hers had started to gray. Cerulean eyes shifted from tranquil waters to sharp ice with one wrong word. She wore the deep purple of their house with gold accents in the embroidery and her crown of diamond and rubies nestled in braided hair.

Brenna looked down to avoid inspection. Freja was all smiles and grace as she spoke, a lifetime of crafting silver words for the court, "We were just getting ready for dinner tonight. We shouldn't tarry."

It was too late. The queen already focused on Brenna. She strode forward, tapered fingers lifting Brenna's chin as she pursed her lips. "Did I raise you to frolic about in the muck?"

"No ma'am." Her jaw hurt from clenching, something her mother could undoubtedly tell being so close. Brenna used mud and dirt to obscure her features whenever she went out as Tatterhood. Everyone knew what the princesses looked like, and no one looked at a dirty face twice.

"How did I raise you?"

"To be perfect." It only came off a little bitter. Brenna should have been awarded for keeping most of her thoughts in check.

But her mother heard it and that was all that mattered as blue turned to ice and fingers twisted to nails against her skin. "To be a princess."

That wasn't right. Freja had been raised to be a princess, to dazzle the court and dance through the politics. Arne had been raised to be king, to be strong and courageous. Brenna had been raised to be forgotten. Do not speak. Do not draw attention. Do not be herself. She hated it.

"It's a masked dance," the queen said, taking her silence as defeat. It was always a masked dance.

"Makeup is a must," she continued. Makeup was always a must as well. "I don't want a hint of red."

As if Brenna would ever want to be so exposed to the queen's court. The queen dropped her hand and Brenna dropped her chin in submission. "Yes ma'am."

"I'll not have you disgracing this family."

No, Brenna already accomplished that with her birth. She kept her face blank and empty, saying the only words the queen would accept at this point. "Yes ma'am."

"If anyone mentions your....disfigurement, there will be consequences." Consequences such as being confined to the castle and additional lessons meant to teach her refinement and propriety.

"Yes ma'am."

"And no dancing. You'll remain seated and refuse any offers. Politely."

A spark of anger slipped through. "So I can't tell someone to shove—"

"I'll help her get ready." Freja interjected, still smiling, her hand on Brenna's arm tight as a warning, squeezing bruises she wasn't aware of. Brenna hid a wince. "Don't worry, mother."

The queen hummed, studying Brenna's face for any sign of disobedience. "Very well. Don't ruin this for your sister, Brenna."

Because that was all this was for. A dinner to solidify Arne's relationships, to smooth his way to be king. A dance to test Freja's matches, to find her a husband that would strengthen their political ties. Brenna had no place in them except to fill a seat. As the queen left, Brenna stuck her tongue out at her retreating back.

Freja rolled her eyes and pulled her along to their room. Despite their parents' insistence that they were separate people, that the sisters would do well with their own space and own tutors, the sisters did not agree. They stayed in one room with two beds and shared secrets and hardships together. On truly bad nights, Arne joined them.

But they each had their own dedicated space. Brenna pulled on browns and greens and blues that reminded her of the tranquility of the forests that surrounded the city. Gifts from grateful citizens littered her bookshelf. Simple items like handwoven scarves, eagles carved from wood, runes of protection etched into stone, the Aworynian symbol done in careful embrodiery.

Freja opted for a more royal look with delicate embroidered pillows and bolts of purple and gold. Her bedspread always tightly tucked in the corners and each thing in its designated space: her embroidery kit in the basket by her bed, her preferred perfume of lavender and honeysuckle in bottles along her vanity, her bow and arrows carefully hidden in her closet.

Brenna slumped in front of her own vanity and huffed. "First chance I get I'm ditching the crown for good."

True to her word to their mother, Freja placed a basin of water filled with flower petals in front of her. "And what? Live your life as Tatterhood?"

"Why not?" Sounded like a dream to her. She spent every spare moment walking the streets with her cloak. She liked helping people, she liked doing something worthwhile.

"It's just a hood, Bri," Freja said with a sigh, the familiar argument creeping into her voice. "It's not who you are."

But Brenna never felt more herself except when she donned the hood. When Hilde told her that she could be Tatterhood, that she could continue the legacy that brought hope to her people and starred in childhood stories, it felt right. She was Tatterhood as Hilde had been before her. And she would forsake her birth name and title long before she ever gave up the chance to be a hero.

Silently, Brenna washed the dirt from her face, feeling exposed even in the safety of her room. She stared at the mark that distinguished her from her twin, a curse if her mother was to be believed.

"Yikes. What died in here?" Arne asked, stepping into the room with a scrunched nose.

She looked up at him in the mirror, cracking a smile. It was tradition for the three of them to gather before a big dinner or event, a gesture of solidarity even as their parents tried to pull them apart.

"That would be our lovely sister smelling like the backend of a goat," Freja said, crossing her arms.

Brenna scowled. "I fought a draug, they don't exactly smell like røsslyng."

Both siblings stared at her in horror. "You what?"

"Oh, hadn't I mentioned that?" Brenna asked, swiping off the last of the dirt in complete innocence. "Must have slipped my mind."

Of course it was Freja to react first, fear and worry making her voice shriller, too much like the queen. "What the Norns were you thinking?! We have soldiers for a reason!"

And because it felt too much like the queen, Brenna reacted in kind, speaking over her, "Yes, and they're overworked and stretched thin!"

"And they have more training," Freja continued as if her defense was nothing.

"They wouldn't have made it in time and it's my duty as Tatterhood to—"

"Tatterhood is just a name!"

And there was the issue. More than anything else, Freja hated that she went out as Tatterhood, hated that she enjoyed it, hated that it took her away from her. Brenna clenched her fists. "Hilde chose me to do it!"

"Well she can choose someone else!"

Brenna flinched at the truth of the statement.

Arne stepped forward, putting a hand on Brenna's shoulder, ever the diplomat. His steady brown gaze meeting her stormy blue eyes. "Okay enough. Bri, are you hurt?"

She looked away, petulant, and unwilling to admit how sore she was. "Some bruises, I'm fine."

"Promise not to do it again?"

She crossed her arms, the ludicrous statement rolling off her harmlessly. As if she was the only one doing something the others hated. "Only if you promise to stop going to the Sticks."

"Well that's—"

She wasn't done. After all, Arne wasn't the only one with a vice. "And if Freja promises to tell off the next 'nobleman' whose hand accidentally slips during a dance."

He frowned. "Wait, who—"

"It's called diplomacy and tact," Freja snapped, still angry. "Try it sometime."

"Aren't you three supposed to be getting ready?" Three heads swiveled to the spectator of their argument. Anger faded in the stern gaze of Hilde. She raised an eyebrow, looking at each of them in turn.

Brenna squirmed under the unflinching gaze of the woman who raised her. Instinct blurting out the first words to minimize damage. "Arne spent all day in the Sticks."

"Traitor!" he gasped, then pointed back at her. "Bri fought a draug!"

Hilde's face barely twitched at the news as she turned to the last royal sibling. Freja crossed her arms and stuck her nose in the air. "Neither of them invited me."

"Brenna, Freja you're 16 years old and ladies. Act like it. Arne, you're well past age for petty bickering at 22." She entered the room fully, hanging Brenna's dress on the changing divider.

Brenna looked over at her brother and sister, the argument forgotten in the light of sibling solidarity. "Nope."

Unamused, Hilde gave a *hmpf* and put her hands on her hips. "Freja, attack the bird nest your sister calls hair. Arne, you have duties with the queen before the dance tonight."

He slumped. "Can we switch?"

The answer was no and he was shooed out with a swat. He smiled sadly at Brenna, an apology and comfort rolled into one. None of them particularly enjoyed events like this, but she was often the object of their mother's ire when things went wrong. Arne always made sure she knew he was on her side, not her parents. It's part of the reason she knew he would make a good king one day.

Hilde began tidying the room as Freja's soft fingers worked through the knots and tangles of red hair. She smoothed Brenna's hair out with herbal water and then braided a few pieces away from her face. Tradition would dictate that all unmarried woman keep their hair down, which Brenna preferred as she could use her hair as a curtain to hide behind if needed.

Their eyes met in the mirror, an apology exchanged. Freja's voice was quiet as she worked. "You shouldn't let mother dictate how you feel. Your worth isn't found in her opinion."

"I know." Most days Brenna really couldn't care what their mother thought. She made something of herself despite her mother's insistence that she was never meant to be born.

Freja finished up her hair and rested her hands on her shoulders, repeating a statement from earlier. "It's just a piece of cloth. It's the person underneath it that's amazing. And I'm lucky to be her twin."

Brenna gave a half-smile. "Thanks Freja."

Hilde helped her into the dress and Freja helped her with the makeup, covering the red stain on her skin with practiced ease, before offering a plain white mask. They walked out arm-in-arm, finding their brother and presenting a united front in the shadowed corridors of their home. They wouldn't be close to each other for the rest of the night, with Arne politicking through the guests and Freja dancing through the suitors.

It didn't matter what their mother said. It didn't matter what rumors whispered through the court. Brenna had family in her brother and sister, she had purpose in Tatterhood. She needed nothing else.

II

Like barn leker best

Similar children play best

$\mathcal{T}$he Sticks had been aptly named for the place outside the city walls where the buildings shifted from stone to wood and the roads turned to dirt. It was where the poorest of the city inhabitants dwelled, finding community and refuge in the haphazard, leaning buildings. As those from the border towns fled the darkness, the Sticks grew until it was nearly a city in its own right. Dwindling resources and safety led to increased crime and desperation.

It's also where Arne spent the first years of his life.

No matter how many years he spent in the castle, Arne would always feel a little bit at home in the Sticks. Brenna understood this somewhat; she understood him defying their parents to visit even more. What she didn't understand was his insistence on bringing her or Freja along on occasion.

"Mother gave me death glare number three," she said.

Balls were meant to foster connection and facilitate normalcy as the world around them crumbled. For Brenna, it meant a night where her face was covered under makeup and a mask. She never danced, just floated on the edges. Arne danced and flirted and negotiated with vaguely important people while Freja fluttered and danced and laughed with variously single men. Since Brenna and Freja's fifteenth birthday, their parents had pressured Freja in dancing solely with people who could make promising marriage alliances. Last night was not a special occasion, but it still left Brenna prickly and Freja withdrawn.

"You get that glare at least twice a week." True. It had lost some effectiveness over the years but it's the thought that counted. "It wasn't that bad."

A fog had settled in the night and had yet to dissipate in the now early morning. The city and its inhabitants huddled under the thick ethereal blanket. Brenna shifted the basket of food on her hip. Maybe he brought her out here to avoid their parents' wrath. She hated dinner parties. "Weaseldork left screaming."

"He always does," he said with an easy grin. "It's part of the reason we call him 'weaseldork'."

Her voice lowered to a whisper as she admitted the part that really got to her last night. "She told me to think about my place in this family."

Brenna didn't have to go over the implications. They all knew what the queen meant behind that statement: think about if she belonged in this family. All because one member of the court insisted on dancing despite her protests. It wasn't her fault the man couldn't take a hint. The only proper reaction to untoward advances was a swift and well-placed kick.

Arne stopped walking to face her, pain and sympathy framed in kind, brown eyes. "Bri…you belong in this family."

"You're just saying that because you're adopted." The queen struggled with being barren, only conceiving Freja and Brenna through magical means. It was why they adopted Arne to be their heir when he was a child. They had no hope of continuing their line and they needed someone to succeed them, someone they could train in their beliefs. And despite his reluctance, Arne was a good prince, a good successor. Brenna was proud to call him family, to know he would be king someday.

"Well yeah." He smiled, letting the tension ease with a tease. "If anyone has the right to say that, it should be me. Look, we all know Freja is the favorite. That's not going to change anytime soon. But you're Freja's favorite."

"Whatever," she mumbled, although that did make her feel a little less weighted. "Why are you dragging me out to the Sticks again?"

"Idunn demanded I bring you the next time I came." He was such a bad liar. "And I really don't wanna be in the castle after that dinner fiasco."

"Ha! You admit it!"

Arne rolled his eyes but grinned as she relaxed. He gently bumped her arm as they walked along the quiet street. "Why are you wearing the hood?"

"So no one recognizes me obviously. You don't exactly scream crown prince yourself."

He hummed, thoroughly unimpressed with her logic. "I'm wearing plain garb and ditched the crown. That's not the same as creating a whole new persona for myself."

"I'm not doing that." The statement came out mumbled and defensive, fingers instinctively gripping the edges of her cloak. She was not going to ditch her cloak.

"Sure, Tatterhood." The name came out as a tease and she glared at him for mocking it.

"It's a symbol. People see it and know they can ask for help." She had been running around as Tatterhood for the past year. Before that, Hilde would go out and deliver food and money to those in need in the Sticks. Maybe Brenna took it a step farther by chasing down some thieves and fighting a draug or two, but it still meant something to people. And it meant Brenna was more than the unwanted product of a shady deal with a hag. As Tatterhood, she mattered.

He rolled his eyes again. "You know there's this amazing new word people can use if there's danger. Have you heard it?"

Her eyes narrowed, suspicious of his tone, and shook her head. He smirked. "If there's a fire or thieves or monsters, people scream 'help' and like magic people appear to help."

"Shut up."

Her command went unheeded as he chuckled. "At least put the hood down. You can keep the cape on. No one's gonna see us in this fog and I don't want to explain to mother or Hilde that you tripped because you were too stubborn to look around."

The fog had settled in thick around them and the hood obstructed her periphery vision. And yet. "I'm not going to trip."

"So you're a coward?"

"No!" How could he think she was afraid? She fought a draug yesterday! She wandered the streets helping their people in ways her parents never dared. Just last week she stopped four thieves and three brawls.

He shrugged. "I mean only a coward goes around refusing to show their face."

Brenna glared at him and pulled the hood off her head with a snap of her wrist. "I'm not a coward."

Despite her anger towards him, he snorted. "Sure. Next step is cleaning that mug of yours. I know you didn't go to bed with the dirt."

"I have a little more distinguished features to hide. I'm not plain and boring like you," she snapped, diverting attention from the mark hidden by mud just as thoroughly as it was last night with makeup. She covered it so often that seeing her washed face in the mirror caught her off guard at times.

"Sure, we can use that excuse." His tone light as he stuffed his hands in his pockets, looking ahead. She pursed her lips.

"Oh hush."

He laughed as they continued, his steps quickening as they wound through leaning houses and muddy paths. Though it was still early, Brenna felt eyes on her from slated windows and dark corners. They were in the original part of the Sticks, the place where Arne once called home. As such it was more patched and ragged than the hood she donned.

Arne didn't notice. His steps gained a bounce, his eyes brightened. She often forgot how happy her brother was when outside the castle, outside the burdens placed on him. Her lips twitched into a smile as the bad mood from the disaster of an evening faded.

He bounded up to a door that did not fit within its frame, large triangular gaps on the sides as the entire building leaned precariously, and threw it open. A young woman with pale hair and blue eyes smiled at his entrance, her grin growing wider as he beamed and rushed to embrace her with a kiss. "Ah! My dearest Idunn!"

She laughed, a bell-like laugh that made Brenna jealous, and returned his kiss before shoving him away. "Sap. Hey Bri. How was the dance last night?"

"I'm ranking it as one of the top ten. The queen was in a fine mood."

Arne snorted, arms around Idunn's waist as he buried his face in her shoulder. They had been childhood friends, living in this very house with two other families as children. Idunn was the reason Arne was constantly scolded for leaving the protective walls of the castle.

Brenna stuck her tongue out at him. "No one asked you."

"Has Arne been behaving?"

"Does he ever?" Brenna asked in response, setting down her basket and sitting at the table. "I don't know why you'd ever allow him in your house."

"Mainly for the free home repair," Idunn said with a wink. "The view isn't so bad either."

"How did I end up the bad guy?" Arne frowned, casting a mock glare at his sister.

Idunn smiled and patted that arm around her waist. "I'll explain it to you later."

He gave a dramatic sigh and pulled away with great reluctance. "Fine. Since I'm here, what needs doing?"

"The roof is still leaking."

He dropped the act and nodded. Arne was that way, goofy and playing in one moment, until there was a need, then he would do whatever needed doing, no complaints or questions. "I'll see what I can do."

Hilde often said that while the royal siblings did not share blood, they shared the same heart. Brenna wasn't sure where that came from—certainly not from their parents—but she could see it. They all had a desire to help, to be useful, to do whatever it took to make their home a better place. Arne went to the Sticks and did home repair. Freja ensured every servant employed by the royal household had enough food to take home to their families. Brenna masqueraded as Tatterhood.

Idunn turned to her the moment Arne disappeared into the house for repairs. "Alright, what's wrong?"

Brenna blinked from her musings, defensive. "Nothing!"

But Idunn knew them, because her brother wanted his siblings to see this side of him, the non-castle life that ached in him some days. So Idunn knew them, as surely as they knew Idunn. She folded into their patched family as an older sister. "Arne isn't subtle. He only drags you out here when he thinks you need advice. So what did you do?"

Which meant she had another sibling nagging her about safety and caution. Her mouth twisted into a scowl: she should have stolen away to the stables this morning and not returned until after dusk.

"Oh, that's not a good face. You have to tell me now."

Rolling her eyes, Brenna shrugged and said as nonchalantly as possible, "I fought a draug yesterday. Two. By myself. Right before the dance. They may be upset with me about that."

"You…"

Yeah, nonchalant was not working for her. She rushed to defend herself before the lecture could start. "It's not like I planned it. I didn't ask there to be monsters lurking at the castle walls or for someone to ask me to help them." She huffed as she frowned. "And I'm worried about what it means. We've never had such monsters so close."

"The darkness is closer today," Idunn murmured, fingers making the lines for the rune of protection over her chest. She leaned back, her gaze distant as fear settled on her shoulders.

"But the sun still remains," Brenna said, completing the typical greeting, then peered out the window where the fog settled into a white wall. "Somewhere up there at least."

Brenna shook her head and opened the basket, inviting Idunn to take a break and eat with her. It was a tradition of sorts to always bring food when visiting the Sticks. When they were younger, Arne would pile the basket as high as he could and waddle down, dropping rolls like crumbs in his wake.

He was a little better now, but only because the cook had to report large amounts of missing food. If allowed, Arne would have the royal cook follow him here and make a feast for all those starving in the lower town.

"Can I give you some advice, Brenna?" Idunn asked as she picked the smallest sweet bread, calloused fingers tearing into the soft food.

Brenna missed the significant use of her full name, something rarely done outside her parents or serious conversations, too busy thinking about whether her mother would notice if she stuck tacks to the bottom of Weaseldork's shoes. "Of course. You're practically our older sister. Still could be if Arne finally sticks it to our parents and proposes."

She did not miss the pain in Idunn's smile, the obvious acceptance to an unwanted fate. "It will never happen."

"It could."

"It won't." Idunn's smile turned into a sigh and there was pity in her gaze as she explained, pity that made Brenna's skin itch. "Arne, as much as he likes to pretend, no longer belongs in this world. And I don't belong in yours."

"That's—"

She held up a hand. "Do you want to hear my advice?

"…do I?"

"You can't change fate," she said softly, gently, kindly. But underneath the gentle demeanor lingered hurt and resignation and defeat. Brenna hated it. "Arne's destined to be king. I am not destined to be queen. Is Tatterhood your fate? Because you can't be Tatterhood and Princess. You cannot forsake the crown while still clinging to it."

Brenna's heart clawed to her throat, choking her. She couldn't choose. Her family or her freedom? That wasn't a choice she could make. "I…"

She donned the hood because she wanted to help, to make a difference to her people. When her mother told her she was worthless, Hilde told her she was needed. Brenna couldn't do anything as the shameful secret the queen was desperate to hide, but Tatterhood could.

She was saved from answering by a scream tearing through the air like a knife. In an instant she stood, flicking the hood over her face and rushing out.

The fog hadn't lifted and the cry reverberated on the haphazardly placed walls and buildings. She twisted around, trying to pinpoint where it came from when the cry rang out again, anguished, hurting, desolate. Left. The sound definitely came from the left.

"Bri, wait!" Arne said, reaching for her, but she was already moving.

The fog enveloped her, barely offering to show her path, until she nearly fell over a woman kneeling in the mud. With no obvious sign of an attack, Brenna knelt by her, placing a hand on her shoulder. "Are you okay? What happened?"

But whatever happened left the woman incomprehensible in her grief. She made no other sound but the wail, tearing at her clothes, tears clearing paths down her cheeks. Brenna hesitated.

As gently as she could, she said, "I can help. Please let me help."

A hand touched her shoulder and she looked up at Arne, not even out of breath from chasing after her. Brown eyes closed off and careful as he whispered, "You can't help, let her be."

What?

He pulled Brenna up gently, enough to get her to step back from the poor woman. Others ventured out now, investigating the commotion. Friends, neighbors, family surrounded the distraught, never asking why, simply pulling her inside from onlookers, closing doors that did little to muffle the sobs.

"I don't…I don't understand," she said, looking around as the streets emptied. "What happened? Why'd you pull me away?"

"Her kid's been conscripted," Idunn said as she came up on Arne's right, her voice quiet, careful not to carry to the too close houses. "He's gone."

"Conscripted? We don't…"

"How many?" Arne asked, his mouth in a harsh line.

Idunn sighed and put a hand on his arm. "One a week for the past few months. "

He pulled away and Brenna watched as the carefree boy from the Sticks dissolved under the weight of the crown prince, showing a man of hard lines and harder decisions. Her hands clenched at the pain in his voice. "Why haven't you told me?"

"There's nothing to be done." Arne's shoulders slumped as she spoke in a flat, toneless voice. It made Brenna want to scream and fight. She wanted to punch a wall, but the walls here would simply give way and leave a family without shelter. Idunn continued, ignoring the pain and anger in front of her, "You're not king, Arne. And this is how it happens in the Sticks. You know that."

Brenna's jaw clenched so tightly she felt her teeth scream under the pressure. She shook her head. "No. Not today."

The guards would bring him to the nearest barracks, located at the edge of the capital, so Brenna pursued, ignoring her brother's call for her. In the back of her mind, she gratefully recognized that he called for Tatterhood instead of her name. At any other time, she would have listened.

But now she had a duty and that went beyond sibling affection.

Just as she guessed, she found two guards leading a young boy to the barracks at the south wall. The boy was crying, but he kept his head up, even as the soldiers gripped tightly on his arms. He couldn't have been more than ten years old.

She ran in front of them and stopped, forcing them to take notice of her. She kept her stance wide, her shoulders back, her knees bent. Her hand rested on the sword at her hip. A clear threat: she wasn't leaving here without a fight. "Let him go."

The guards barely blinked, viewing her as a nuisance. She would gladly correct them on that. The guard on the left said blandly, "Out of the way."

"He's just a boy!" she hissed. The boy in question sniffed and looked up at her, a dying light of hope in his eyes as he took in her cloak.

"Ain't yer business. Get lost." The guard shifted, inconvenienced but hovering into annoyed. One wrong push and he'd be drawing a sword. She couldn't let him do that with the boy so close.

"We don't kidnap kids to play soldier. There is no honor in that." No matter the darkness eating away at their lands and their people, Ayworn would always have honor and pride.

The guard stepped forward, getting in her face, but keeping a hand on the child. His foul breath reeked of cabbage and fish, making her want to cough. She held her ground as he spit. "You have no honor. Step aside or accompany us to the jail."

Fine. She could use a good fight after last night. Shifting, her hand tightened on the hilt of her sword.

A hand gripped her wrist before she could draw her weapon.

She jerked, shocked to see Arne holding her, flicking her a warning glare as he pulled her wrist away from her weapon. Even more shocking was the atrocious accent he used as he spoke, "Sorry 'bout ma sister. She didn't mean no harm."

For a moment, everyone held their breath. The guard flicked grubby eyes between them, deciding if it was worth the time and paperwork to cause an incident. Then he slouched back, relenting with a grunt. "Keep her on a leash."

"Aye, sir. Sorry, sir." Arne kept an iron grip on her arm as he forcibly dragged her out of their path, sending her a hard look to stay quiet as he did so. She remained quiet out of surprise more than a desire to obey, unused to seeing her brother look so fierce.

The spell broke once the guards disappeared in the fog, their booted steps becoming fading echoes. She ripped away from him, convinced he left a bruise. "What the Norns was that? How could you let them take him?!"

"What did you expect me to do? They were acting on orders." He ran a hand over his face, suddenly looking older than she had ever seen him. Not that it dampened her anger.

"You're the crown prince!"

"Not out here!" His anger rose to match hers. Arne rarely got angry, but Brenna had a special talent in bringing it out. "Challenging the king's authority in public would do nothing but sow discontent."

"You are the same authority! It wouldn't be a challenge."

He leveled her with a scathing look, crossing his arms. "You're not that dumb, so don't act like it."

"Do you agree with a draft?" she demanded, anger rolling off her like waves on a beach, constant, inevitable.

"Of course not."

"Then challenge it!"

"It's not that simple!" He tugged at his hair, a habit of childhood that their parents corrected harshly. Then the anger dropped from him like a snuffed candle, leaving the smoke and ash of regret and exhaustion. He let his hands fall to his sides with a low curse. "Idunn was right. I've forgotten what it's like."

Brenna shifted, uncertain with the sudden lack of rage. "What?"

He looked down the road, where the guards disappeared, sorrow etching into his eyes like cracks in dry earth. "My brother was conscripted."

"Brother? What?"

He looked back at her and smiled. It was the same resigned, sad sort of smile that Idunn wore, an expression born from facing grief and heartache every day and continuing regardless. "He's the reason I got adopted in the first place. Pushed me in front of the king's horses."

"You... you've never talked about him before." Her world felt unsteady, uncertain. Arne didn't keep secrets, not from her and Freja. They were united, together against the oppressive force of the castle. He wouldn't keep this from them. He wouldn't.

"He died within weeks of being sent to the front. Fodder for the darkness." He sighed, running his hand through messy hair, which hung loose around his shoulders. He looked so far from the prince their parents wanted, unpolished, disheveled, hurting. What would Arne's life look like had he stayed in the Sticks? "I didn't find out until years after."

"What did you do?"

He shrugged. "I raged. I yelled at our parents. I demanded the draft be stopped. I foolishly thought it was over."

"I'm sorry. I didn't….I didn't know." She didn't know. He never told her. Her brother, her family, had been hurting for so long and she didn't know

"When you're living in the Sticks, you can't afford to hope. You just survive. You keep your head down and you don't complain when things get rough; you don't share when you're hurt." She knew he was trying to explain, trying to ease the hurt, but all she could think of was her brother who faced this awful reality while she did nothing.

"It's not right," she stressed.

"It's not. But that's life."

She shook her head. She could not help her brother as a child, could not soothe those lingering aches of grief, but she could still help this child, save one family from that loss. "No. I refuse to accept that."

III

Sjaldan er ein báran stök

> *There is seldom a single wave*

Brenna often wondered what made her so different from her siblings. She wondered if the magic flower her mother ate to get pregnant, disobeying the instructions the witch gave her, had somehow cursed Brenna to be an outcast. Arne could be explained as he spent his first few years on the streets, learning wisdom and lessons she couldn't fully understand. The hardships he went through made him kind, grateful, strong. Freja, on the other hand, navigated life like calm, smooth waters, never revealing the myriad of complexity hidden in her depths. Both mastered the art of wearing a mask and maintaining the status quo.

Brenna? She was kindling in a drought, waiting for a spark to set her aflame. And once the fire raged, it was difficult for her to put it out again.

This fire made her see red and blinded her to one purpose; make things right. Tact and diplomacy meant nothing in a world filled with such injustice. And what purpose did she have as the king's daughter if not to eradicate injustice? If she had to fight her parents to do so, then so be it.

She stalked through the halls of her crumbling home until she found her parents' study, a room with polished wood and well-cared for tapestries and dusty tomes meant for reflection and decisions. Her father sat at his desk, parchment laid out in front of him, as her mother lounged in a chaise embroidering.

She didn't wait for permission or a greeting. "Child soldiers? Have we really stooped to such depravity?"

The queen looked up at her outburst, unamused as she took in her daughter. Her eyes traveled up and down her figure and spoke, sharp and commanding, "What in the five realms are you wearing? This is not befitting your station."

"Answer the question," she demanded, even as she flushed. She had always been so careful to put her cloak away when she entered the castle. And now she risked her parents discovering what she did in her free time. Stupid mistake.

But the king and queen didn't react like they recognized the cloak that their people whispered about, so maybe all was not lost. Instead, the queen merely looked at her husband, telling him to deal with his unruly child.

Her hands clenched. While her mother did not miss an opportunity to voice her displeasure in her daughter, her father was the opposite. He rarely spoke with her, to her, about her. No, any significant conversations were held with his heir or his beautiful daughter who would solidify an alliance one day. He had no time for a child that served no purpose but to distract and disappoint.

True to form, the king sighed and shifted the papers as he spoke to someone behind her, "Arne, you said you were talking with your sister about her recent behavior."

"Yes sir." Brenna hadn't even noticed Arne following her. He didn't look at her as he answered, keeping a perfect mask in place that betrayed no emotion or preference.

"And that entailed?" Although there was no blood relation between king and son, they truly did look the part. The king had the same brown hair and broad shoulders, the same deep voice. Sometimes it was hard seeing her father ignore her, as if one day it would be Arne looking at her with detached annoyance instead.

"I thought she might be more receptive on a walk along the nearby streets. We ran into a few guards accepting new recruits."

"It was a child!" Brenna didn't bother correcting him about where they were. No, those confessions were for Hilde and Freja only. "No more than ten."

"Nonsense," the queen said dismissively, attention returning to her sewing. "The guards have explicit instructions. Boys and girls must be twelve years or older to be part of the guard."

"That's hardly better!"

Queen Beret continued as if Brenna hadn't spoken, pausing to look up once more with cold grey-blue eyes. "And while we needn't explain such complex things to you of all people, the families are given compensation. And recruits that show promise are rewarded."

"What? With their life?"

"I grow tired of your childish tantrum, Brenna." Queen Beret picked up her embroidery once more, a clear dismissal.

Except Brenna wasn't done, wasn't ready to be pushed back in the shadows to smolder quietly. "Our kingdom was founded on honor, bravery, courage. Sending children to die at the hands of the darkness goes against all that we stand for!"

"Enough." The king's dark gaze met hers, commanding obedience in a single word, a single look.

Brenna startled at her father's raised voice, shock breaking the anger gripping her heart. At least momentarily. "Father—"

"It is not your place to question our leadership. We are not just your parents, Brenna, we are king and queen. It is our duty to lead, not yours."

She opened her mouth to speak, to explain if they would just give her a chance, she could lead, she could shine, she could do better. But as she did, a tremor ran through the castle, strong enough to knock her off balance. Arne caught her arm, alarm breaking through his carefully cultivated mask.

The royal guard filtered in as the ground steadied itself. Harald, the head of the guard, stepped forward with a shallow bow. "We are currently under raid, your majesties. I must ask that you move to the inner safe room until the danger is passed."

Well, that wouldn't do. Blood still running hot, Brenna found a new target to work out her frustrations. Before any could stop her, not that her mother would try, she slipped out the doors. Once again, Arne dogged on her heels.

"Arne, you're the heir, you need to go with the guard," she said as she raced down the corridors to the barracks situated along the outer walls. Raids happened occasionally, often by magic users. Protocol dictated royalty evacuate to hidden rooms within the castle. Thankfully, raids only focused on supplies, never people.

"I've had training just as you and this is my home too."

She really couldn't argue with that. At least Freja had enough sense to stay within the castle walls. Freja abhorred picking up a sword as she claimed the bow a superior weapon. As if.

Brenna skidded into the armory and didn't bother removing her cape, simply buckling on the armor over her clothes for efficiency. Arne did the same beside her, picking up a broadsword before facing her. Nerves skittered down her spine. She had training, but she rarely used it so openly.

"Stay safe," he commanded with every bit of authority due the heir of a kingdom. "Freja would kill me if anything happened to you."

"Same to you." She tightened the wrist guard and met his gaze fiercely. "Let's protect our people."

With a crooked grin, he led her to the outer walls.

A troll hung on the tallest spire like a child playing house. A troll. Not just magic users. A troll attacked the castle, permeating the air with the stench of rotting fish and stagnant swamp. The creature stood nearly as tall as the castle, with skin like mud. She grimaced as some of the mud-like skin fell to the cobblestones with a sickening 'schoop'. First she had to fight off draug and now a troll raiding her home.

The guards focused on the troll, rightly so considering the damage it could cause, but that left few to manage the five or six others gleefully raiding the castle for rations through the new giant hole in the storeroom wall. Well, Brenna could handle that. Her eyes darted, counting the team attacking her home, marking the guards and their weakness, taking note of the flashes of magic charging in the air. Only one magic user made themselves known in the group, flinging spells in merry abandon as his friends loaded bags with food and coins.

"Arne, help the guards. They need to drive that troll back. I'll help shore up the defenses," she said with more confidence she felt. Her father had trained her in swordwork, but he wanted her as a spy rather than a soldier. Something she didn't quite argue against. She was more comfortable in the shadows.

Arne gave a salute and raced off. She did her best not to think of all the ways he could get hurt. No wonder they reacted so badly when she told them she fought a draug.

Squaring her shoulders, Brenna ran off to help protect the stores. She may not be the best swordsman her father employed, but her fervor and dedication made up for any lack. Dodging through the fallen rubble and torn up road, Brenna joined the half a dozen soldiers attempting to stop the raiders who paid them no mind, protected by the one casting spells.

All the training in the world meant little against magic. Her people typically had very little use for magic that spilled out from the Lost Isle. The king had a court magician that strengthened wards and blessed farms but he was worthless when it came to fighting. Their solution to magic users was a swift end.

She lifted her shield in time for a flash of light aimed at her. Her shield sprouted daisies and she scowled at the offending opponent: a boy her age with stark white hair and a rag tied over his eyes, with a pointed nose and manic smile. As if feeling her glare, he offered her a cheeky salute. Oh, no. Brenna was not going to let him steal from her so smugly.

But despite the obvious impairment, the boy moved quickly and confidently away from her. The ground shook once more as the troll fell back. Steadying herself, when Brenna looked up, the boy was gone, hiding behind a wall or disguised by magic. She raced around the castle where the troll was, just in time to see the band of thieves gather together, magic building in the air, then disappear in the blink of an eye, leaving rubble and injured in their wake.

With a sigh, she found one of the captains and helped with the mess left behind, moving stone and scattered food.

"We were very fortunate," the captain said

Brenna frowned, taking in the half dozen injured and significantly emptier store room. "Fortunate?"

The captain nodded as she straightened and looked around. "Food can be replaced and the injuries were minimal. They could have stripped all resources and left swathes of dead."

Brenna shuddered at the thought of so much damage. While her people had runes and protections, magic remained passive in Ayworn. Something she preferred. Only those that traveled to the Lost Isle dealt with the chaotic nature of magic and the fae.

"I'm going to check on my family," she said, her heart racing as she couldn't find Arne in the rubble. The damage may have been minimal but she didn't believe they came away that unscathed.

The captain waved her off and Brenna wandered through the halls. She let out a shaky breath as Arne came into view, helping move injured to undamaged rooms to be treated. He looked up at her approach, eyes skating her length. "You hurt?"

"Bumps and bruises, what else is new?" She offered a tired smile. "Freja is probably out of her mind with worry though."

They walked to the throne room together to find it empty. A few servants directed them to Brenna and Freja's room. Curious and just a tiny little bit worried, she exchanged a glance between her brother and hurried through the halls. Brenna stopped short just inside the door. Guards cluttered the space, making it difficult to navigate inside. They shifted once they recognized Arne, revealing the queen in a foul mood. Why was their mother glaring at her as if Brenna committed treason against the crown? She hadn't committed treason this morning, despite her best efforts.

Then the people shifted again and Brenna slapped a hand over her mouth to keep the laugh in. Beside her, Arne froze.

Freja had a cow's head on her shoulders instead of her perfect face and hair. Freja had soft, red fur and large ears that stuck out and brown, brown eyes that made her face nearly unrecognizable, inhuman. If not for her body, which remained unchanged.

"What—" Brenna clapped a hand over her mouth in an attempt to stop the small hysterical laugh bubbling out, horror and absurdity clashing. "What happened?"

Despite the bovine features, Freja was able to accurately depict her frustration at the situation with a baleful look. "This is my punishment for attempting to help."

"You…" Arne blinked, looking around the room for answers, finding none, then settling on Freja. "You were helping and got turned into a cow?"

"Just my face. Stop laughing!"

Brenna was doubled over now, wiping tears from her eyes. "I'm sorry, I just…You have a cow's head."

"Brenna, that's enough." Leave it to the queen to douse the joy like water to a fire. Brenna's laughter died as she straightened, but she couldn't quite wipe the grin off her face.

"We'll get it fixed. Runar or someone will know what to do." Brenna paused, trying to read her sister's expression beneath the fur. "What?"

"Runar's been by, he couldn't fix it." Further proof that their court magician had zero redeeming qualities.

Runar unable to fix her left much to be desired; Freja couldn't be stuck with a cow's head. "How did it even happen? You were supposed to stay inside."

The animal features and fur did little to mask the sullen and defiant look her sister sported at her question, conveying just exactly what she had been doing: helping out. Freja would hold her tongue with their mother in the room. She had been helping, most likely with a bow and arrow in her hands. "I wanted to see the progress and one of the raiders spotted me before I could get back inside."

"White hair? Blindfold?"

Freja blinked at her, large eyes strangely empty. "Yes, how did you know?"

"I had a run in myself. Glad I had my shield because otherwise I'd have a daisy for a head." This mysterious magic user would be able to reverse his own spell. A rough plan began sketching itself out in her mind. Magic belonged to the Isle. All they had to do was find this boy on the island and force him to reverse the spell. Arne was going to be so mad at staying behind, but they couldn't let Freja go around part bovine. Had Brenna been the victim, she could have bought more time as she was already disfigured and shoved aside. Their parents may have even considered it an improvement.

Before she could ruin her brother's day further though, Captain Harald entered to give a report. He gave a quick bow and said, "Everyone has been accounted for, your majesty. We have two dozen injured along with three deaths: two soldiers and a staff member."

Fear crawled across her skin like a spider, leaving a trail of gooseflesh in its wake. "Who?"

Harald looked to the queen for permission and bowed his head at her nod. "Madame Hilde Björnsdóttir. She was escorting other workers out of a collapsing corridor and didn't make it out in time."

No.

Her breath stuttered in her throat, caught by the sudden stone lodged there. The air plunged to ice. Brenna felt her heart cracking.

A hand gripped her wrist. The queen spoke empty words. No. Anyone but Hilde. Anyone but the only one who could claim to be a parent to her. She met the strange unfamiliar eyes of her sister and fell to the ground.

The hand on her wrist shifted to arms around her, then another pair as soft fur grazed her cheek. Brenna had no tears as it couldn't be possible. Not Hilde. Not strong and sure and constant

Hilde. She trembled and she couldn't tell if it was because she was shaking or if it was one of her siblings falling to pieces. It didn't matter, the pain was shared.

"She will have a burial befitting a member of the royal household," Arne said, uncharacteristically stern to the queen. Brenna didn't hear the response.

In a blink, the room emptied save for the royal siblings who clung to each other as lifelines. Brenna let the pain settle deep in her bones before pushing away. She had a plan. She had a sister to restore. She couldn't fathom…couldn't linger on the death, on the pain choking her.

"I have to pack," Brenna said, her voice detached and coarse as if she had been screaming. Had she been screaming?

"Pack? Where would you possibly want to go right now?"

She gave Freja a look and gestured to her face. "You have fur instead of skin, remember? I said I would fix it."

Freja gaped, an expression that looked absolutely ridiculous on a cow, but Brenna had no urge to laugh. The world dimmed without Hilde's steady light. Arne put a hand on Freja's arm and sighed. "She's right. We need to get you fixed sooner rather than later."

Before their parents started talking about their poor daughter who was now useless to them. Brenna grew up with the queen's disdain and learned to ignore it, Freja had not. And she planned on keeping it that way.

"How do you expect to fix it? And why can't it wait?" Freja asked as if Brenna didn't want to linger. Of course she wanted to stall, to wait, to pretend the world hadn't crashed around them.

Hilde died. Hilde was gone. Brenna took a short, stuttering breath and shook her head to clear it.

"Because I'm going to track down the one that did this. And the longer we wait, the harder it'll be to track him down." She stood and grabbed a canvas bag from her closet.

"I'm going with you," Freja said, pulling out her own bag.

"Obviously." Brenna couldn't imagine going anywhere without Freja. A smile tugged at her lips, a brittle, fragile thing, so she let it drop. "Sorry Arne, that leaves you with the horrors."

He shrugged, resigned. "I suppose someone with common sense needs to stay."

She bit back a quip, not in the mood to make things light and breathing easy. Instead, she pulled travel clothes and her favorite weapons out. Focus on the task at hand and let all other details slip away. If it was important, she would remember later.

"It would be better to wait for first light though," he said and she could feel his eyes on her back. She didn't turn to see the ache of grief, the raw shock of loss, didn't need to know how it mirrored her own soul. "Journeys always have better luck when beginning with the dawn."

"It's two days to the docks. And then another day on the water to get to the island," Brenna said, her hands jerking as they stuffed travel clothes in the bag haphazardly. "We shouldn't waste the hours we have left in the day."

Freja stared at her too, but instead of demanding details as she would on any normal day, she turned to their brother. "It'll be easier to slip away from the city now, in the aftermath of the attack. And we'll be able to get back sooner."

Brenna threw her sister a grateful look.

"Alright, I get it. There's no stopping you." He moved to sit on the bed to look them both in the eye and said, "Just promise you'll make haste in your return."

"We're not strolling through the moors," Brenna said with a roll of her eyes. It wasn't a vacation or pleasure trip. Although a small spark of excitement at sea travel, something she had never done, lingered in the back of her mind, but that spark languished under the weight of everything else.

"I'll keep her focused."

He nodded. "I'll do my best to keep the parents from declaring you dead, then."

"Your sacrifice is noted." Freja patted his arm with a small smile. For a moment silence enveloped them like a comforting blanket, grief permeating the air like a fragrance. Then Arne stood jerkily, gathering his sisters in a hug and leaving them to it without a word more.

With a sigh, Freja headed for the door as well, pulling a hood around her to cover her face. "I'm going to get rations from the kitchens. Meet you in the stables?"

She hummed confirmation as Freja left for supplies. Brenna stared at the last item to pack: a tattered, mended cloak, as an unnamed pain settled in her chest. Hilde was gone. She would do this alone.

Maybe not completely alone. With a *mmrp*, Signe, one of their mousers, wound through her legs and jumped up on the bed, making herself comfortable in Brenna's bag. While the castle had its fair share of cats in the nooks and crannies, Signe alone frequented their rooms for pets. With a flick of her dark brown, bushy tail, she met Brenna's gaze and dared her to move her from the bag.

She pursed her lips. "You are, under no circumstances, coming with us."

Signe settled deeper in her clothes, shedding long hair on the fabric. "It'll be dangerous. You could get turned into a mouse for your troubles. And I won't be catching your dinner on the trip."

She purred and slid her eyes closed. Brenna sighed and scratched the top of her head. "Silly skogkatt."

Closing up the bag, she let Signe burrow her head out of an opening and settle before pulling it on her shoulder. The cat gave a *mkgnao* of protest before once again closing her eyes and letting it happen.

As usual, no one paid her a second glance as she wound her way to the stables. She pulled the cloak tighter around her; the cloak Hilde wore and patched herself when she was Brenna's age, the cloak Hilde settled around her shoulders and told her to do good in the world. She let out a tenuous breath as the scent of hay and leather surrounded her.

Signe offered another protest as Brenna set the bag on the ground to get Hrolf, her steed, saddled. "Keep complaining and I will leave you here. Don't think I won't."

Hrolf shook his mane and she smiled. "Not you, darling. I wouldn't dream of leaving you behind."

He stamped his feet and his teeth caught a bit of fabric hanging in the corner of the stall, tossing it at her. She caught the old cap she had made as a child that Hrolf liked to wear. It had taken her weeks of feeding him sugar cubes to get him to wear it, now he loved the hat. "Sorry, bud. Maybe later."

She stuffed the cloth in the saddle bags and got him fitted out for the journey. It would have been smarter to take a less conspicuous horse. Glossy black and prim as any royal steed, Hrolf wasn't above sabotaging the stables and following after her if she left him here. The stablehands didn't need his drama.

Plus, Brenna wanted the comfort of familiarity.

"Please tell me you're leaving the ridiculous hat behind."

Brenna turned and grinned at her sister. "He thinks he looks dashing in it."

"It was funny when we were ten and pretending he was a goat, but is that really how we want to present ourselves to strangers?" Freja put her hands on her hips, lips pursed.

Brenna smirked and pet him on the nose. "Don't listen to her. You be a goat if you want."

Freja strapped in her bag, glaring at Signe who had the audacity to glare back at her. Despite the jostling, she still didn't jump out and leave. Brenna held out a hand and helped Freja settle behind her on Hrolf. And so, the two princesses made their way out of the castle, dodging ruins and refugees from the most recent attack.

Freja, uncharacteristically, kept her hood up, covering the evidence of magic left on her face. Brenna did the same out of comfort, letting the familiar weight of a tattered hood remind her of better days. A hollow sort of pain settled in Brenna with each step of Hrolf's hooves. They moved forward, steadily, quickly, and behind them, burial arrangements were made.

IV

Bra vind i ryggen er best

A fair wind at our back is best

"*F*irst time out at sea?" A young woman approached Freja and Brenna. Gold paint adorned her dark eyes and turquoise beads dotted her black braided hair.

The twins found a boat that offered charter between Ayworn and the Isle for a hefty sum. It may not have been so exorbitant had Brenna not insisted their animals be given passage as well. Or if she had not threatened a crewmate with death should harm come to Hrolf or Signe.

Thankfully the ride to the port had been calm and easy, with nothing of note beyond sore muscles and tired eyes. Brenna had a weight on her chest she refused to acknowledge and Freja hid her face as much as possible. When they first left the castle, she never imagined how dull sea travel could be. Ayworn dwindled out of sight quickly, leaving nothing but open sea and harsh sunlight for miles. She expected other ships. She expected storms and high seas. She expected…more.

"Is it that obvious?" Brenna asked, shifting to keep Freja behind her, to hide the fact that her sister had a cow's head. Neither of them were sure of how others would react to the clear use of magic. Her eyes roved over the modest ship they found themselves on. People and goods of all sorts tucked themselves into corners and rooms, avoiding conversation and prying. All the better for them. Brenna really didn't want to be recognized on this trip. If their luck held, they would return home without any injury or incident.

"Those going to the Cursed Isle are always appropriately nervous the first time," the woman said, sitting on a box near them as they crouched by the railing of the ship.

"Cursed Isle?" Freja asked, her voice barely carrying across. Her head was bowed, keeping her face in shadow. "I've never heard it referred to that way."

The woman hummed. "What else would you call it? Lost? It is not lost. It is the source of all calamity. After all, the fae are responsible for the black stain that now plagues us."

Trade between the other countries all came by sea, the darkness cutting harsh black lines between the sister kingdoms. Even worse, all ships had to stop at the Isle in order to pass on to the other kingdoms. Any attempts to reach the others, even such a short distance from Ayworn like Denwes or Nolpa, resulted in sunken ships and horrific deaths. The darkness vanished from sight at the shoreline, but it remained just as deadly. Could the fae have devised such horrendous borders?

"They say the fae queen once stood against the darkness. That it was her death that caused it to spread," Freja argued. Rumors about the fae queen varied with each person. Some claimed the fae king ate his queen's heart to spread the darkness. Others declared the queen's heart broke and through her tears, saved their lands from total destruction. No one actually knew, but in a secret vault in the Aywornian castle, a jagged jewel was kept in reverence and called a heart piece.

"The fae are responsible for this darkness. You'd do well to remember that as you enter their lands." The young woman, apparently finished with the conversation, stood and walked to the other end of the boat.

"I miss home." Freja slouched forward, the hint of a snout pushing past the hood.

With a sigh, Brenna leaned over, lending strength and comfort where words failed. "We'll be home soon enough."

Brenna missed Arne and the castle and the people she helped as Tatterhood, but going home meant facing Hilde's death, it meant facing her mother's scorn and her father's indifference. If it were not for Arne and Freja, she would have run away years ago.

"You'll be wanting to step away from the edge, lassies."

She blinked and turned, staring at the grizzled sailor, tuft of silver hair sprouting from dark skin, lines carved into his skin from sun and salt. She frowned as she looked at the vast emptiness around them. "Is there something wrong?"

"Bit of a shock for freshies. Entering the port."

"Uh..." Brenna looked around again at the empty sea, not a port or land in sight. Not even a seagull to give hints of their journey stopping soon. Was this the sunsickness they were warned happened on long journeys?

She shared a look with her sister, but the man had already left. Freja took a step away from the rail. "Odd. Perhaps we should find another place to wait."

"Oh please, there's nothin—ack!"

In the span of a blink, the serene seascape disappeared. In its wake, a port bustled with noise and chaos. Sailors yelled as they threw boxes to each other, ships groaned in their confines, seagulls demanded attention and bread in squawks and dives. Sea salt lingered in the air still, but now traded spices and leather and sawdust shifted in the winds. And over it all, a scintillation teased the corner of her vision. An unnamed element that made Brenna's skin itch and her breath catch. Her shoulders rose in tension.

"Magic," Freja breathed beside her.

A shudder ran along her spine. That was it. Magic. Chaos. Change. Brenna couldn't decide if she liked it or not, but it didn't really matter. Once her sister was put to rights, she would put this tiny island behind her and think nothing of it.

Unfortunately there were so many more people than she expected. The port had twice as many inhabitants as the Sticks back home and none of its privacy. People did not hide in lopsided buildings and shadows here, but lived on top of each other in stacked homes with open doors. Keeping a hand in Freja's to keep from being jostled away, she wound down to the port with the other passengers, and waited quietly as their things and animals were brought out. Only a few minutes on this island and Brenna was already longing for the cold glares of her mother.

Brenna took hold of Hrolf's reins, grinning as he headbutted her gently in retaliation for leaving him in the swaying underbelly of the ship. Patting his nose in consolation, she offered a sugar cube for forgiveness. He huffed, but accepted. Signe stared at them from the saddle, her tail flicking dangerously. With a flat, unimpressed look, the cat hopped down and disappeared into the crowds.

Well, cats were fae in disguise. Signe would be fine. Probably.

Looking around at the mess of people, magic and chaos, Brenna got the nearest sailor's attention. "If we were looking for someone or for information, where would we go?"

The sailor hefted a bag of grain and shrugged. "Googin's. You got questions, he's got answers. For a price."

"Right. Thanks. And where…"

The sailor waved them off with vague directions to a tavern. Brenna wasn't too sure about it, but they had no other lead. If this Googin couldn't help them, maybe another magic user would. She looked at Freja and shrugged, hopping into Hrolf's saddle. "Let's get your head back."

"Still not funny." Freja scowled, but accepted her help in the saddle behind her.

"It's a little funny." Brenna pulled out the bundle of cloth from home and smirked. "As is this."

Brenna reached forward and pulled the hat on Hrolf's ears. He pranced in delight as he now donned handmade, curling, stuffed horns. He looked nothing like a goat, but in a place that thrived on the absurd, she thought it fitting. And it didn't matter what anyone said, he liked pretending to be a goat.

She could practically feel her sister roll her eyes. Apparently that required a full body motion. "You're ridiculous."

"This place is ridiculous."

The road they were on seemed to shift from cobblestone to packed dirt to polished marble at will. Stalls of vibrant color called to them from the shadows. Brenna couldn't tell what they were selling, only that the color defied explanation or name. And what was that smell? Divine nectar, sweet and tangy and tantalizing. Better than anything the cooks ever created in the castle. While the people around them seemed humanoid in shape, some shifted form in the shadows, growing fangs or claws, fur or feathers. She shuddered at the unnatural beings around her, her heart hammering a little too loud.

And the noise. A thousand conversations overlapped with too many people in too little space. Like the Sticks that grew overnight, but ten times worse. It was enough to make her almost miss the dull monotony of the ship, if only to get the quiet back.

She looked back at Freja. It was harder to pick out expressions with the large brown eyes and fur covered snout, but she knew her sister, cow or not. Freja reveled in people and opportunity. As Brenna learned to not be noticed, Freja learned to work a crowd. Brenna could see her sister's fingers twitching to see how court politics and machinations translated to this bed of conversation and disarray.

Googin, a roughly middle-aged fae, set up in a stall about a half mile from the port. Few people milled about his stall. Several books were opened in front of him, pages turning of their own accord as his eyes darted to each one. Nothing about him screamed dangerous or even magical with his brown cropped hair and short pudgy stature. The only thing marking him as a fae were his tapered ears.

He looked up at their approach and Brenna had to reassess. His eyes held wonders and worlds she would never understand. It wasn't the color, which she couldn't quite place between blue and green and, inexplicably, purple, but the light that shone out of them and swirled inside. A shudder ran down her spine.

Carefully dismounting, they approached his booth. Brenna took a deep breath. "Are you Googin?"

"Yes'm. Whatcha need?" His eyes fell back to his books and relief rushed through her.

"We're looking for a magic user."

"Magic users are defined by their ability to use seidr. There are 546 such beings on the Lost Isle alone and are categorized by type of magic and willingness to deal. Out of 546, only 113 are willing to deal with humans. The Lost Isle only has 19 human magic users currently residing on its shores." He pulled out a quill, scratching out something on parchment, as he spouted off facts so quickly it left her dizzy.

"No," Brenna interrupted, desperate to stop the flow of information. "We have a specific magic user in mind."

"Mind magic is dangerous and tempestuous and nearly always fatal to humans. Statistics show that 76 percent of all—"

"He's young, has white hair, wears a blindfold and just got back from a raid on Ayworn," Brenna said all in one breath, patience running low at the barrage of useless information. Freja squeezed her arm in warning to keep her temper.

Her outburst met with silence as Googin went back to staring at her. The magical charge in the air sparked along her skin, pulling at her in a tease, but she kept her chin up. She fought a draug and lived, she wouldn't be intimidated by an irritating record's keeper. His gaze shifted to her right and then back. "Can you pay the price?"

She pulled up her coin pouch, mentally calculating what they would need to get home, but he sneered. "I deal in value, not gold."

"Gold is value," she said, annoyance creeping into her voice. He gave away information like a waterfall before, but now that they wanted something specific he asked them to pay? She should have grabbed her knife instead of her money.

But Freja held onto her and stepped forward to de-escalate as she always did. "What sort of value?"

"Memories, time, sacrifice. I have no interest in skilled make or expensive craft, only what value it has to the beholder. No value, no attachment, no deal." As he spoke, weapons and jewelry and cloth of tremendous craftsmanship shimmered on the counter then puffed away like smoke. "A prized possession. Not a prize."

Silence stretched between them until Freja nodded. "My sister has a set of knives given to her by a beloved caretaker. They were gifts of freedom, courage, independence. Would these suffice?"

"Freja!"

He grinned sharply. "Bring them out and we shall see."

"If we show them to you and they meet your satisfaction, we have a deal?" She held a hand against Brenna's protests. Brenna scowled. How was it her stuff being bartered? She wasn't the one that ended up with a bovine for a face.

"As you say."

Freja's eyes narrowed. "You will reveal all that you know?"

"I will answer one question fully per item," he said evenly, his face placid as the ethereal light continued to shine from him. At least he focused on Freja and not her. Silence fell once again as the deal settled between them as awkward and unsteady as a newborn colt. Slowly, Freja turned to her and nodded. Brenna's eyes narrowed. Really? They had to use her stuff to solve this?

Of course they did. Freja didn't bring anything she held dear and Brenna always had her knives on her. It was a simple conclusion. Freja tilted her head. Brenna let out a huff.

For a moment, Brenna contemplated offering a different weapon, but eyes that shone like stars would see through the deception. With great reluctance, she slid a dagger from its sheath and stabbed the wooden counter with a little more force than necessary. It didn't make her feel better.

Hilde gave her that knife, put it in her hands and told her she had the strength to wield it. Hilde trained her with that knife, showing her the best way to curve her arm to strike fast and true. Hilde would never gift her with such kindness again.

Googin nodded. "The deal is struck, what is your question?"

"Who cursed my sister with a cow's head?" Brenna demanded, frustration from the entire conversation leaking through. Freja glared at her.

There was a pause as he tilted his head dramatically to the right, the shine of his eyes dulling for a moment. "His name is Einar. He is a blind magic user that has no color to him. He cursed your sister three days ago at the Aywornian castle with a spell designed to be a prank from the fae. He is eighteen years old and has no known relations."

Googin stopped as his head righted itself and the glow returned. He raised an eyebrow in mute query and Brenna scowled in return. She procured another knife out of the set and stuck it next to the other, letting Freja ask the next question.

"Where would we find him right now?"

His head went left this time and Brenna wasn't sure it was an improvement. "I do not have all sight. He has many residences but, after a raid, Einar and his troupe are often found at O'Malley's tavern to share in their victory until their spoils run out and they must raid again. O'Malley's tavern is six streets away."

"Can someone else break the enchantment?" Brenna asked in a rush, hoping maybe he would be bound to answer in whatever weird trance he was in. Alas, he returned to normal and gave her a flat look. She scowled at Freja; there was no way she was giving up the last dagger unless absolutely necessary.

Freja sighed. "That's all the questions we need answered."

He nodded and moved to take her beautiful weapons, but Freja shot forward, putting a hand on them and meeting his gaze with an unimpressed look. "What do you think you're doing?"

"You made a deal," he said, his eyes narrowing.

"Yes." She raised her head and straightened her shoulders, a glimpse of the queen beneath the fur. "The deal was to show you our wares. If you found them pleasing, you would provide information. We never promised to give them to you."

Oh, that was sneaky. Brenna glanced between them, holding her breath as Googin evaluated them. Would he claim the deal false? What were the repercussions to dealing falsely on an isle belonging to the fae? She bit her lip and shifted, slipping the last of Hilde's daggers to her hand, just in case.

He grinned sharply. "I see your sister is not the only one marked by the fae. Careful lest the fae king keep you."

"Marked?"

Brenna instinctively pulled the hood lower. There was no way he could have seen the mark on her face.

"That would be another deal," he said, his grin never fading, his eyes shining inexplicably brighter. "And my eyes are open; you won't trick me twice."

It was Brenna's turn to curb her sister's curiosity. Perhaps being marked by the fae was a saying or phrase common among magic users. It could even be an insult; she felt insulted. No matter the meaning, nothing good could come from making another deal. She pulled Freja back to Hrolf. They had a destination and a goal and should focus on that.

Once out of earshot, Freja turned and glared. "We could have bargained with him again."

"Let's just revel in the success of one deal," Brenna said, carefully tucking her knives back in their sheaths.

Frejav rolled her eyes. "Have some faith, I was never going to let him take your weapons."

"Yeah, and I didn't know that!" Like dry kindling waiting for a spark, anger Brenna didn't know she had burned through her. The fear of losing connection to Hilde raged through her and spilled out now that they were alone. Well, as alone as they could be in the hive of magic and movement.

Turning to pet Hrolf, Freja said dismissively, "It's not like I was bargaining your cloak. I may have let him keep it if I had."

"Don't." She bit off the word bitterly and Freja jerked at the tone, turning back to her in surprise. Brenna clenched her fists as grief laced each word she spoke with pain. "You had no idea if that would work. And they are not some trinkets for you to test your ability to negotiate."

"Bri, I wasn't—"

"Hilde gave me these! It's all I have left of her." She was gone and it hurt and Brenna wanted to hide in her room with the hood tight around her, pretending everything was fine. Today would have been the day of the funeral, her pyre blazing to match with the pain in Brenna's soul and maybe they should have waited. Maybe if they had waited, the fire could have burned off the worst of the ache.

Freja wrapped her arms around her. "I miss her too. I'm sorry. I didn't mean…"

"It's fine." Brenna sniffed and pulled back. They were on a mission and emotions were best pushed aside until they were safe at home. "Let's find this Einar and get you fixed."

V

Bara döda fiskar följer strömmen

Only dead fish follow the stream

$\mathcal{B}$efore the darkness first descended, the Lost Isle did not allow humankind to wander its beaches. Back then the island had a name and smaller islands surrounding it. The Isle belonged to the fae and it was treacherous for even the most seasoned adventurer. The nature of being off limits made it even more enticing and lured daring heroes eager to prove their mettle, but few returned and none left unchanged.

While a king ruled over the small kingdom, there was no queen. The most prevalent rumor was that she had been lost to the darkness. The first casualty. The queen had once been human, a girl tossed to the sea by cruel family and found by the fae king and given mercy. For those that still remembered among the fae, they spoke of her kindness and gentleness, foreign concepts in a people ruled by chaos and mischief. She had been well loved.

Brenna knew none of this as she was too young to remember anything before the darkness. Only stories drifted down from a time of light and free travel, inspiring the next generation to hope and wistfulness. She had foolishly thought that the Lost Isle had been unaffected by the darkness, so far from the black walls that bordered her home.

After all, the fae must have benefited. Perhaps even orchestrated the whole thing. Their kingdom thrived in the dark, in the desperate.

She was forced to reevaluate those thoughts as they now wandered the Isle. The further they moved from the port, the more the people and buildings closed in. Away from the salt of the sea, the underlying scent of sewage and filth that came with not enough space and too many bodies permeated the air.

"There's O'Malley's," Freja whispered from beside her, gesturing to what must be the tavern. Had the sign not claimed it as such, she would have kept walking.

There was no stall for Hrolf, so she tied him up on a post and patted his nose. "You have my permission to bite anyone that comes near."

He huffed and swished his tail as he stamped. Message delivered. She grinned and gave him one last pat before turning to the dilapidated lean-to parading as a tavern.

"No weapons inside."

She stepped back and looked down. Two goblins were glaring at her as they sharpened makeshift blades that gave off a green tint. Her eyes narrowed; there was no way she was going around without protection.

"Do all your patrons check their weapons at the door?" Brenna asked with a raised brow.

"Yes. O'Malley's rules."

She looked back at Freja for her take. Freja shrugged and stepped forward. "If we release them to you, do you swear to return them to us?"

One of the goblin's pouted, the younger one if she had to guess. The other studied them for a moment. "We swear."

"You swear to return them to us the moment we leave this tavern in the same condition we present them to you?" Freja pressed, meeting their gaze with fierce demand.

It was the other's turn to pout. He sneered at them and spat, "We swear."

There was a spark at his words, a deal struck in magic. Did that happen with all fae or was it the magic of the Isle that caused such a tangible reaction to oaths and deals? Satisfied, Freja turned and nodded at Brenna, then pulled off her bow and arrows. The younger took them and stuffed them in a bag that was definitely too small and yet fit them with ease.

With a sigh, Brenna unhooked the scabbard at her back and the two knives at her waist. With a flick, the daggers on her forearms came loose and were added to the bag. The goblin glared at her impatiently and she scowled back as she pulled the small knives in her boots. She crossed her arms and gave them a flat look.

Freja cleared her throat and she pursed her lips. With a huff, Brenna pulled the hidden knife from her boot heel. It fell with a clank into the bag.

They stretched their lips over their yellow, pointed teeth. "Enjoy O'Malley's."

Freja pushed her through the door before she could offer a quip. Probably for the best. Any hope that inside would be calmer than out was dashed the moment they crossed the threshold. Like the magic that kept the Isle hidden until the last moment, the tavern had magic that stretched and expanded the space beyond the limits of the shack it embodied. Inside was a two story tavern as big as their grand dining hall at home.

Unlike the hall at home, this space used every available inch to fill with people and chatter and magic. Freja and Brenna were jostled and shoved aside as busy waiters pushed to fill orders and tired customers searched for an empty seat. Brenna grabbed her sister's hand and wove her way to the stairs.

Peering above the crowd, she looked for white hair. There! Tucked in the corner the snarky magician was laughing as a small imp jumped from shoulder to shoulder. The troll that had towered over their castle and reduced halls to rubble had shrunk and just barely had to crouch to fit. It was probably for the best that the goblins took her weapons as she would have stabbed the lot of them already. It wasn't completely off the table yet, just a little more difficult.

"Keep calm, Bri. Threatening them will not get us what we want."

Brenna offered an emotionless smile. "I'll ask nicely."

Before Freja could add further stipulations, Brenna hopped down the stairs and stomped over to Einar. As she came up to their table, she swiped a foot under his chair and grabbed the front of his tunic before he could hit the floor. In a low snarl she demanded, "Fix her. Now."

His blindfold was off. Seeing him this close, Brenna understood better what Googin had meant when he said he lacked color. From his short white hair to his milky, pale eyes, Einar was whiter than a corpse. Most corpses didn't smirk though.

"Who, what, when, where, why?" His smirk smoothed into a 'who, me?' look. "You probably can't tell, but I'm a poor blind boy. I have no idea what you're talking about."

"You cursed my sister with the head of a cow. Change her back," she growled, not buying the innocent act for a moment.

The troll gave a 'heh, heh', completely unconcerned by his friend's predicament. Einar grinned, unrepentant and unconcerned as he hung from his shirt. "That was a pretty funny trick. Personally, I think she's better this way."

Pursing her lips, Brenna released his shirt abruptly, satisfied in the thunk and 'oof' he made as he collided with the floor. No one moved to help or defend him. She dusted off her cloak and smiled sweetly. "I'm sure we can settle this in a civil manner. Change her back and I won't draw and quarter you for raiding our country."

With a whoosh of air and magic, Einar twirled back in his seat. He propped his chin in his hand in facsimile of rapt listening. "Fascinating. You know, I don't think we will."

"You doubt my sincerity."

"Well, weapons are not allowed at O'Malley's and if you held the beautiful well of magic within yourself, you would not be here." He leaned back, completely at ease, as he spread his hands out in a 'what can you do' gesture.

He was right. She had to check her weapons at the door and she couldn't use magic to threaten or coerce or fix. But he was also very wrong to assume she was harmless because of those things.

Brenna gave a sweet smile, which made Freja sigh and step away from her, then grabbed the nearest thing to her: a wooden spoon. With one swift motion, she whacked him upside the head and then rammed the handle against his neck. She leaned into his face again, all her rage and pain and grief bleeding through.

"I lost someone very dear to me in your funny, little raid and the only reason I'm not ramming this down your throat is because you serve me better alive than dead." She took a ragged breath, glaring at him. "So fix her and we'll be on our way."

The tavern around them faded to background noise as the table waited for the next move. Either Einar was gifted in magic and therefore Brenna was not a true threat to him or no one really cared about him one way or another as none of his companions moved to help. Maybe a little bit of both. Or they were all drunk out of their minds and everything passed in a haze to them. It didn't matter. They had one goal here and wondering about Einar's raiding troupe was not part of it.

Einar mouth set in a thin line as he gave a short nod. "Lemme up, I'll fix her."

She held the spoon against him for a moment more before stepping back and crossing her arms. "Just as she was. No other tricks."

"Yeah, yeah, lighten up. It was a joke." He rolled his shoulders and cracked his fingers. "You're twins right? Easy peasy, I'll just copy your face onto hers."

"No!" Brenna's outburst caused him to stiffen, though she made no move with her makeshift weapon. She scowled. "We're not identical."

"You sure?" Einar tilted his head as if studying them, a rush of cool air washed over her. Magic. "You feel identical. I mean, bovine parts aside."

"I'm certain." She glared at him. "Can't you just undo whatever you did before?"

"*Can't you just undo what you did before?*" he mocked, shaking his head. "Ugh, mundane people are so naive."

Maybe Brenna could ram the spoon down his throat anyway. He didn't need to talk to do the spell and, really, the world would thank her for removing his ability to speak. She clenched her jaw and asked, "What do you need, then?"

"Well, obviously, I'm blind so I have no idea what she looks like." He tapped a pale finger on his chin before snapping them. "Got it, we'll just take a copy from your memory. Picture what you want your sister to look like clearly, I'm only doing this once."

Brenna closed her eyes and imagined her sister with her red hair braided up in the high fashion, with the sprinkling of freckles she always got in the summer, with her clear blue eyes that were the same color as hers but mimicked a calm lake rather than the raging sea. She took a deep breath and fixed the image in her mind. "Okay, got it."

"Done."

"What? Really?"

She opened her eyes and blinked, turning to Freja, who slowly lowered her hood. Relief rushed through Brenna. There was her sister. Her flame-red hair, her sea blue eyes, her freckles from the sun and wrinkles as she frowned in worry.

"Well?" Freja asked, eyes darting around the group. "It feels like my normal face. Is it right?"

"I wouldn't know," Einar drawled, but Brenna rolled her eyes.

"You're perfect," Brenna smiled. "Back to normal."

Back to normal. Which meant they would need to head back to home. As much as Brenna wasn't a fan of anything this island had to offer, the thought of returning to heartache and normalcy in a crumbling palacemade her blanch. It had only been three days but she had gotten used to the lack of her mother and her constant disparaging remarks.

"What? No gratitude?" Einar asked with a raised brow.

Brenna glared at him. "If it weren't for you we wouldn't be here in the first place."

"I still say it was a brilliant joke."

"I still say you deserve a worse punishment."

Freja took her arm before she could follow through on her threat. "Let's go home."

The weight of grief pressed on her and she nodded. They turned for the door.

"I am sorry for your loss," Einar said, serious for the first time since their meeting. His voice quiet and solemn. "Our raids are meant to be victimless."

Her whole body tensed, rage filling her vision red as Brenna looked back at him. Her sister's hand on her arm preventing her from shoving the spoon down his throat. "You brought a troll!"

"And a fine fighter. He knows how to watch his feet."

"And his club?" she demanded, facing him fully again. He leaned back, holding up his hands. "And what of those who will go hungry because of the food you stole?"

"Hey, we're all hungry." He crossed his arms, thought better of it, and let them fall to his lap, fingers tapping his leg. "Best your friend have a swift death now instead of the torment waiting the rest of us."

Brenna lurched forward but the grip on her arm kept her back. "What's that supposed to mean? I should be thankful she's—"

"As the rest of us face starvation or are consumed by the darkness, yeah." Einar slouched in his chair, as relaxed as a coiled snake and just as deadly. "I get Ayworn isn't as desperate as the rest of us but even sheltered royalty can't ignore the signs."

The darkness was closer today.

Brenna knew it was getting worse with how the Sticks doubled in population overnight and the ever present threat of black walls filled with monsters and horror. But that was their norm. It wasn't that bad…right?

She stared at him, anger and disbelief and fear warring in her. "That's just fearmongering. The darkness hasn't really gotten closer."

"Tell that to Faldinn. It was consumed a couple years back."

No. That wasn't possible.

While Faldinn was not their direct neighbor, they shared the sea with Ayworn and three other kingdoms. Faldinn belonged to the land of the strong, where leaders were born. They said that the royal family rose to greatness by defeating a horde of dragons with naught but their own skill. Rich veins of ore ran through the mountains of Faldinn that shone like none other, and its people made jewels and weapons alike from it.

And sure, she hadn't heard from those traders lately but she was kept out of such business. For her own good, of course.

Could such a stronghold truly fall?

Freja pulled her aside and leaned in from spying ears. "I know what you're thinking. Don't. We cannot help Faldinn."

"How long before it's our people that face that fate?" she asked, her tone just as low, though the din of the space hardly allowed for eavesdroppers. "Do we not have a duty to them to ensure their prosperity?"

"We have no indication that things are as bad as he claims."

"I fought two draugs mere steps from the castle." If that wasn't proof then what was? Such foul creatures had no place far from the abyss they called home. They should not be close enough to terrorize the capital. And yet Brenna had the bruises to show for their presence.

Freja faltered in her conviction. "It's…unusual. But not enough to cause a panic. We're needed at home."

"To gladhand the courtiers?" she asked, weary, desperate. "To hide in the shadows waiting for a day we can finally do something? What if, by then it's too late?"

"Bri…"

Freja hesitated, giving into the logic of striking at the source rather than managing the effects. They could not maintain their kingdom with the incessant raids and loss of land. Waiting until Arne accepted the throne may be too late to save their people. Freja knew that. Whether she liked it or not.

Freja sighed. "Okay. We'll see if it's possible. I'm not promising anything until there's a sizable lead to follow."

"Of course!" Not waiting for her to change her mind again, Brenna charged back to the table for Einar.

"Never gonna happen," he said with a laugh, his back to them. "Give it up, wonder duo, and go home."

"You were listening."

"Obviously." He swiveled in his seat and leaned back on his elbows. "I'm blind, not deaf."

"I bet you hear a lot of conversations," Brenna said casually, crossing her arms. "I mean, this is the best locale to hear rumors and gossip."

His head tilted cautiously, as if scenting the wind for danger and said slowly. "Sure. People forget you when you don't match up with their ideal."

Oh, there was so much to unpack there. Something resonating within her. Later. "Even the fae?"

"The worst gossips." Einar rolled his shoulders, leaning back against the table. "Never trust them with a secret. As soon as you whisper it to one, it's being told to another."

"Sound advice." She looked over at Freja, who quirked an eyebrow at her, a silent gesture to hurry things along. "And being so immersed in magic, they must have theories, poems, songs even, of how to defeat the darkness."

"Ah, ah, ah." He waggled a finger at them. "I am not getting involved. No matter what I may or may not have heard."

Brenna smirked at his confession and leaned forward. "So you have heard of something. Do you not have a commitment to the greater good? Do you not have a responsibility to help those in need?"

He scowled at her and stood straight, matching her in height. It was a strange thing to stare at a boy whose eyes never met hers, clouded and unfocused. Had he been born blind? "Look, Double Take, I'm out for my own interests. I help when I can and get by. I leave the dangers of 'hero'ing to lesser men."

There would be no appealing to his sense of justice and decency for he had none. She should have known trying that track was a dead end. She frowned for a moment. He was the closest lead they had and if she didn't get something from him, Freja would drag her home. She wasn't going home just yet.

"Then in payment of the debt you owe."

"What debt?"

Brenna put her hands on her hips and kept her voice as level. "You took a life from me. I demand restitution."

He stilled, mimicking marble. "That's only for death of family."

"She may not have birthed me but she was my mother." The words burned coming out but Brenna didn't let the pain show. "And as such, I call on the life debt you owe me."

"One could argue that I fulfilled any debt in restoring your twin," he said, holding his hands out in a 'what can you do' manner.

Her shoulders slumped. That could be a convincing argument and would be enough to allow him to wriggle out of helping. Demanding his help to rectify the goods he stole wouldn't work either. He could easily claim his right to the supplies as he bested them in combat, even if he did cheat with his magic and a troll.

"She was my mother as well," came a soft reply. Brenna looked at her sister, who smiled with pain and resignation. Freja pushed back her hood now that she was fur free, revealing fine lines of stress around her eyes and red hair braided in a rightful crown around her head.

Einar tensed, opening his mouth to speak but Freja beat him to it, channeling all the lessons of ruling and diplomacy in her manner and bearing. "You cannot claim helping me to satisfy both our loss. You owe me your life, magic user."

A spark in the air charged at her words, like that moment when speaking with Googin, a promise of magic, an oath declared, a contract binding. His face folded into a scrunch as he felt the magic settle around him. His troll friend laughed again.

"Ugh, fine, what do you want?"

Freja offered a pretty smile that proved disarming and mischievous. "Service. You will join us in seeking out a cure for this darkness."

"Yippee," he said, deadpan.

Brenna flipped her hair off her shoulder and grinned. "Now, what do you know?"

Einar pushed off the table and sighed. "Some fae would claim that the darkness can only be broken by 'the heart being restored'. Bunch of fanciful nonsense. It's a lost cause trying."

It would be nonsense, for those unaware of what lay in the deepest parts of each kingdom. Brenna looked at Freja, who nodded gravely.

VI

Ber er hver að baki nema sér bróður eigi

Bare is the back of a brotherless man

As heirs to Ayworn, Brenna and Freja knew their lives were not their own. One day, Freja would be bartered off as a bargain piece for peace and Brenna would be relegated to shadow work for the crown. Their childhood was filled with lessons and training to this effect. Lessons on history, on the pitfalls of a crumbling kingdom, on the secrets lurking in the shadows, on how to attract attention and how to slip away. One such secret belonged to a mangled piece of stone that emanated a deep ache of pain and heartache, an insignificant looking pebble that the king called a heart piece and held in high regard.

If Ayworn had a heart piece, it would make sense that the others would have something as well. It would just be a matter of collecting them. Brenna glanced at Freja and knew she was thinking the same thing.

"You two are being weird." Einar tilted his head and she wondered just how he knew. they were looking at each other. Maybe he wasn't as blind as he claimed. Perhaps it was a gimmick to get others to underestimate him.

Brenna sighed and checked her sister for permission. "A precious stone was given to our family for safe keeping, called a hear piece. It makes sense that the other royal families would have one as well."

"I guess, yeah," he nodded. "Five kingdoms, five pieces. The fae like odd numbers, makes things lucky."

"But Faldinn has been lost," Freja pointed out, yanking back any hope for their venture. "Even if it were possible to venture into that land, we'd have no way to find it."

A manic grin that offered no comfort spread on Einar's face. He snapped his fingers. "Well, good news for you, I got just the man you need."

His grin and tone made her immediately tense. He may owe them a life debt that kept him in check, but she wasn't about to trust him with anything of value. "Who?"

"A royal such as yourself," he said, the grin not dropping. "You said the royals had these pieces, right? And Faldinn was lost but one lonely royal scuttled out at the last minute. He should be at the Middle Court tavern. He is most days."

"You say that like we know the place."

"It's location is in the name. It's at the middle of the island." Einar waved her off, turning back to his table as if they were done with their business. Freja stepped around him and settled her hand on the table to keep him from joining his crew.

"As simple as that seems, I'm grateful we have a guide who knows these parts to keep us from getting lost."

He pursed his lips and tapped his leg. "Are you sure you don't belong to the fae?"

"We're human," Brenna said with a roll of her eyes. Why was that even a question? Obviously they had no magic running through their veins. "And as far as we know, we are not 'marked by the fae' although I'm still not convinced the queen didn't bargain with a hag."

"Bri, let it go."

"No, no, I'm on the edge of my seat here." He leaned his chin on his hand. "I'm all ears. Did she haggle with the hag? And what was she wanting so desperately?"

"You were going to show us to this tavern." Unwilling to wait for Brenna to get the hint, Freja turned her towards the door and grabbed Einar's coat to drag him along. "I'd like to get home before old age hits so talk and walk."

Brenna grinned at Freja. She didn't often lose her patience but when she did Brenna remembered that they were more alike than different. It also reminded her that Freja was not a clone of her mother, perfect and shining and serene. So maybe she pushed those buttons to get her out of that mood, but hey, that was a sibling right?

Ready to launch into the woeful tale that was her birth, she led the way out of the noisy tavern and into the slightly less cacophonous street. The goblin greeters sneered at her outstretched hand and procured her weapons. She looked them over and nodded. "We're good, let's get Hrolf."

"They just gave them back to you?" Einar demanded, following behind.

"Freja got a promise out of them." Brenna pulled out Hilde's knives first. Freja slung the bow over her shoulders as he looked on, mouth agape. "What?"

"The fae king would drool to meet you."

"No thanks," Brenna said as she tucked the last of her daggers out of sight.

Hrolf waited patiently at the post, chewing on the cloth of some unlucky thief that ventured too close. Brenna patted his nose affectionately. "Did you have fun, Hrolf?"

Hrolf huffed and dropped the chewed up fabric, tugging on the ropes still tied down. She rolled her eyes at him and checked the bags to ensure nothing was taken.

"You named your horse 'wolf' and dressed him as a goat," he said, flatly, unimpressed by the hilarity of that statement. So much for enjoying a good joke. Said horse whinnied and glared at the newcomer, determining friend or foe.

She pet his neck in consolation. "He likes being a walking contradiction. Insult him and he'll chew your hair in spite."

Einar took a step back as Freja untied him. "Ignore her. He'll leave you alone as long as you don't try taking the horns off. He gets his personality from his owner."

Rolling her eyes, Brenna took the reins. "Lead the way."

"You really want the blind man to lead you anywhere?"

"Apparently you can see better than you let on." She raised an eyebrow. "Unless you'd rather give directions from the saddle. We'll make sure you don't get trampled on out here."

"Such a tempting offer, but no." He dusted off his tunic and tied a rag over his eyes. "Alright Double Vision, keep up then. I may be in your service but that just means I'm your problem now."

And he took off, staying just out of arm's reach of them. With a look, Freja climbed in the saddle while Brenna led the reins. While she would have preferred the saddle, Hrolf did not let anyone lead him but her. Well, and Hilde. That was just out of self-preservation. No one disobeyed Hilde.

Working their way to the middle of the island was slow work, despite Einar's warnings. Some roads crowded so bad that bodies pressed against her and jostled her forward without consent. Pickpockets attempted to take advantage but received a sharp prick for their troubles. When the crowds eased, people still spilled from buildings and alleys.

But then they passed some invisible barrier and that all fell away. It was as if they stepped in another dimension where silence reigned and demanded stillness. The cobblestone gleamed as if untouched and the buildings, leaning and twisting in creative ways that made no sense, had breathing room between them. The people they now saw had pointed teeth and pointed ears and dark secrets glittering in colorful eyes.

"Einar," she hissed, unwilling to speak much above a whisper lest she attract attention from the strangers around them. He kept walking but turned his head back in acknowledgement. "What happened? What is this?"

He stopped to let them catch up. "It's the Middle Court. What?"

"It's empty."

That wasn't entirely true. Fae and a few scarce humans still milled on the streets, but compared to the tightly packed streets of before, it may as well have been deserted. Einar shrugged. "The fae king only allows certain visitors in his court. Congratulations, you passed."

Freja scowled at him. "Are you saying if we hadn't, you would have left us behind?"

He put a hand on his heart as if offended. "I would have never considered such a thing. It never crossed my mind that you wouldn't be accepted."

"Uh-huh," she said, utterly unconvinced. Brenna just shrugged, nothing for it now. "Where's this tavern?"

Freja dismounted now that they had room to walk as Einar continued on. Gleaming eyes watched in silent judgment as they followed. Hrolf's hooves clattered and echoed in the empty spaces.

Einar disappeared in a large black building hewn from stone rather than wood. Opaque windows dotted the surface and strange runes decorated the threshold. There were no goblin keepers and no stalls for horses. Brenna was even more reluctant to leave Hrolf, but there was nothing for it. She couldn't bring him inside and she wasn't leaving Freja alone. Silently she tied him to a post and patted his side. He would be fine. He had to be.

Taking Freja's hand for solidarity and comfort, she stepped in with her.

The dark theme continued inside, but the large windows allowed enough light that Brenna was impressed rather than oppressed. The walls were the same black stone of outside but a closer look showed specks of diamond and ruby and sapphire catching the light. A polished, light wood stretched out on the floor, decorated with tables and chairs of the same construction. Mage lights dotted the walls and floated in the air, shifting colors with no pattern or reason.

Conversation created a soft hum in the air and scents of exotic wine and foods tempted the nose. Most tables had at least one patron at them with enough space for privacy; a sharp contrast from where they just left.

Something about the space was familiar and not at the same time and it settled on her like an itch she couldn't scratch. She shifted from one foot to another.

"Welcome to Middle Court," Einar said with a grin, his voice quiet in respect to the space. He leaned against the bar as he waited for them to adjust.

Brenna took a deep breath and focused. They were here for a reason. "Where's this guy you said could help?"

"Who are you looking for?"

They turned towards the bartender and she could hear Freja's breath catch. For good reason as the man who asked the question was, without a doubt, the most handsome man Brenna had ever seen. The trouble was, she couldn't quite pinpoint why. Perhaps it was his dark hair, perfectly tousled, covering pointed ears and looking soft and inviting to the touch. Or maybe it was those dark eyes that were warm and enticing and secretive. Long, tapered fingers wiped down a counter, pale even against the light wood.

Staring at him stole her breath and words away, leaving her feeling as if she were staring down a cliffside with the undeniable urge to jump.

"We're looking for Tapio," Einar said, unaffected or used to this man. "Is he here today?"

"In the corner as usual." The bartender nodded in the right direction, still studying them. "I'm afraid we haven't been introduced."

"I'm Freja," her sister said, only slightly breathless. "And my sister, Tatterhood."

"Geez, your parents didn't give you much of a chance, huh?" Einar mumbled.

Brenna glared at him, grateful Freja didn't give out her name. Only her parents used her full name casually and she hated it, like it was a curse. Tatterhood settled much better on her shoulders.

"A pleasure to meet you both," the barkeep said. His gaze settled on Brenna for a moment and she could swear she could feel him staring at the mark on her cheek, even as it was covered in the shadow of her hood. But he said nothing as he moved on to Freja and gave a secretive smile. "Welcome to the Isle."

Unwilling to linger in this man's presence longer than necessary, Brenna tugged her sister's hand, pulling her towards the corner he indicated. Einar looked faintly disappointed as they walked away. But his face smoothed out to what was becoming his trademark smirk as he said, "Let's get this show started."

Brenna narrowed her eyes but wound over to the table where a lone man sat with a dozen empty glasses. He was her age and she remembered faintly from history lessons of her youth that the Faldinn royal family had several sons. If she remembered correctly, the oldest had been born six years before her. Had they ever traveled to Ayworn for diplomatic missions? Arne had traveled to their neighbors once before it had been deemed unsafe. She really should have asked Freja what she remembered before they entered this tavern.

Too late now as they approached. The young man had dark hair in small braids and dark skin and scruff on his chin. He had broad shoulders and thick fingers. A gold signet ring gleamed from his right hand with the Faldinn crest; a bear paw holding a black diamond. Other than that, he wore ill-fitted, plain garb. He did not look up at their approach.

"Heyo bear-man," Einar twisted a chair and sat opposite him. "Want another drink? You'll need one after these two start chattering."

What an introduction. She looked to Freja for damage control. Freja sighed and stepped forward. "Good evening. My name's Freja. This is my sister, Tatterhood. Do you mind if we sit with you?"

Tapio's head rose slowly, black eyes lined red. He looked at them each in turn and leaned back. With a voice of gravel and mountains, he said, "Sure."

They sat, and Freja nodded at Brenna to take the lead. That was fair, she supposed. Brenna was the one that instigated all this. She sat up straight and met his eye. "My sister and I are heirs to the Aywornian throne. And we came here originally to fix a magical attack, but seeing the state of our world we see there is no other choice but to act. We're going to reunite the heart pieces entrusted to each kingdom and lift our world out of darkness."

He blinked at her and tapped his glass on the table. The cup filled with a thick honey liquid. Why did he have so many empty glasses on the table if he could refill them at will? Or was there a limit to each glass? She shook her head of those thoughts as he took a sip. "Okay. And?"

"Einar said you were from Faldinn."

"I was."

"From their royal family."

"Also true."

Brenna pursed her lips. Tapio was being purposely obstinate and maybe they'd be better off trying their luck in the fallen kingdom themselves. Freja tapped her leg under the table, a call for peace. "Then you must know where the heart piece lies and can help us navigate the darkness to restore your home."

Tapio hummed and took a longer pull from the glass, setting it down with a slight tremor, but his voice was clear as he said, "No."

"What?"

Einar chortled beside her, doubling over as he tried to keep the noise down. Tapio's expression didn't change as he huffed. "I don't think I can make it any plainer."

"Welp, we tried." Einar clapped his hands together. "Good effort all, but I'll be going back to my previously scheduled debauchery now."

"Don't even think it." Freja put a hand on his shoulder and forced him to sit.

"Why not?" Brenna asked Tapio, baffled. "You of all people should know the cost of doing nothing. You lost everything."

"I also know exactly what you're facing." His voice gained an edge at her poor choice of words, but she didn't back down. "I'm not going back to the darkness."

"You have a duty," Brenna hissed, hands clenching as she leaned forward. "To your people. To your homeland."

"My people are dead and my home consumed. And thank you very much for being so sensitive to that." Tapio disappeared behind his glass and she reached forward and knocked it away, glass shattering on the pristine floor.

He glared and she glared back. "I'm trying to keep others from facing the same fate. Would you not spare them that?"

Brenna kept her stance, demanding action, demanding honor. No, she had not been to Faldinn before, but she knew the stories, knew the strength that stemmed from that land. She would make him see sense, make him take up the strength his people were renowned for. She would settle for nothing less.

But before either could act, Signe jumped on the table. Brenna stared at her cat, who had somehow gotten a collar of laurels on whatever adventure she was on. Her fluffy tail flicked and she curled in Tapio's lap, before staring at him with amber eyes. He blinked and sighed. "Yeah, alright."

"What?!" Einar cried.

Tapio shrugged. "She's very convincing."

"Who?" he demanded, gesturing wildly at Brenna. "The cat or Copycat?"

Tapio pulled Signe into his arms, who began to purr. "We'll need supplies and a plan of action. We'll need all five pieces to make it work."

"We'll start with Ayworn," Freja said, ignoring Einar's squawks of protest. "It'll be the easiest to procure."

Brenna scowled. "Or we could leave that last."

Her sister gave her a look that made her slump in her seat and keep her mouth shut. Brenna knew the logic behind it. They would need a small victory to start their journey, rather than tackling the worst first.

Einar stood and huffed. "You plan. I'm going for a walk."

"You're in our service," Freja reminded him.

He waved her off and walked for the door, calling out, "Put that on my headstone, why don't you? I'll be back."

"He's right," Tapio said quietly as Einar disappeared. "It's highly likely one or all of us will die on this venture. The heart was broken for a reason, a reason we don't know, and there are protections in place to prevent it being whole."

"We have to try." Brenna had hope for their success.

But they needed more information. She knew vague history on the heart piece in Ayworn's care, but as she was not in direct line to inherit the throne, her knowledge was limited. Arne may know, but she had a sinking feeling they would have to speak with their parents one way or another.

"Do you know who the heart originally belonged to?" Freja asked. All the stories they knew simply said the heart pieces were given to the kingdoms in time of great peril to ensure peace. No one talked about the time it was whole.

Tapio shook his head. "That knowledge would have been lost when Faldinn fell. Or possibly when the darkness first descended."

"The fae are long lived," Brenna said as she looked around, frowning. "Would there be some who lived in a time before the darkness?"

"None that would be forthcoming."

Brenna sighed. It was a longshot anyway and she had no desire to continue bartering with the fae. They had enough close calls anyway. "Let's get Einar and set sail. We'll have several days to plan the next step before we reach Ayworn Castle."

Signe jumped out of Tapio's arms and trotted out the tavern as if she owned the place. Tapio reached behind him and Brenna only had a moment to wonder if he planned on attacking before he brought out a staff of rough hewn redwood. Her eyes widened as he used it to stand and walk, his left leg unmoving and unsupportive.

He raised an eyebrow at her staring. "No one escapes the darkness unscathed. Something to keep in mind as we head into this quest of yours."

But fear only made her stronger, only made her want to fight back all the more. She kept her back straight and her head high. "It's not just my quest. I'll sacrifice what I must to protect my people."

Brenna walked out with more courage than she felt, trying not to think about how the thud of his staff sounded like the mourner's drum.

VII

Línur bartskerí gjörír fúín sár

Mild physician — putrid wounds

"There's no way I'm getting on that sorry excuse for a boat." Brenna stared at the floating piece of debris Einar claimed was his ship. It was long and thin in the old style with what she assumed was an attempt at craftsmanship with a carved helm and aft. No shields adorned the side as custom would dictate, trophies of battles won. An upper deck allowed for a captain's quarters and deep belly provided storage.

Beyond that, half the railing was missing and the wood was stained in different colors that accentuated the splintered and warped places.

Einar shoved past her and clambered up on his death trap. "Fine by me. Swim alongside, for all I care. Maybe a marmennlar will cure me of your presence."

"Bri, let it go," Freja said as she followed Einar aboard.

Brenna sputtered, waving at the obvious and multitude of flaws in the boat. As she gestured, a hanging board from the boat dropped into the water with a *plonk*. "Freja, that thing is a hazard. I'm shocked it's even floating."

"This is the finest Ealish handicraft you'll find on the sea." Einar scowled at her, patting his ship as if she were insulting it rather than telling the truth.

"That explains a lot." She caught her sister's arm. "*Ealish craftsmanship*, Freja. Ealic can't build a sailboat worth its salt."

Einar raised an eyebrow. "And what kind of boat did you get here on?"

Brenna tilted her chin up and crossed her arms. "A respectable, sturdy Aywornian ship. Can this flotsam even make it out of the harbor?"

He snorted. "More like Aywornian dead weight. This baby glides over the waves like silk."

"Freja, we can find a better boat and a better captain."

Freja patted her arm in sympathy, unmoved by her logic. "Einar is fulfilling his life debt and is offering his boat and saving us money. You'll be fine."

"Einar easily gets out of his life debt if we're all dead," Brenna reasoned, once more gesturing to the boat and its many, many cracks and poor build. "Ealish craftsmanship!"

But her sister had clearly been bewitched when Einar cured her. She shrugged and walked to the death trap. "He has more sense than that. Come on."

That left only one to support her position. She whirled on the surviving prince. "Tapio, back me up here."

Her hope fled as Tapio shrugged. "I don't really have a head for sails. And I trust Einar's self-preservation skills."

"You're all mad," Brenna muttered. Everyone knew how you started a journey dictated its success. They were starting this quest on a boat that was likely to fall apart in the first storm surge. Although, if it sank she would not have to face her parents and all that awaited her in Ayworn. With a resigned huff, she led Hrolf on the boat and to a small stall below deck. She patted his mane as he settled into the rhythm of the ship.

Hrolf nipped at her shoulder, getting cloth instead of skin and she sighed. "I know. Not my first choice either."

Signe yowled at her from her feet and Brenna glared down. "Take it up with Freja. I already tried telling her this was a horrible idea."

With a tail flick, the cat led the way above deck. Brenna planted herself by the railing for quick diving access should the boat rip apart and prayed for a quick journey.

It was not quick.

The boat lurched and rocked at every small wave. Brenna yelled. Einar yelled back. The boat managed to dock on Aywornian soil, but not without hitting the dock. Twice. Brenna resisted the urge to stab anyone as they secured horses for the capital. And to add insult to injury, Einar refused to shorten the journey with his teleporting trick he did during the raid.

"You're just being obstinate and contrary," Brenna growled from the back of Hrolf, knuckles white as she gripped the reins. They were halfway to the capital by now and she wanted to pitch Einar in the nearest ditch.

Brenna could understand his reluctance to help. Einar hadn't volunteered for this quest, having been tricked into it through the life debt. But surely he didn't want to prolong it more than necessary.

"Sorry, can't teleport goats. I don't make the rules." He shrugged from his horse.

"He's not actually a goat." Hrolf protested with a shake of his mane and she patted him consolingly. It wasn't his fault the magic user was being ridiculous.

"Enough," Freja said with a sigh. "Bri, take lead with Tapio."

In other words, get some distance and cool off. They had been sniping at each other since leaving the Isle. With a huff, she snapped her reins. Hrolf trotted forward to be level with the gentle bay Tapio rode.

He looked over at her with a raised brow and offered a sip of his flask. She pursed her lips and took it. The alcohol burned on the way down and made her cough. She didn't feel better.

"He probably can't transport over large distances," he said. Signe rode behind him on the horse and flicked her tail in agreement.

"I saw him do it."

"You saw him leave," he pointed out. She gritted her teeth. "You didn't see where he went. They probably had a camp outside of town and left with their loot as most smugglers do: with everyone else."

That did not improve her mood. Brenna slumped forward, glaring at the space between Hrolf's ears. If they had been a little faster in response, they could have caught them before they launched out to sea. And while she was glad to have found a mission and purpose on the Isle, she could have done away with all the rest.

"How do you know so much about magic?" Brenna grumbled. As far as she knew Faldinn did not have a magical stronghold either.

Tapio shrugged. "You pick up things on the Isle. The main thing to know about magic? There's always a price and always a limit."

"Einar seems to get by just fine."

"Well, yes, that's just because he's male. We pride ourselves in making things look easy, especially when they're not." Tapio grinned and took a swig, but the grin was as bitter as the drink. She hadn't seen him truly smile during the entire trip.

"I'm still not convinced he's fully blind," Brenna muttered, utterly done with her companions. Einar did not act as if he could not see. Even when he wore that stupid blindfold, he walked around confidently and turned to whoever spoke easily.

If she was completely honest with herself, part of her agitation had nothing to do with the company. Being home, surrounded by familiar forests and voices, had put her on edge. They hadn't even gotten to the castle and she could feel the weight of her mother's judgment settling on her shoulders once more.

"So, I know your parents didn't name you Tatterhood, and I'm not calling you those ridiculous names Einar comes up with," Tapio drawled, raising an eyebrow. So far Einar's favorites included 'copycat', 'thing one', and 'first draft' with Freja having, of course, corresponding nicknames.

"Is there a question in that?" Brenna wasn't fond of the nicknames Einar came up with either but it could invariably be worse. She made no qualms about them ever being friends.

"What do I call you?"

She rolled her eyes. "Tatterhood is fine."

"That's not a name." Tapio gave a pointed look and she resisted the urge to chuck something at him. She really needed to get her agitation under control.

It wasn't a name, but it was hers. A reminder that she was more than what her mother believed and better than her father expected. Tatterhood gave her purpose and courage and strength.

She sighed as he continued to watch her, waiting. "My parents named me Brenna but if you ever call me that I will stab you."

"Freja calls you Bri, how about that?"

Pursing her lips, she shifted in the saddle. Hrolf threw his head back to look at her and she patted his neck in reassurance. "Freja is my sister, we have a bond. You, sir, are a passing stranger."

He snorted as he rolled his shoulders, facing forward once more. "That's really not helping my problem of what to call you."

"Just because you don't like the option I provided doesn't mean I'm required to offer you another." The words clipped at the end. She was not doing a very good job at curbing that anger. Einar was definitely going to be stabbed at this rate.

But her anger didn't seem to phase Tapio. Signe jumped his horse to hers, demanding attention. "I suppose I'll have to fall back on court etiquette and refer to you by your title, Princess."

Her nose scrunched. That was not a better option, but his smirk said he wouldn't be changing his mind anytime soon. Any protest would be met with gleeful continuance. So Brenna lifted her chin and threw him a haughty look. "As you like."

It was hard thinking of Tapio in the same way as the courtiers of home. While she did not remember meeting any of the other royal families, she had met plenty of other nobles and ambassadors. He didn't act like them. He was not arrogant or proud or determined to be right in every way.

There was the drinking of course. No courtier she knew would be drinking to excess, to let it be a crutch as much as his staff was. Not in public where others could sniff out weakness like a bloodhound. And while he bore himself regally, grief weighed down on him, providing a contradictory stance of proud and humble. If she studied his face, his hands, she saw the young man not much older than herself, but when she met his eyes, there was an age, an experience, she could only hope to understand.

She shook her head of those thoughts. She wasn't much of a typical noble herself.

"Oh tireless leaders!"

Brenna scowled. She may end up with Tapio's drinking habit if she continued in Einar's presence.

Turning in her saddle, she snapped, "What?"

Freja threw a cautionary glare as Einar grinned. "I just thought we might find a place to rest. Seeing as the sun is rapidly falling."

She pulled Hrolf to a stop and glowered at her companion, mumbling, "You apparently can't see."

The hope of sleeping in an inn and bed dashed, Brenna dismounted and led the group off the road to make camp. Once her and Freja's tent was set up, she entered it with the determination not to interact with anyone else until the sun made its appearance in the east.

Thankfully, for Einar's safety and Brenna's sanity, they passed the night and next day without incident. Freja ran interference when needed and Tapio watched in amusement with a biting remark. They were all glad to see the capital in their sights.

Mostly glad, at least. The castle peeked out over the town, the main tower missing half its bulk in the latest raid. With its crumbling state and haphazard slap-dash nature of the Sticks, Brenna's home looked more like a pile of rocks and sticks a child built and declared their town. She was almost embarrassed to show it to these people who, she supposed, made up a team. There was little grand about it.

In the distance, smoke from a pyre lingered. Hilde. Brenna's hands shook as she looked away. They missed the funeral. They missed the rites. Grief fell on her shoulders as if the Sticks collapsed on her.

Brenna pulled Hrolf up short just as they reached the outer wall that separated the Sticks from the main city, then slid off. She took a deep breath, ignoring how it caught in her throat. Freja looked at her, head tilted in an unspoken question.

"I'm going to see if anyone needs help." Brenna checked her hood. She had kept it up the entire journey, unwilling to bare herself to their companions. "I'll meet you at home."

Freja pursed her lips, but didn't argue. Not that Brenna gave her much of a chance. She turned on her heel and hurried through the leaning alleys of the Sticks, her cloak nipping at her ankles.

Brenna wandered through the alleys of the Sticks. At this

point in the afternoon, people milled about in front of houses and around wells to gossip and trade. Eyes followed her, but no one approached. Conversations dropped to murmurs if she came close, but no one called her name.

No one asked for Tatterhood.

Some days were like that. When she first started going out as Tatterhood, Brenna faced scrutiny and distrust. Hilde rarely walked the streets when she had the cloak, unless she was making a delivery. But Brenna took the cloak as an opportunity to be free of her parents. In the beginning, she strolled through the streets, interfering in petty squabbles and tripping the odd pickpocket.

As her reputation grew, people began calling for her if they needed help, sometimes even seeking her out. Like that little girl whose farm had been destroyed by draug. But there were still days like today, where no one trusted a stranger who refused to show their face to help.

Her feet fell into a familiar route that would wind her through the majority of the city. Whispers followed in her wake, clinging to her like cobwebs. Her name fell from lips like the sighing of the trees, but never loud enough for her to pinpoint. Maybe it was simply the wind whistling through the cracks of the city.

Brenna took a slightly longer route through the city. She did not want to go home. She was not ready for life to return to some semblance of normal or acknowledge the gaping hole left behind by Hilde. She did not want to face her parents, who would tell her to return to the shadows of the throne. They would tell Freja to review marriage candidates, uncaring of how Freja felt about the whole affair. They would tell Arne to take on more duties of the throne, restricting his access to the one woman who made him laugh freely.

Sighing, Brenna stopped at a well and pulled her hood back. Tangled red hair came loose as she pulled water up and splashed her face.

"Tatterhood?"

Tapio's quiet voice made her jump out of her skin as she whirled around to face him. He was leaning on his cane, a bit out of breath. How had he snuck up on her so quietly? "Have you been following me?"

"Freja seemed concerned about draugs of all things. Figured better me than Einar." He raised an eyebrow in challenge. Fair point. If Einar had snuck up on her, she might have thrown a knife.

Brenna huffed, spilling more water on her to remove the grubby travel dirt. "She needs to let that go. It was one time."

"Wait. Hold up. You actually fought a draug?" Tapio walked over, resting his cane on the well so he could grab some water of his own to drink. Her eyes drifted to his lame leg. She could just see a patch of skin around his ankle, black like tar, several shades darker than his natural skin tone.

Now that the terrifying reality of fighting a draug was a week distant, the giddiness of not only surviving but coming out triumphant wrapped around her like a well-loved cloak. She fought a draug alone. She fought a draug and survived. She fought a draug and won. "Two, actually."

"Wait, is that blood?" He gestured to her face, alarmed, shifting forward as if to reach for her.

Brenna pursed her lips, knowing exactly what he was staring at and knowing there was nothing for it. She had kept her hood up and face shadowed on their trip here, keeping the illusion that she looked just like her sister, but he would have found out eventually. "It's not blood. It's a…birth mark I suppose I should call it."

Curse mark would be a better fit. She didn't look up to see his reaction, didn't study the silence that followed.

"Okay." That made her react. That was it? Tapio shrugged at her incredulous look. "You ready to head to the castle?"

With a sigh, she flicked up her hood, letting the comfortable weight settle over her hair.

"Is this a common pastime for you?" He walked beside her. "Draug fighter, princess. Now on a quest to save the world."

"Someone has to help." It always boiled down to that. Someone had to help. Her mother had no other use for Brenna except to hide, so who better than her? If Brenna had to sit in the muck, wash off the blood, work out her own bruises, well, better her than another.

A sound that may have been a laugh huffed out of Tapio. "You don't do anything by halves, do you?"

"You're on the same quest," she reminded him as they neared the castle. He peered up at the stone walls with a twisting grimace.

"So it would seem." He stopped and rolled his shoulders. "Well, one princess delivered safely and not a draug in sight. I'll take my leave of you."

Brenna waved him off and wound through the familiar halls of her home. She stopped abruptly as sounds and smells of the kitchen wafted over her. Hilde. She scrambled back and passed through the outer corridors towards her room. Clanging steel and thunking wood as soldiers tested their skills never felt more a comfort. Brenna paused by a window to watch the soldiers work out their paces with each other.

Had the conscripted child been sent to the borders already? Would he share the same fate as the runaway, bleeding out and dying of infection? Brenna wasn't going to linger any longer than necessary in the castle which meant Tatterhood wouldn't be there to help. If he tried running and got hurt, she wouldn't be here to ensure he got healing.

Or she could sneak him out now.

"Don't even think about it."

She startled at the voice, looking up at Arne. Had it only been a few days since she last saw him? It felt like an age. She resisted the urge to hug him and never let go. Instead, she pulled her hood down and said, "You have no idea what I'm thinking."

"I don't have to," he said, stepping up to her and studying her closely as if memorizing every detail. He wrapped an arm around her. If it was tighter than normal, a thread of desperation in them both, well, neither of them mentioned it. "It's just best to head off most of your ideas when you have that face."

"I don't have a face."

"You do."

"I don't!"

Arne raised an eyebrow. "Are you telling me you weren't thinking of something dangerous and possibly illegal?"

Sometimes Brenna wondered why she was so fond of her siblings. They knew her far too well. Or maybe she was just that easy to read. Still, he didn't have to be so obnoxious about it, pointing out her flaws like that.

Arne tugged her away from the training session and said casually, "The boy isn't here."

"What boy?"

"The one that was conscripted. He just turned eleven and he's back home." Brenna stared at him as if he had grown another head and he chuckled. "I called in a favor from his commander."

"You went against our parents and got a kid out of the ranks?" she asked, bewildered. "You did? I mean, Freja may be convinced to cause a stink, but really, you?"

"Your confidence is uplifting. Yes, I did." He shook his head with a smile, leading her towards their rooms. "Frontal attacks aren't the only option, you know."

Brenna rolled her eyes. How often had she heard that? From Arne, from Freja, from Hilde. The barracks instructors always told her that she needed to be more defensive, less offensive. She was too quick to take the first opening she saw at risk of her own safety. Thing is, it's worked for her so far.

"It's an option sometimes," she said, crossing her arms.

"There's a reason we send patrols out in groups," Arne chided, then took a deep breath. "Freja said you were plotting a mad scheme."

Brenna opened her mouth to defend her plan but then frowned. "It's only slightly mad. And if it works…"

If it works there wouldn't be such a need for Tatterhood, children wouldn't be sent off as fodder for the darkness, there wouldn't be the ever growing dread of being consumed by something no one had seen. If it worked, trade would be open and land would be reclaimed. The tiny fractured kingdoms would be whole once more.

But she couldn't encompass all that in words. Thankfully, she didn't need to. Arne stopped at her door and faced her, solemn as a vow. "What do you need from me?"

"An audience with the king and queen?" Brenna asked, peeking at him. "And maybe a rune of blessing. I have a feeling they aren't going to listen."

"I can help with the first. I'll see what I can do about the second." With one last teasing shove, he left her to brood while he rounded up their parents. She slipped inside her room and leaned against the door to close it, shutting her eyes for just a moment.

VIII

Inga träd växer till himmelen

No trees grow to the sky

"**W**hy are you soaking wet?"

Brenna opened one eye as she leaned against the closed door. Freja shed her traveling cloak, back to the pristine image their mother demanded, and had her hands on her hips as she stared. Brenna rolled her eyes. "I'm not soaking."

That didn't seem to comfort Freja as Brenna expected. "You can't speak to our parents looking like you were dragged through the sea."

"I'm going to change. Give me a minute." Brenna closed her eyes for a moment, relishing in the quiet tranquility of their room. Then tensed as Brenna realized why it was so quiet. "You've left Einar free reign of the castle?!"

Freja waved off her very justified concern. "I had Captain Harald be his escort. I don't think it'll be necessary. I introduced him to Runar and they were in the middle of discussing magical contracts or something."

Brenna scowled. She would rather have him wait in the dungeon while they sorted all this out, but she supposed that wasn't the most hospitable of her. As long as no one ended up with a cow's head, she wouldn't fuss. Too much. "I saw Arne on the way."

Freja hummed, pushing Brenna into a chair and pulling out a brush. She began to drag the brush through Brenna's hair. "I told him it was your venture so you had to explain it all."

"Coward."

Freja sniffed and gave a haughty look. "Diplomat."

"Same thing." Once Freja released her, satisfied Brenna's hair was at least knot free, Brenna walked to her closet. She sighed in relief as she stepped into another traveling dress of sturdy, clean cloth. It wasn't fit for a princess or for an audience with the king and queen, but she didn't plan on staying long enough to change again. Best to be prepared for a quick getaway. "Arne said he would gather mother and father so we can make our plea."

"Did you tell him the plan?"

"He didn't ask." He didn't usually ask. Arne was a firm believer in knowledge arriving in its time and not a moment sooner. Survivors didn't ask questions, they simply made due. "He's not going to like us leaving again."

Closed borders and limited sea travel meant the royal family had no need to travel beyond the capital. Occasionally, their father would go out to the borders, taking Arne with him as he got older, but as the danger grew, the trips lessened. With this quest, Brenna had no idea how long it would be before they were all together again. The thought made her skin itch. Even these few days had left her aching for family in ways she hadn't expected.

"If Einar was a bit more trustworthy, I'd leave it to him to handle." Freja hustled her back into the chair and braided a section of Brenna's hair, letting it fall down her shoulder instead of pinning it up. "Or Tapio if he were willing."

"It was my idea. I'll see it through." As much as she hated being away from Arne and home, she needed to do this.

"You won't be alone for it." Freja finished one more braid, then pulled her towards the door. "Let's get the first heart piece."

Such a simple statement, a simple task, as if they were asking for an extra sweet at dinner. There was no doubt in Brenna's mind that their mother would take advantage of her asking for something. As a rule, she did her best to never ask her parents for anything, to never give them leverage against her. If she knew where the heart piece was kept, she'd steal it instead.

All too soon they were back in a small room meant for private discussions and deals. Or reprimands, in Brenna's case. Their parents sat united in matching regal chairs made of oak and inscribed with runes of honor, pride, and etchings of eagles. Arne stood to the side, shooting her an encouraging smile as they entered. Her returning smile was only slightly queasy.

"Freja, my darling," their mother held out her arms in welcome, angled just enough to exclude Brenna from the gesture. "What a joy to see you restored to us."

Freja smiled and gave a curtsy of respect. With grinding teeth, Brenna followed suit. There was no point in poking the hawk before they asked. "Thank you mother. I'm glad to be back to normal. I'm grateful Brenna was able to take care of me."

The king's eyes flicked over to Brenna, a barely there glance, the only greeting she received from her father as he smiled as Freja. The queen pursed her lips, staring at the undressed and uncivilized manner Brenna presented herself in. Honestly, she would have preferred if Freja hadn't even mentioned her.

"We will have to take care to ensure it does not happen again." The queen smiled cruelly as if she signed an execution. "You will have to accompany us anytime there is an attack. Only then can we be assured of your safety."

Say nothing of her other two children. Freja must be adored, protected, cultivated. With their attention focused on her sister, Brenna shared a commiserating look with Arne. He offered a resigned shrug in response.

"Actually, that was why we requested your presence." Freja turned to Brenna expectantly. "Brenna has a plan to ensure raids and losses at the border are nearly eliminated."

Brenna stepped forward, falling into the stance the soldiers drilled into her for the past year; legs wide, shoulders straight, head high. She had no scabbard to rest her hands on so she clasped them behind her back.

Her mother's eyes narrowed, annoyed at having to address her least favorite child. Her father raised a bored brow and asked, "And what is this plan?"

"While on the Lost Isle searching for a cure, we came across a fae legend." Brenna picked a spot just above their heads as she spoke. While she would have preferred to face Arne while talking, she knew how to improvise. Her eyes fixed on the rune of honor and protection etched just above her father's head and traced it over and over as a silent prayer. "There is a rumor of a way to defeat the darkness. If all five heart pieces from each kingdom are united, our lands and people will also be united. We would no longer have to fear black walls that produce unspeakable monsters."

Brenna let the words settle in the air. Arne sucked in air a little too sharply but said nothing. When no one spoke, she continued, "I believe it is in our kingdom's best interest to see this done and humbly request Ayworn's heart piece for safekeeping."

"Child—"

Her mother cut off as her father stood. The king pressed his hands behind his back, the soldier's pose to match hers, to remind her of her place, his gaze calculating and measured. "I have heard whispers of such things, but you are unprepared and untested."

"There is no other more dedicated to our people than I," Brenna argued. "And Faldinn has already been consumed. We have no time to wait."

"Each piece will require sacrifice."

Brenna shook her head before he completed his warning, unwilling to back down. "Have you not taught each of us that being a royal means sacrifice? I am not afraid of what it may cost."

Brenna met his gaze, unflinching. But instead of speaking, of granting her request, he turned to the queen. The look they shared spoke of a thousand conversations and held the weight of her sentence. She dared not breathe lest she tip the scales out of her favor.

Her father tipped his head and her mother now stood. Her eyes were not cold and icy as she expected but gleaming with satisfaction. Brenna nearly took a step back in response as fear curled in her gut. "You may take the heart piece to restore it with the others, but you will pay a price."

"What price?"

"Banishment." Her mother did not smile, her lips not so much as twitching upward, but warmth infused her tone, betraying her joy at the decree. "Take the heart and you will not step foot in Ayworn again."

"What?" The word came out in a near whisper. Brenna felt as if the draug knocked her back, breathless and dazed, but with a desperate need to get back up and fight. If only she could remember how.

"High price for a high request."

As if her mother hadn't jumped at the chance to get rid of her. She finally found a convenient excuse for something she dreamed of since Brenna's birth, a chance to rid herself of the disfigured daughter she never wanted. Brenna couldn't breathe, couldn't feel her hands. Cold despair settled on her shoulders like her beloved cloak.

"Mother, no!" Freja's voice cracked. Oh. Beautiful, perfect, tactful Freja actually spoke out against their parents. Brenna must be in a vivid fever dream.

"I must protest as well." And Arne. Their adamant defense broke the cold that settled over Brenna. "Surely another price can be asked instead of banishing a member of the royal family."

"The price is set."

Her fingers trembled behind her back. The king watched, impassive, immobile as a statue of the old kings, uncaring, unmoved at his children's anguish. Brenna licked her lips. When had they gotten so dry? "You must swear to provide the true heart piece."

Her siblings stared aghast at Brenna, appalled that she would even consider it, but she stared at the queen, a woman she would never grace with the title mother ever again. The queen raised a perfectly sculpted brow in challenge. "I swear."

The king nodded, adding his own declaration, not interfering any further into the negotiations. He would follow his queen's lead.

"In addition, you will allow Arne to marry whomever he wishes, royal or thrall."

The queen pursed her lips. "You are hardly in a position to haggle this. I have set the price, either accept or refuse."

But Brenna breathed fire and grit, and she met the queen's disregard with passion and ire. "I accept it on my terms. You can be rid of me as you've always wished or I can be a bigger nuisance than the darkness. I think you would be surprised how much I have been holding back."

If Brenna was going to be forced from her home, she had conditions. If she wouldn't be here to see things set right, she would put it in motion now. And her siblings came first. Just as she faced off the draug, Brenna did not back down from the queen, did not turn away. She set her shoulders and kept her knees bent and waited for the next strike.

"Arne may have his choice in bride," The queen acquiesced, turning as Brenna waited for the world to settle. She pulled back a tapestry behind the thrones, revealing their family crest etched in the stone. She blocked her movements until the stone gave way to her touch and revealed a small wooden box.

The red wood gleamed under the mage lights as the queen set it on the desk. She looked up at Brenna with obstinate determination. "You leave the castle within the hour."

Freja stepped forward, distraught, towards the king, as if he would stop this madness if she begged enough. "Father, you can't—"

"Deal." Brenna took the box and twisted on her heel to the door. She had no further goodbyes to offer the people who claimed to raise her. The only parent that mattered to her died. Freja and Arne's protests to the king and queen faded as she walked down the hall.

Her feet stumbled as she stopped in her room, the browns and blues and grays surrounding her like a forest at twilight. She collapsed on her bed, hands still shaking, breath shuddering in her lungs. With a deep breath, she opened the box in her hands. A wave of melancholy washed over her as she stared at the small, jagged rock that let off a soft light, the color shifting from red to orange to purple. It tumbled in the box at the movement, glittering like a broken jewel.

"Bri."

Arne stood at the door, weighed down by dismay and heartbreak for all that he stood tall and regal.

Brenna closed the box, shutting out the strange power that came from such an insignificant stone. Her voice came out in a harsh whisper. "I don't regret it. And I'm not changing my mind."

"No, of course not." He stepped inside and sat on her bed next to her. "It's not right."

"When has it ever been right?" For all that Arne was the adopted one, Brenna was the one they wished to be rid of. The king and queen hardly held back their disdain or disappointment. She stood and pulled a bag from her closet, then stopped. What did she want to bring? What could she not live without? Her eyes flicked to her brother. No, he wouldn't fit.

"You'll stay in touch." He said quietly, demanding, a hint of the king he would be. Her heart ached that she would miss it. "And when you save the world, we will meet at the newly restored border and you will tell me everything."

Her lips trembled and Brenna tried to smile. "Of course."

Arne stood abruptly and pulled her in a tight hug. "I love you, Bri. This isn't goodbye."

"Of course not," she said, choking on the words, sniffing as she pulled back. "And if you don't go down to the Sticks and propose to Idunn today, I'll figure out a way to smack you. We're traveling with a magic user, don't make me use him."

Freja entered at her declaration, storms swirling in her eyes like Brenna had never seen. She met her gaze and the turmoil stilled for a moment. "I'm having Einar escorted to the stables. The horses should be ready for us."

"Mother—" Brenna stopped herself, pursed her lips and asked, "The king and queen are allowing you to come?"

"As if they could stop me." She raised a brow, looking at Brenna, then Arne, daring them to object. Best to move quickly before the guards caught on to Freja's escape then.

Arne rolled his eyes and reached out, pulling Freja into a hug with the three of them. Brenna did her best not to think about it being the final time, relishing in the moment, memorizing how Arne's hugs felt like sunshine and hope and perseverance.

"Right." Arne cleared his throat and pulled back again, shoving his hand in his pocket and pulling out a worn rune stone. "It was my brother's. I think you two will need it more."

A rune for luck. Brenna took it and traced her thumb over the black etching.

"What? Are we doing something reckless and impossible?" Brenna asked, lightening the air between them.

Arne shook his head. "When are you not? I feel sorry Freja's drawn the short straw keeping you out of trouble."

"At least I've had practice," Freja said. Silence settled over them, heavy with so many unsaid things before she shook her head. "What else do you need to pack?"

Brenna had clothes, had her favored weapons, had her sister at her side. She put the stone in the bottom of the pack and looked around for anything else of meaning. Signe had wandered in at some point and jumped up on the vanity, sitting on a plain wooden box she didn't recognize. She frowned as Signe *mrrp*-ed.

"What's this?"

Arne shifted, grief once more overtaking him before he cleared his throat. "A few of Hilde's things. She left things for each of us."

The lump in her throat returned with vengeance as she shooed the cat off and stuffed the box in her bag without looking through it. Later. Today was enough of a battering ram as it was. "I think this is it then. Unless we want to raid the treasury before we go."

"We're not raiding the treasury." Freja had no sense of fun.

"I would just be collecting my due," Brenna reasoned. "A sort of early withdrawal on an inheritance I'll never receive."

Freja did not find that logic sound. "I want to get out of the castle without armed guard. And you may not have to deal with the consequences, but I do."

"You don't need to raid the treasury," Her own brother, the traitor, said. He held up a large, heavy pouch with a smirk. "This should be enough for your journey and then some."

Brenna snatched it with glee. "You're my favorite brother."

"I know." Arne pulled her into another swift hug. "Now get going. I have a girl to propose to."

With a wink, Arne disappeared. He didn't say goodbye, because that would be admitting something final. No. This was merely another parting of another day. And Brenna swore right then on all the old gods that she would see her brother again, somehow and someway. This wasn't goodbye. This wasn't the end. They were family and nothing would ever change that.

Signe gave another *mrrp* and turned for the door, beckoning them forward with a swish of her tail. Well, it was time to go.

Einar stood in the stables, arms crossed and shoulders at his ears, surrounded by attentive and exasperated guards. The captain of the guard gave a nod and left quickly at their arrival, either to be rid of his charge or because word already spread about Brenna's banishment. Brenna sighed and went to Hrolf.

"Did you get the heart piece? Can I be rid of you yet?"

"We got it," Freja said, pulling her horse forward. "And you can be rid of us once our journey is over, not a moment sooner."

Brenna patted Hrolf's nose and slipped on his goat horns again. She needed something to smile about. Signe jumped up in the saddle. "Where's Tapio?"

"I thought he was with you."

Brenna frowned. "We parted at the castle doors. I assumed he would find his way or stay near the stables."

Einar's eyes narrowed as if judging her, then shrugged. "He'll have found the nearest drink then."

Brenna should have stayed with him or ensured that he was looked after. Tapio probably had his own demons to haunt him. Did Ayworn look like the home he lost? She ran a hand over her face. "Freja, you and Einar check out the taverns on the west road. I'll take the south. We'll meet at the South Gate."

She took Hrolf's reins and the reins of the bay Tapio rode in on. With a decisive nod, she left the stables and the only place she ever called home. Brenna did not look back.

No one matched his description at the first tavern. The second tavern earned her a shrugged response and drunk mumble from its customers. At the third, many of the patrons knew the man she described as he stood out with his limp and flask companion. One tavern offered a tankard to the man but he had apparently refused and continued on. No one heard or saw him at the following three. Brenna neared the edge of the city when she found him, sitting up on the outer wall, flask held loosely in his right hand.

His eyes were glazed as he looked out over the city. She stopped just under him, unsure. "Tapio?"

"Looks like home." Tapio's words had a slight slur, but he did not sway as she knew some men did when laden with too much ale. With only slight hesitation, she climbed up and joined him on the ledge.

Brenna looked out over the city with an undeniable ache. From this wall, she could see from the castle, the tallest tower hobbled by the raid, to the Sticks, precarious wooden buildings crammed in every available inch. The city sprawled out before her and she knew it intimately. If she wanted, she could point out every corner she helped someone as Tatterhood, could name each street she skinned her knees on as a child. And outside the walls, the trees grew tall and proud, a forest of protection with only dirt roads to cut through.

She leaned back, her hands brushing against something soft. An eagle feather. Her eyes immediately searched the skies for the noble bird with no luck. Her fingers traced the soft edges. Honor. Pride. Dedication. A symbol of a home she no longer belonged to.

"Does the ache go away?" Brenna asked quietly. "Do you ever miss home less?"

She would never miss her parents, but she would miss this place. She would miss Arne. She would miss the memories embedded in the stones themselves.

"No."

Brenna sighed. Probably not the best question to ask. Tapio obviously wasn't moving on. She shifted to move down.

"But you carry it differently," he said. She paused, looking at him. He scanned the streets for something missing. "Some days, it feels like you're barely carrying anything at all, like you're used to the weight. Other days it crashes into you and leaves you breathless."

No need to ask what day Tapio was experiencing now. His fingers tapped the flask and he shook off the heaviness. "Did you get it?"

Brenna nodded. "I have been banished in recompense. When all this is done, maybe you can buy me a drink and teach me how to cope."

"No point in delaying." Tapio held the flask out to her, his gaze serious and understanding. She was not losing her home to the darkness, but the loss was no less painful. Brenna took the flask, the offer to make the pain dull for just a moment. She could feel the burn already.

But she shook her head and handed it back. "Later. We have a world to save."

She pulled a string of leather from her bracer and tied the feather into a braid, a reminder of home, of hope, of courage. Once satisfied, she stood and offered a hand. He was slow to take it, slow to stand, but held her gaze the entire way. He looked at her as if he didn't entirely understand her but he found her no less valuable. Her feet shifted on the wall as a slow smile, small and fragile, lifted his cheeks and lightened his eyes.

"Sounds like a plan. Let's go, Princess."

Warmth unrelated to ale burned through her and lingered long after they left the capital behind.

IX

Man må hyle med de ulve man er i blandt

One must howl with the wolves one is among

The Middle Court Tavern was not Brenna's preferred place to be as they planned their next step. Of course, it was not the worst option, but if she had her way, they wouldn't leave the boat and she wouldn't have to set foot on the Lost Isle ever again. She could, begrudgingly, admit that there was logic in docking and stocking up on resources. They needed a plan, maps, information.

There was also the pesky detail that, while the walls of darkness disappeared from sight on the ocean, they still impacted any who dared cross. No one could venture to the other kingdoms without first traveling to the Isle.

So the Middle Court it was. At least it was not jammed with people and noise. The bartender, an older fae with long pointed ears extending out of black hair and unnatural green eyes and a permanent smirk, waved them to a table as they entered and offered drink unasked. Brenna did not like the faint disappointment Freja showed when the previous bartender did not show. Nor was she impressed with this new bartender's predatory smile. They sat at the table in the far back and she claimed the seat by the wall.

The boys entered, Signe leading them, and Einar dumped scrolls on the table. "Maps for my overlords."

Freja rolled her eyes and grabbed the first scroll. "Your reluctant service is noted and ignored."

"I strive to be an inconvenience," Einar said, dropping in a seat and leaning back so only two legs of the chair rested on the ground.

Brenna pulled a map towards her and unfurled it. But instead of neat lines inked on the parchment, an intricate and rude scene was painted. "What the—"

"Oh? Something wrong?" Einar asked innocently. "Probably shouldn't have sent the blind man to find pictures on parchment."

"That's why Tapio went with you."

"I don't need a babysitter."

"You can't complain about us giving you a task while also complaining of receiving help."

Einar tilted his head and grinned. "I think you'll find that I can."

Brenna growled but Tapio stepped in before she could stab Einar somewhere vital. "They're all maps but some are quite old. I don't know how much use they'll be."

Taking his cue, Freja found a map to her liking and spread it over the table. This map showed the five sister kingdoms surrounding the Lost Isle. It predated the darkness as it showed all five whole and undivided. The edges of the map cracked under her fingers and ink faded to near illegible in some places.

Brenna's heart tightened as she looked at Ayworn unravaged by an unknown evil with towns and places she hadn't known existed. She had forgotten there had been a coastline on the other side of the land, that there were countries that lay beyond the wall of black. They were so cut off from the world.

Shaking her head, she helped spread out maps of the individual kingdoms. They had one for Faldinn, pre-darkness, Nolpa, Ealic, and Denwes. They wouldn't need Ayworn.

Tapio stared at the map of his home with the same distance and heartache Brenna felt looking at Ayworn. He cleared his throat. "These may not help. We moved the capital closer to the sea as the darkness moved."

"We'll have to assume these are out of date anyway. This just gives us an idea." Brenna frowned and grabbed a charcoal stick.

She marked the highest edge of the darkness in Ayworn as a reference point, then used that to make a circle through the kingdoms. They didn't know how the darkness worked, but it was safe to assume the worst and be surprised later. Her fingers faltered at Faldinn, her eyes darting up. Tapio offered a short nod. Pursing her lips, she dragged dark lines of charcoal over Faldinn and the outside of the circle.

"If we save Faldinn as last, that leaves Nolpa, Denwes, and Ealic. Have you been to any of them, Einar?" Freja asked, fingers tracing the three kingdoms.

Einar tensed. "If you're insinuating that I have raided any of those kingdoms, I vehemently deny it."

Brenna rolled her eyes, pulling the appropriate maps closer to her. "Save your defense. We just need to know if you'll be useful in planning the next step."

"Sure, right." He tapped his foot. "Denwes is probably the best next choice. Those people are completely gullible. I mean, uh, kind."

Brenna glared at him for a moment then looked at the other two: Tapio shrugged and Freja sighed. "Yeah, we'll put that as last then."

"Don't ask for my advice if you're not going to take it."

"Freja asked, not me."

"Enough," Freja snapped, glaring at each of them in turn, waiting until they both slumped in their seats before continuing, "This is going to be difficult as it is without constantly badgering each other. If you can't be friendly, at least be civil."

Brenna scowled at her, unwilling to back down. Pursing her lips, she turned to offer a truce to Einar when he sat up straight, eager and excited. "I'm leaving you all for someone of infinite more worth."

"You're still in our debt," Freja reminded him as he stood.

Einar waved a hand dismissively as he left. "As if you'd let me forget it."

Brenna watched as he met with a young girl with straight black hair and slanted eyes by the doors. Her hands gestured wildly as a greeting and he slung an arm around her, leading her to an empty table. As if sensing her gaze, Einar turned his sightless eyes with eerie accuracy to her, then positioned them so his back was to her and he hid the girl.

"At least we might get something done now," Freja said as she turned back to the maps.

"You realize he's probably plotting to betray us."

The look she received told her just how idiotic that statement was. Brenna crossed her arms in defense as Freja spoke, "Bri, the girl looks twelve, what could she possibly be plotting?"

"Maybe he's enlisting her help to get the heart pieces for himself, to sabotage us getting them." Brenna knew plenty of sneaky twelve year olds. It was the best age to do nefarious things. She was twelve when she started raiding the kitchens.

Tapio looked over to the girl in question and shook his head. "That's Delja. She's not the plotting type. And she's not twelve. I think she's fifteen."

"You know her?"

Tapio shrugged. "I basically lived here for the past year, you get to know the regulars."

"Which proves my point," Brenna stressed. "No one that frequents this place could ever be trustworthy."

He raised an eyebrow at the mark against him, and she winced. That wasn't what she meant. Although, could she trust Tapio? He agreed to join them readily enough but what made him linger in this place? Why choose somewhere so dissimilar from his home?

Before she could offer an apology or explanation, Freja nudged her. "Looks like you'll have a chance to find out. Be nice."

Einar slouched as the girl dragged him over, nearly skipping as she did. As they approached, Brenna noticed the slight point to her ears and red irritated skin along her arms and side of her face. She stopped at the table and waved, then nudged Einar.

He scowled. "I am not being selfless with them. I have been forcibly dragged against my will about it."

The girl nudged him again and he gave a dramatic sigh. "This is Delja. Delja, this is Stumpy, Thing One and Thing Two. They all have a horrible affliction of playing hero. I'm afraid it's terminal."

"Or," Freja said with a kind smile. "I'm Freja, this is my sister, Tatterhood, and Tapio. It's nice to meet you, Delja."

The girl's grin somehow got wider and her hands twisted as she signed quickly. When no one spoke, Delja looked to Einar to translate. He crossed his arms. "She says it's a great misfortune to meet you and you should all be ashamed of tarnishing my name."

"No!" she croaked, the word coming out cracked and painful, like clay drying out in the summer heat. She looked between them frantically. "No. Nice to meet. Einar!"

"It's okay," Freja said, as the only diplomat amongst them despite almost all being royals. "We know Einar likes to exaggerate."

"How do you even know what she's signing if you're blind?" Brenna asked, once again confused just how his sight supposedly didn't work.

He offered a lazy smile and spread his hands in a facsimile of surrender. "Magic."

Brenna rolled her eyes and went back to studying the girl, who shifted uncomfortably under her gaze. Delja's hair shifted to hide her face, one hand rubbed her other arm self-consciously. Or was it a tick to show her lying?

Maybe Brenna was being too cynical.

"How do you know Einar?" Brenna asked, unwilling to trust that easily. Even if her presence in this fae-heavy location wasn't suspicious, being friends with Einar was. It's not like he hid his immorality.

Delja glanced at Einar, her hands moving slowly, her eyes narrowed, as if daring him to misinterpret. He scowled and nodded. "She says it's a long story. Although it's not as long as you'd think. She helped me out of a tight space with some of the fae and I did so in return. Now I'm stuck with her."

Unlike most of Einar's snide remarks, this was said without bite and his hands brushed Delja's arm as if in reassurance. How peculiar to see him considerate, soft almost. Delja smiled at her, bright and innocent and kind, and Brenna began to understand. Such pure, unadulterated innocence must be protected from all that is evil in the world.

"Einar said," Delja said, her words were slow, careful, cracking, "you are fighting the darkness?"

Freja nodded. "That's the idea. I'm still not convinced it's possible."

Delja tilted her head, studying the maps and then each one of them in turn. Brenna could see the fae in her when she was quiet and contemplative. Her childlike demeanor grew ageless and her eyes shone like a cat, but then she smiled and returned to looking no older than twelve.

Delja turned to Einar and signed rapidly. His face contorted as he signed back, his fingers slow and clumsy compared to hers. It went on for several minutes before he gave up on hand signs and growled, "No, you are not."

Delja set her lips in a firm line and turned to them, hands on her hips. "I want to join. To help."

"I don't know," Brenna said before anyone else could accept. While it would be amusing to say yes just to rile up Einar, she wasn't sure they needed one more person on this journey. "It'll be dangerous."

Delja's smile dimmed until Tapio took a sip and said, "Odd numbers are safer though."

Einar snarled at him, but Freja asked, "Have you been to any of the five kingdoms?"

"Nolpa," Delja said with a nod. "Grew up on coast."

"That could be really beneficial. And we may need help from a fae," Freja said, looking to Brenna with a smile, ignoring the squawk of protest from Einar.

Brenna gave a dramatic sigh. "Alright, pull up a chair."

It quickly became apparent that Delja's strengths were not planning or preparing or anything related to adventuring. Einar played translator, which resulted in biased interpretation at best and wild accusations and lies at worst. Despite her friendship with a dubiously moraled guy, Delja seemed incapable and unwilling to lie so it was very obvious whenever Einar was not being truthful.

In addition to the difficult communication method, Delja had very little insight into what they should do.

"I don't see what the fuss is about to plan," Einar drawled, leaning back in his chair so only two legs rested on the ground. "We travel to the capital of each kingdom, raid their treasury, and split. We've got supplies, we've got a slightly helpful map, what else do we need?"

Brenna thumped her head on the table. She would not strangle him. She would not strangle him. She would not strangle him.

Freja put a hand on her shoulder and spoke for her, "First, we are not stealing anything, we will request each heart piece as we did in Ayworn. Second, we have no idea what the price will be for each piece. And third, we have no idea the consequences of taking the heart pieces and joining them."

Einar offered an exaggerated yawn in rebuttal. "Sounds like a lot of talking and not a lot of doing. Tell me, will I finish my service before I'm old and gray?"

Freja let out a slow, controlled breath like a hissing cat, the only sign of her frustration. She smiled, brittle and waning. "We have a route mapped, but I'd like to find out more about the lore of the heart pieces. This is the best place for that knowledge."

Delja signed quickly, eyes sparking with sudden interest. Einar huffed. "She says ask the bartender."

Her sidelong glance suggested that was not exactly what she said but the statement was simple enough. Brenna frowned. "Why?"

"This is the hub of fae activity and as a bartender, he will have heard all the stories that filter through."

That was surprisingly sound logic. Brenna shared a look with her sister, who nodded. "Alright, we'll ask. Signe's in charge while we're busy."

The cat in question jumped up on the table at her name and groomed herself. She fixed a glinting stare at Einar, which proved Signe was wiser than most humans. Brenna gave her a scratch in approval before heading over to the bar with Freja.

"They're not the enemy, Bri," Freja said softly as they moved out of hearing from the table.

Brenna sighed. "I know."

Freja raised an eyebrow in silent rebuke. "And until we resolve this ridiculous quest, they are our team. Whether you like it or not, we must have some measure of trust."

"I know," she mumbled again, then pursed her lips. "I'll do better."

The only reason they were on this venture was because of Brenna. She knew that. And if she wasn't going to put in the effort to make this mish mash group work, then they would be doomed before they began. She would do better. The fate of their people, of their home, of their lives, depended on their success.

So she didn't scowl when they approached the bar, but kept her face arranged in a neutral expression and allowed Freja to take the lead. Freja was, after all, better suited for delicate conversations and subtle persuasions.

Freja smiled at the older fae. "Good morrow, sir."

"To some, perhaps," he hedged, ethereally bright eyes studying the pair in healthy suspicion. "How might I help you?"

"We hoped to learn about the darkness and how to rid ourselves of such horror." Freja's eyes were wide and innocent, her tone casual as one would ask on the weather. With a small smile, she wore innocence and honesty like a cloak, an act, carefully crafted and cultivated under her mother's guidance.

The bartender said nothing for a long time, weighing the words and sincerity behind her inquiry. "Information does not flow freely under the fae king's court."

"Don't even think about it," Brenna whispered to Freja under her breath. She was not bargaining her knives again. That trick only worked once on unsuspecting victims and this man was far from unsuspecting.

Freja broke her character enough to shoot her a quelling look and then smiled at the man as if Brenna said nothing. "We understand, sir. Perhaps a trade of information? You provide knowledge we do not know and, in turn, we provide knowledge you do not know."

A question for a question. A dangerous gamble in the hands of the fae. Brenna shifted in place, eyes darting from her sister to the bartender, whose name had not been offered. He licked his lips and dropped his gaze as he wiped down the counters with a gray cloth.

"I know a good many things," he warned.

Freja's smile grew a slight edge, visible to only those that knew her. "We will continue to provide information until we can satisfy the deal."

Quiet for a breath. Two. He raised his gaze slowly. Brenna tried identifying the color of his irises. Gold. Gray. Blue. Green. The color shifted so subtly that she didn't notice until it was already a new color. The corner of his mouth lifted and revealed a hint of sharper teeth beneath. "The deal is struck. Ask your question."

Freja leaned forward. "Tell me all you know about the darkness and the heart pieces said to cure it."

"A hefty request," he murmured, the words rumbling like thunder in storm clouds. He hummed. "Uniting all the heart pieces will free the lands of the black disease, that is true. Each heart piece will require sacrifice to obtain. In five hundred years, many have attempted such a feat, none have succeeded. It is in the darkness that monsters are born and it is only through magic of the fae queen that it has not consumed us all."

A shiver ran down Brenna's spine like a scattering mouse running from a broom. Of course others had tried to do something. It only made sense. She was not the only one honor and duty bound to help, to save, to do something about the black mark on her home. And yet, the odds were never as bad as they were now. Faldinn had been consumed. If those before her failed, what hope did she have?

Freja reached over and squeezed her wrist, likely guessing her thoughts. "What spurred the darkness? How did it come to be?"

No one knew. No human life spanned centuries, and written histories only spoke of great calamity that occurred when the darkness spread, cutting off their kingdoms, staining their maps like ink spilled over parchment. But the fae were longer lived and escaped the worst of the damage. Some even said it was the fae that were responsible.

His eyes narrowed for a moment. "There are many stories regarding it, passed down through the years, distorted and twisted by time and malice. The truth lies in the fae queen's grave."

He made a gesture then, a rune that she didn't recognize wholly but knew the signs of grieving well enough. And at his mention of the queen, every fae in the room fell silent and made the same gesture. Brenna shared a look with her sister, who offered a small shrug.

They had heard many tales of the fae king, of his ruthlessness, of his chaotic nature, of his desire for human flesh, but rarely the fae queen. Clearly she had been well loved and long lost.

Before Freja could ask more, the bartender straightened. "Your turn. Give me your true name."

Brenna's mouth ran dry. Names in the hands of the fae meant power and control over oneself. She looked over in panic but Freja simply smiled, relaxed. "Our brother once convinced the cook to make a feast despite there being no special occasion to mark it. Left with all the food, he then invited everyone he met to eat with him."

What?

Brenna remembered vaguely the feast, but why was Freja bringing that up? She glanced at the bartender who looked just as befuddled and a little annoyed.

"That was not what I asked."

"No," Freja said, still calm and at ease. "But I did not promise to answer anything you asked. I promised you information you never had before. If you already heard Arne's story, I'm sure I have other things to offer to satisfy our deal."

Oh, that was tricky. Brenna studied the bartender but he didn't look angry. Still, she slid a dagger to her hand and shifted her weight to her back foot, just in case.

After a tense moment, the bartender huffed. "As you said. If you wish to know more, a new deal will need to be made."

"I'll keep that in mind." Freja turned and pulled Brenna away from the counter, back to the table, back to relative safety. The bartender's gaze lingered on them.

"You are insane," Brenna hissed quietly. "You can no longer complain every time I do something dangerous and stupid because clearly you are worse."

Freja rolled her eyes. "They underestimate humans and the queen raised me to be shrewd and manipulative. I can handle myself."

Brenna knew that was true, knew that all the lessons the queen taught her daughter about how to glide through court with a light touch and winning smile would equip Freja to navigate the fae deals, but Norns that was such a gamble. Her heart thrummed in her ears and her hands shook as they got back to the table with the tidbits of information they gleaned.

What was worse, worse than being in this slippery, uncertain place, was how Freja so quickly adapted and belonged in a world of chaos and deals and words. Her sister told the group of their deal with a satisfied, smug look even as Einar scowled. Her sister thrived in the fine art of negotiation. Brenna desperately tried ignoring the feeling that it would be her doom if left unchecked, tried ignoring the hungry gleam in the bartender's eyes as he watched them.

One thing was for sure, she was never leaving Freja alone while they lingered among the fae.

X

Ju senare på kvällen, desto vackrare folk

The later in the evening, the more beautiful the people

"**U**nless we're planning on spending the night here, we'll need to make our way to the boat now," Tapio said quietly over curled maps and scratched out notes. "The inner circle is not safe for humans after dark."

"You ruin all my fun," Einar complained. "They would've been fine."

Tapio raised an eyebrow as he helped roll up the fragile papers. "You know the gates lock at dusk."

Brenna frowned and checked the nearest window. It was hard to tell just how much time had passed since arriving. The window had a dark covering that made outside seem like a perpetual twilight. "What happens at night?"

"Nothing meant for our sensibilities," Tapio said, refusing to elaborate. Given the amount of time Tapio spent in this tavern and the amount of drink he normally partook in, he probably witnessed more than a few nights with the fae.

The fae were naturally nocturnal beings, all the stories said. They danced under the stars and stole children in the dark. The darkness was associated with the fae for their love of the night. Surely, they wished the world to be plunged in eternal darkness. Brenna shuddered and stuffed all their plans into her bag quickly.

"Leaving already?"

Brenna yelped at the bartender suddenly standing next to them, hands in pockets, looking much less wrinkly than he had when they first entered. Did night grant youth to the fae?

Delja shrunk behind Einar. He put an arm around her protectively in a rare display of common decency. Freja stood and nodded to the bartender. "We are. We thank you for your hospitality but must continue our journey."

He nodded. "May Lady Magic light your paths."

That sounded more like a curse than a blessing. Brenna was not a fan of magic and the chaos it spawned. She shuffled forward with the group, letting out a breath she didn't know she was holding once they stumbled outside.

The light waned around them, ducking behind buildings and elongating shadows. By her estimate, they only had about an hour of daylight left. Their group tightened around each other and walked quickly through the fae section of the island, ignoring the maniacal grins and whispered promises that nipped at thier heels. Brenna kept one hand in Freja's and another on her knife. She did not release either until they were safely ensconced on Einar's disaster of a ship.

"I hate this place," Brenna muttered as her sister moved away. Tapio offered his flask in commiseration. She offered a stink eye in return. "Ale doesn't solve everything."

"Of course not," he said with a bitter grin. "A good fight solves the rest. Would you rather spar?"

"I'd rather not step foot on the Isle ever again." Brenna leaned against the ship railing, facing towards the unending sea, tinged orange in the fading light.

"It grows on you. Like a fungus."

Brenna leveled a glare at him."Lovely. I'm finding better company."

Pushing off the rail, Brenna went below deck. Tapio had enough common sense to not follow. Hrolf greeted her with a tossed mane and a snort as she entered the stable. He was the only horse on board, the only one to fit in the small stable below deck. She had refused to part with him. Signe slipped in behind her. Brenna patted Hrolf's nose in commiseration. "Poor Hrolf. We'll get you out tomorrow. Promise."

"Horse has horns?" A scratchy voice called from behind her.

Brenna yelped, whirling around to face her shadow. "Delja! Make some noise when you follow someone."

"Sorry." The girl raised her shoulders to her ears and offered a sheepish smile, lowering her age to seemingly eight years old. Seriously, no one had any right to look so young and naive, not someone who considered Einar a friend.

"Ah, Norns, it's okay. I'm sorry. You just surprised me." Delja hadn't done anything to earn her ire. Brenna did promise Freja to do better with their companions. She smiled in what she hoped was an apologetic way. Something tugged at her hood, pulling it around her shoulders and she turned to glare at Hrolf. He nickered softly.

"Like me?" Delja bounced on the balls of her feet, which Brenna just realized were bare.

"Huh?" Signe wound between her legs then jumped up to an overhanging board to preside over them.

Delja grinned and bared her arms to her, showing off red patchy skin on the soft skin. Unlike the mark Brenna bore, Delja's marks looked dry and angry. "Better around water. Bleeds sometimes. Because I'm half."

"Oh. Uh, no. Mine…mine doesn't bleed. It just…is. Like a wine stain or…I don't know." Her mark never bled, never bothered her more than attracting stares and whispers. Brenna touched the rough skin under her eye, frowning as she looked at Delja.

Delja's brow furrowed, eyes studying her face like she was a puzzle to solve. "A fae mark?"

"I don't really know." With all the attention and guesses from the Isle, Brenna was beginning to wonder if it meant something more. On Ayworn, it was a constant reminder of her mother's failure, of Brenna's failure, but perhaps there was more to it than that. Perhaps like the hood, it was a mark of something greater.

"Fae king might remove fae marks," Delja said, tilting her head in thought.

Oh, what an offer. If there was one thing the fae could tempt her with, it would be to be free of her curse mark. But they would require a deal. Brenna sighed. "I…I wouldn't have anything of equal value I'd be willing to trade."

"Oh."

Brenna didn't know what to say after that. Signe stared at her from her perch, judging and uncaring all at once. Delja shifted on her feet, looking around at the decking of the ship.

"Your voice sounds better." It didn't sound so rough and painful, as if she had been coughing and gone without water for days, as if sandpaper coated her throat.

Delja nodded, then shrugged. "Better on the water. But not welcome in it."

"Because you're half human? And half water fae?" Brenna guessed. It was easier to tell now, either because of the approaching night or the proximity to the sea. Delja had gained an ethereal look to her youthful face. The hair on the back of Brenna's neck raised slightly, her body recognizing a threat despite knowing she wasn't in danger.

But the girl was either ignorant of these changes or indifferent to them. Delja merely nodded again and stared at her bare feet. "Lost human mother to the darkness. Never met fae family."

Oh. Delja was alone. She was hurting. She was unwelcome in both worlds.

Brenna knew that pain. If she did not have Arne or Freja growing up, would she have turned bitter and raging, lashing out at anyone that came near? Or would she have accepted anyone that showed the slightest kindness? Even if it came in the form of an obnoxious, blind magic user with a vague moral compass.

"Maybe you can teach us the hand signals?" Brenna said, offering a smile and friendship. "I mean, if Einar can learn it, it can't be that difficult."

The grief and pain disappeared like smoke and Delja beamed at her. "Now?"

"Uh, sure, why not?"

They sat in front of Hrolf's stall, the sweet scent of hay mixing with the salt of the sea surrounding them. Hrolf watched with one eye on them and another on the door, even as he snacked. Signe hopped down and stretched out between them, glaring if fingers dared attempt to stroke her soft fur without the appropriate accolades and begging.

Delja taught patiently so Brenna attempted to be an eager student in return. She couldn't deny her relief when it was finally time to retire though. She assumed it would be similar to the hand signs that soldiers used in battle but it was much more complex, a language unto itself. Brenna never had a knack for languages, not like Arne or Freja. Still, the pleased look on Delja's face every time she got something right kept her going.

That night she dreamed in silence with cruel kings looming over and dangerous magic pulling her towards the shadows.

When she awoke, the boat rocked and her stomach rolled. Brenna went above to find Freja scowling at Einar at the wheel, his blindfold in place as he steered through the water.

"You can't just make those decisions without us," Freja snapped as Brenna got close.

"We're going to Denwes, right?" Einar asked, a slight edge to his voice. "It's my boat. So I get to decide when we cast off. The tide was with us and I wasn't sleeping."

"Anything could have happened and you would have doomed us all to a watery grave." Her sister's voice was sharp and harsh.

She was not a morning person and dealing with Einar would give anyone a short fuse.

"What happened?" Brenna asked, forcing Freja to turn her glare to her. Freja huffed and crossed her arms.

"He decided to launch us to sea while we were all sleeping. We're an hour from the Denwes port." The wind off the sea pulled at her braided hair and she swatted at loose strands, agitation making her movements snap and her words bite.

They did not grow up on the water, they did not know the intricacies of the sea. They only knew the dangers and horror stories. Brenna knew what she was fearing but there was nothing for it now. And she trusted that Einar had no desire to die anymore than they did.

Sighing, she pulled Freja away from the magic user. "Have you had something to eat?"

"I am not having a hunger-related fit," Freja hissed.

Brenna held up her hands. "You get cranky in the mornings before breakfast. We're near port, we can't change what happened, so grab a roll and cool off."

Freja glared at her for several long moments before finally relenting and stomping below deck to the galley. That left Brenna with Einar and she attempted to keep out as much annoyance out of her voice as possible. "You should have woken one of us."

"Nothing happened," he said flippantly. "Although I had no idea Copycat had talons."

She smirked. Not many knew the sharp edges Freja hid behind flowing flattery, her soft tones were an ornate scabbard meant to distract from the blade within. Brenna was of the opinion that

Freja didn't show her true danger enough, that she allowed the courtiers to become too comfortable around her.

"Something to remember as I won't be kind enough to distract her the next time you anger her." With that, Brenna flipped her hair over her shoulder, found a spot on the ship furthest from Einar, and attempted to quell her rolling stomach by fixing her gaze on the horizon.

Tapio saw her lurking along the railing and joined her. "Morning. Any idea why Freja was mending a coat as if it wronged her?"

"Needlework calms her down." Which could not be said for Brenna. If anything, needlework made her more likely to snap and rage.

Tapio snorted. "You two are so eerily alike and different at the same time."

"How so?" Brenna asked, frowning. She knew the characteristics she shared with Freja but wasn't sure what that had to do with needlework.

Tapio's eyes crinkled in amusement as he looked at her, nearly unburdened from the grief he wore as a cloak. "You both find relaxation in stabbing something."

She laughed, letting the movement ache in ways she didn't want to think about. Taking that as a cue to get comfortable, Tapio leaned his back against the railing and sat down, stretching out his bad leg with his cane then resting it across his lap. Probably wise. She could easily imagine it rolling off the rocking ship.

They didn't speak for several moments, letting the air be light and easy for a small sliver of time. Brenna rested her head on the railing, eyes scanning for anything beyond blue waves and blue sky. She didn't think she'd ever be used to sea travel, exposed and alone in a wide ocean. She missed the forests of home, the shelter of the mountains, the fog enclosing around her.

"Penny for your thoughts, Princess."

"I'm not a princess."

Tapio raised an eyebrow. "So your sister is a princess and your parents are king and queen but you aren't royal?"

"Obviously not," she sniffed, raising her head in a very snobby courtier way, then met his gaze in challenge.

"And how would that work?" he asked, leaning back, a ghost of a smile teasing at the edges on his lips.

"Oh, I'm adopted." The words came out instinctively, an inside joke between her, Freja, and Arne, a way to ease her brother's place in their family.

Tapio squinted at her. "You and Freja—"

"No, no, just me." She offered a wide grin as he attempted to piece together her humor. His eyes narrowed further, scrunching his nose as he did so, which Brenna refused to claim was cute even in the privacy of her own mind. To distract her from the growing horror of distant feelings, she escalated the lie. "Freja was born, as you do, but I simply manifested. Sprung into form, perfect and effortlessly."

She used to bet with Arne and Freja who could come up with the most outrageous lie. On slow court days, they would see how many people they could get to believe in their lie. There were still rumors floating around the castle about Brenna having a taste for goblin fire.

"Right." His voice had gone flat and uninterested as he pulled his flask out. She sighed.

Brenna stood and stretched. "Come find me when you find your humor."

Brenna wasn't about to fight ghosts. She probably could, if she put her mind to it and if the ghosts decided to attack her in the woods, but the memories haunting Tapio were not her responsibility to handle. She had her own grief to manage.

He did not follow after her and did not seek her out in the last hour of their voyage. Instead, Brenna continued to work with Delja on sign language, roping Freja into joining them. Naturally, her sister picked up the nuances quicker and could converse almost fluidly by the time they docked and deboarded.

The Denwes port opened up to a sprawling city of thatched roofs and stone walls and boarded sidewalks over muddy paths. It was vast and spread out, and hungry eyes watched openly from street corners. Stepping off the boat, Brenna knew there would be more than one pickpocket rifling through their things. She could only hope Einar had some sort of magic keeping his boat safe.

She held tightly to Hrolf's reins as Delja skipped ahead. "Well, Einar, you wouldn't happen to know where the capital is, would you?"

"Further up the coast. We should arrive by dusk." He tied a ribbon around his eyes, blocking the strange blank whiteness of his eyes. Brenna pulled her hood lower on her face. They rented horses from the nearest stable. Einar mounted his horse and offered a hand to Delja. She didn't seem thrilled to be on a horse but took his hand regardless.

Brenna followed Einar's lead with a sigh, mounting Hrolf with Freja behind her.

The city seemed to stretch on forever, endless streets with people milling about in threadbare clothes and hunched shoulders. It burned her to admit that Einar was right; Brenna had no idea how bad it truly was for their sister kingdoms. Ayworn had enough to sustain itself for now. Denwes had not been so lucky.

For a kingdom that needed pasture and rolling hills for livestock and farming, with barely there mountains for protection, the darkness was a death sentence.

Once they left behind the city, Brenna wished nothing more than to go back. In the distance, the darkness was a harsh black line, dividing the sky and land with a black shadow. Brenna stared. She had never been so close. The darkness was a starless sky, the deepest shadows on a moonless night. She prayed her eyes betrayed her when she detected movement in the blackness where none could live.

Freja paused with her, studying it in mute horror. Tapio noticed and looked back, his face grim. "It's many kilometers off. We should be safe as long as we make it to the city by nightfall."

But she didn't feel safe, exposed to a grassy lowland with the black borders that felt alarmingly close. Shadows stretched towards them like a low fog. She kept an eye on it even as she spurred Hrolf forward. "You've been in the darkness."

"Bri…" Freja warned but they needed to know. They would be venturing to Faldinn. They had to know what they were facing.

Tapio had turned back around, but his shoulders were tense and one hand lingered near the pouch holding his flask. He spoke tight and controlled, "No light enters the darkness. And there is no warning for attacks. I can offer no guarantees that we will succeed if we must venture through it."

"You survived," Brenna said as gently as she could manage, not sure how much comfort the statement would be in the face of such devastation. "Failing isn't an option anymore."

If they failed, their lands would be consumed. The Lost Isle would not be able to support all the refugees fleeing darkness. She took one more look at the unnatural darkness looming and urged Hrolf faster.

As predicted, they reached the capital just before sunset. The flags of the castle, tattered images of the Denwes crest, hung limply in the humid evening. Einar led them to an inn that had a boisterous dance occupying the main floor. When inquiring about the rooms, the innkeeper offered them any room. Despite the mass of bodies in the main room, none were staying the night. There were no travelers risking the roads and no money in the country to continue trading.

Brenna flopped on the bed with a huff. "Should we ride to the castle to request an audience? We have an hour before dusk."

Not that she wanted to get up from this mediocre bed. The straw was scratchy and the blanket thin, but it was gloriously still and comforting. She doubted the ground would stop swaying before they had to get back on the blasted boat.

"I think we can wait for the morning." Freja set the packs by the wall, glancing at the room with two beds that had to accommodate five people. "We'll be fresher then and better prepared to provide whatever sacrifice they require."

"Which means just enough time for a little gambling." Einar grinned. Delja frowned.

"If you have money for gambling, you have money to spare for another room," Freja said, raising an eyebrow in challenge. Freja was still smarting about him starting their journey without telling anyone.

Wisely sensing her mood, his shoulders slumped. "So what? We just hang around until we pass out?"

Brenna sat up with a grin. "We can play 'I heard a rumor'."

"I assume that's a game?" Einar drawled.

"Something we came up with to pass time in court. The idea is who can come up with the most believable, outrageous lie." Freja smiled in fondness. "I was the reigning champion."

"That's because you cheat." Brenna stuck her tongue out at her. No one doubted Freja when she told them something, which was ludicrous given how often she lied and manipulated to get her way. On the flip side, it didn't matter if Brenna told the truth, people rarely took her words to heart.

"Poor sportsmanship is unbecoming, dear sister." Freja patted her on the arm. "We have no way to track the rumors. We played this game over months so we can't really do it in one night."

"Fine. Any other ideas?" Brenna asked the room. Delja tilted her head, then lit up, her hands a blur of motion. She blinked. "Okay, I am not familiar enough to have caught that."

"She suggested a lie detection game," Einar translated. "We all give out two truths and a lie and the others have to guess which is the lie. But that won't work because we've got Thing One and Two over here who can probably read each other's minds."

Freja rolled her eyes. "If we can't think of something, then Bri and I will sit out for each other's turns."

Tapio shrugged and carefully worked to sit on the floor, pulling his lame leg out in a stretch. "I'm game, better than gambling."

Delja clapped excitedly and sat by Brenna, Freja taking the other side. They all looked to Einar expectantly. He gave a long-suffering sigh and completed the circle. "If we must do this, we're doing it the right way."

He rummaged through the bags and pulled out a green bottle. Tapio snatched it and took an experimental sniff. "Fairy drink. That's a horrendous idea. Let's do it."

"Fairy drink?" Freja asked. She took the bottle and took a sniff before passing it to Brenna.

Looking down the long neck, the liquid sloshed, catching some unknown light that caused it to shimmer. It smelled of wildflowers and summer and sea breeze. For a moment she was transported to a meadow outside the castle where she, Freja, and Arne spent their summers running and tripping and laughing.

Einar snatched it back and the vision faded. "Fairy drink affects emotions and forces truth. If you guess wrong, you have to take a sip."

Brenna blanched. "I'd rather drink Tapio's ale."

"I'm not sharing, sorry."

"You sound entirely remorseful."

"Einar starts since it's his idea to drink," Freja said before they got off track.

Einar tapped his chin in thought. Brenna was at a disadvantage and wished he hadn't gone first. Delja would probably know what his truth was. After a tortuously long moment, he snapped his fingers. "Got it. I was born an only child, I abhor the color yellow, and I have never lost a bet."

Okay, this would be harder than she expected. Sneaking a glance at the group gave nothing away. Well, it gave away that they were all as lost as she was. She guessed yellow as the lie. He was blind, why would he have a preference for color? Tapio guessed the bet while Freja and Delja guessed on his lack of siblings.

"Drink up, Lame Leg and Doubletake."

"You're blind! How do you know what yellow is?" Brenna demanded.

Einar raised an eyebrow and held out the drink. "That's what you get for making assumptions."

Brenna scowled and took the bottle. Nothing for it then. She took a sip. The summery feeling filled her, wrapping her in a blanket like Hilde used to on stormy nights. "I framed Freja for messing with Arne's journals. Multiple times."

Brenna clapped a hand over her mouth. That was not what she expected. Wide eyes met her sister's as Freja cried, "I knew it!"

The game progressed. Einar somehow never guessed wrong. When accused of cheating, he demanded Brenna take another sip for his honor. She did so and told the group of the time she stole lutefisk for a stable boy she liked.

Freja and Delja curled up on the bed after they all went around about a dozen times while Einar slipped to whereabouts unknown. Brenna was still on the floor, letting her head roll back onto the itchy mattress propping her up. "That stuff's weird. I feel all fluttery."

"You can control what truth comes out. Just have to focus on it before you drink." Tapio grabbed the bottle and met her gaze in the darkening room, keeping it while he drank. "I wish we could have met before the end of the world."

Fire raced along her veins, a thrum of desire shooting through her. She took the bottle and hesitated. The bottle settled on the floor with a thud. "If we had met before, you would have never seen me."

Suddenly tired, she crawled into bed with Freja and Delja and pretended to sleep.

XI

Det som göms i snö, kommer fram vid tö

What is hidden in snow, is revealed at thaw

"**I** don't see why I have to tag along to your royal hang out," Einar complained as they waited for an audience with the Denwes queen. "I'm already sacrificing my good name just by associating with you, so I won't be offering anything else in this quest."

Brenna scowled at him. "You're with us because we don't trust you to be on your own."

"We're in the land of the gullible. Is it not my duty to take advantage of such?"

A chorus of 'no's followed with even Delja shaking her head and patting his arm comfortingly. Einar pouted. Brenna rolled her eyes at his antics. It's not like there had been much to steal anyways. The room lacked all pomp and circumstance. A sturdy chair sat in place of a throne and empty walls did not even hold the lingering outlines of tapestries. Anything of value or worth had been raided or traded to stave off the darkness long ago. The castle now was simply an empty shell.

Were the other kingdoms in such disrepair? Was there any hope for recovery?

"Please try to be on your best behavior," Freja asked, smoothing out her dress one last time. She had been nominated as their spokesperson since she looked the part. Tapio probably could have as well but it was apparently a bad day for him, judging by his bleary eyes and hunched shoulders.

"I'm always the best," Einar muttered with a sniff.

Freja chose to ignore him. Wise. Brenna shifted on her feet, eyes roving around the empty room. Why had the guard brought them here? If Ayworn had fallen to such, her parents would have received in the smaller parlor. Anything to hide the weakness. What kind of ruler would they be meeting if they were so open about their lack?

The doors opened and a maid entered with bare feet. She was tall with blonde hair kept up with a strip of fading blue cloth that highlighted blue eyes. Stopping just in front of them, she met their gaze before speaking in a light accent, "How may I help?"

Unfortunately, Einar spoke first. He stepped forward, all smiles and swagger. "We're planning on robbing the treasury. You don't mind, right?"

He even had the audacity to wink. Brenna resisted the urge to smack her forehead. Or him. Definitely him.

"Einar," Freja bit out in warning, pushing him back to the group. "My apologies. We were waiting to speak with the Denwish royal family. It's a matter of great importance."

"Although if you're taking drink orders—"

Brenna shoved her elbow into Einar's ribs to get him to shut up. He glared. She ignored him.

The young woman studied them all once more, something akin to amusement in her light eyes, then turned and made for the throne. With a simple twirl, she sat down on it and tilted her head with a smile. "Should I ask again?"

Oops.

Freja's eyes widened at the social suicide they committed in front of fellow royalty. She dropped into the curtsy that signaled deference to an elder. "Please forgive our assumptions. I am Princess Freja Eriksdóttir of Ayworn and I'm accompanied by my sister and our friends."

Introductions went around. Einar refused to bow, crossing his arms instead, but everyone else paid respect. The queen waited until they were finished before speaking, "We have long since forgone such niceties. I have little to offer, but the need must be great to bring two sister kingdoms to my court."

Freja nodded and looked at Brenna. Freja ached, pained to see their neighbors in such straits. The moment passed and her court mask was back as she faced the queen. "I will be blunt then: our party seeks to restore the heart and banish the darkness for good. All we ask is the piece entrusted to Denwes and your blessing as we strive to restore our lands."

"Is that all?" the queen asked dryly.

"I was ignorant of how desperate our lands have become," Freja said softly, her compassion forcing its way past court etiquette. "Seeing what I have, I cannot turn a blind eye."

Brenna stepped forward and took her hand. "We both were, but with your heart piece, we will bring back our former glory."

"I would expect nothing less from Aywornians." The queen's gaze swept over them as she relaxed in her throne. "I'm unable to give you the heart piece."

Brenna's heart sank. They had been so close and the Denwish queen had seemed so…normal. So different from what she expected from her parents' lessons. This was not a detached leader watching from an ivory tower. No, this was a leader of the people, who gave up the fineries of royal life to better serve those in her care. Someone Brenna wouldn't have minded as an example.

And she wouldn't help them.

"Your majesty, we—"

The queen held up a hand at their protest. "Not because I don't want to, but I'm physically incapable. My ancestors placed the heart piece under protection and all who ask for it must brave the challenge to retrieve it."

Oh. Well, that wasn't so bad. Brenna straightened her shoulders. "We can do it."

"Don't be so arrogant. I know what people say of my country." The queen pinned Einar with a hard look. "I know what they say of the barefoot, crownless queen. But you will not simply walk in and take it. You will not leave unchanged."

"Have you gone through it?" Freja asked curiously.

"I have. And I came out empty handed but alive. Some are not so lucky."

That was encouraging. Brenna looked around the group and sighed. They had no other choice. "I'll go alone."

"To succeed, the entire group must enter as one." The queen stood and walked to the door, turning once a guard joined them. "If you decide to attempt it, you'll find the entrance just behind this castle. Speak with Hajar. He will allow you entry."

And she was gone. They were alone in a strangely empty room with a rickety chair in place of a throne.

"Welp, we're doomed."

Freja sighed. "Einar."

"You're right, you're doomed." Einar crossed his arms. "I'm not going in some sort of judgment trial for a piece of something that may or may not save the world. Life debt or not."

Not that anyone expected him to act with honor. Brenna rolled her eyes and looked over at Delja and Tapio. Delja bit her lip as she looked at each of them. Tapio frowned, his brow scrunching in as dark eyes studied the stonework at their feet.

"Tapio?"

Tapio looked up at her and sighed. "Going as a group is risky, even if we were a proper team. We have no idea what we're facing."

"We know what we're facing if we don't try," Brenna argued. "The Lost Isle cannot hold everyone in the five kingdoms, so who will you condemn to die?"

Faldinn was already gone, thousands of lives lost. And each day someone else succumbed to starvation, illness, the darkness. Brenna had been naive to the pain her people and her neighbors suffered, blissfully unaware of just how bad things had gotten. Now that she knew, she couldn't do nothing. She couldn't not try.

"Ugh, do you ever get tired of being so ignorantly noble all the livelong day?"

Brenna turned her glare towards Einar, dagger in hand with a flick of her wrist. "Just because you lack the ability to think beyond yourself doesn't mean others do."

"Are you going to duel me for my honor?" he drawled, stance loose, preparing for a fight. "You should know by now I fight dirty."

Freja put a hand on her arm. "No one is fighting. I know this isn't ideal, but we've come this far. If we must enter as a group, then we enter as a group."

A tense silence followed her words. Delja frowned and turned to Einar, blocking the signs to speak with him privately. Brenna clenched her jaw and stuffed her dagger back in its sheath. Fighting amongst themselves was only going to get one or both of them killed. As Delja reasoned with Einar, she took a breath and regained control of her emotions.

Einar huffed. "Fine, whatever, let's go. If we die, I'm haunting you all."

"Wonderful." Freja sighed. "We should have asked the queen what this trial would entail."

"I don't think she was in a sharing mood," Tapio said, taking a sip of his flask. Brenna resisted the urge to snatch it away from him. Now was not the time to get drunk.

Despite the ominous warnings, the guards pointed them straight to Hajar, who led them to the mouth of a cave. He offered no advice, simply gave a blank look and a monotone 'good luck'.

Brenna stared at the mouth of the cave, a yawning void of uncertainty. A rustle in the nearby brush had her drawing her sword. Freja stopped her from stepping forward as well as keeping Einar from casting.

"Lynx are sacred to the Denwish. Just let it pass."

Sure enough a large spotted cat jumped up on a rocky outcropping and regarded them all. Amber eyes and giant paws and tufted ears grew still. Unlike Signe, there was no fluffy tail revealing signs of agitation or calm. This cat merely watched them all, waiting for their next move.

"Is it part of the trial?" Delja whispered, staring at it in awe. "Should we pray to him?"

"I don't think it's divine," Freja said slowly, unsure. "We should head inside."

Brenna still bowed her head to the beast in an overabundance of caution as she moved to the cave. Drawn to the movement, the reflective eyes of the lynx watched her until she was out of sight. Once everyone was inside without maiming, she sighed in relief.

"Where do you think the heart piece is?" Brenna asked, looking around what seemed to be an ordinary cave: dark, damp, empty.

Until the opening closed behind them.

"Lovely." Freja sighed. "Einar could you cast us a light?"

"What, having trouble seeing?" Einar mumbled softly and a soft yellow glow filled the room.

What Brenna confused for a typical cave was a hewn cavern filled with runic carvings and lifelike statues dotting the room. Statues of men and fae alike, in various forms of distress that left little to the imagination of how they got there. Nothing like seeing just what their outcome would be for motivation.

Brenna approached the nearest statue, a young man with roguish hair. One hand covered his face, but she could see his eyes between his fingers. Wide. Lifeless. The other hand was outstretched, as if staving off an unseen enemy.

In the middle of the room was a raised dais, which they all shuffled towards, eyes darting around for threats. More runic carvings covered the platform, several runes glowing gold. Brenna picked out the rune of protection and safety. How ironic.

"Anyone read Denwish?" Brenna asked as she took in the local dialect set in the stone. Instructions possibly. Warnings probably. She cautiously reached out to dust off the lettering.

The moment her fingers brushed against the stone, a voice boomed around them, "Those seeking the heart must lay themselves on the altar."

The light shifted from yellow to red as the last echo faded. Brenna shuddered. "We could do without the mood lighting, Einar."

Einar tilted his head. "If it changed, it wasn't me."

"What does it mean?" Delja asked. "How do we get the heart?"

A tense silence followed her question before Einar said dryly, "I'm going out on a limb here and guess when they say altar, they mean human sacrifice."

"It didn't say that..." But Freja's argument died as they all stared at the dais now soaked red, at the statues that surrounded them.

"Good thing we've got two of something." Einar turned to Brenna, his features oddly sharp in the flameless light.

Brenna's shoulders tensed, crowding around her ears as her fingers itched for a knife. "I'm not doing it! If we have to pick someone I don't see why we don't throw you on there. What else are you contributing?"

"You mean, other than my boat, my magic, my knowledge?" he demanded. Magic sparked along his fingertips and Brenna drew her sword. She faced him once, she could face him again.

Tapio stepped between them, using his staff to help keep the distance between them. "Let's all calm down. If someone has to die, let it be me. Perhaps this was my purpose for this journey."

"We need you for Faldinn. Can we all stop throwing names in to die please? We don't know that's what it meant." Freja moved in front, keeping herself between everyone and the altar.

"Oh, my bad. I didn't realize Aywornian royalty were all-knowing," Einar sneered.

"What else would it mean?" Brenna demanded.

The ground shook and a crack formed on the far wall. They were running out of time. Tapio moved toward the altar, but lost balance as the floor beneath them trembled. Brenna dodged out of the way of a spell shot from Einar.

"Hold still!"

"Stop it!"

Brenna leapt out of the way of a statue of an old man as it fell in the unstable room. Underneath the sound of crashing stone, chanting in a foreign language intoned. She hid behind a small bench and peered around. Freja was pulling Tapio away from the dais and Einar was still sending out random sparks of magic, transforming whatever he hit into various plants. And Delja…

Delja was strangely still and calm as she studied the dais, her head tilted as if she were listening for a whisper.

"Oh." Despite Delja's quiet exclamation, her voice carried around the room. "I am afraid of water. I fear fae would kill me because I am only half. I don't carry enough blood for them to care."

At her strange statement, the room stilled. Brenna slowly stood from her hiding spot as Einar turned to Delja. Freja and Tapio pulled apart and frowned.

"What did you do?" Brenna asked, approaching slowly. A few more runes on the platform glowed now.

Delja smiled at them as if they hadn't been fighting over who should die and pointed to the Denwish script. "Trust can mean lay bare. Trust means vulnerable. Sacrifice."

Freja gasped. "Oh! It asked us to lay ourselves on the altar. We have to show that we trust one another to accept the heart. How brilliant."

"How is that brilliant?" It sounded like Brenna's worst nightmare. The last thing she wanted was to tell everyone a secret, especially one she would have hidden from Freja. The room rumbled as if sensing her hesitation.

"Because anyone who approached with selfish intentions would never be so vulnerable."

Before another statue could fall, Tapio bowed his head, his voice thick. "It's my fault my family is dead. I urged them to stay longer, to try one more thing before the darkness struck."

Brenna reached out and put a hand on his arm. The rumblings ceased, momentarily pleased as two more runes glowed: grief and strength. There was a stone where her stomach should be and it was quickly dropping to her toes. She couldn't do this.

Brenna sought out her sister, who smiled sadly. Freja said, "I hate being the perfect sibling. You, Arne, mother, father, you all look at me like I can do nothing wrong, like I have all the answers. The truth is I'm terrified and I have no idea what I'm doing."

Family and duty runes lit. What was happening? Brenna cried out as a particularly violent tremor forced her to her knees, yet Delja, Tapio and Freja stayed standing. Her sword clattered out of her hands and she tried grabbing it, only to find her hands uncooperative. She watched in horror as the tips of her fingers shifted into stone, gray and still.

"Einar, Bri, hurry!"

"I'm gonna throw up," Einar responded with a groan. He took a deep breath and gritted out. "I wasn't born blind or with magic. I stole it from a fae to save my older brother and the fae cursed my sight in recompense. My brother died before I could even try."

The stone was up to Brenna's forearms now and she couldn't move her toes. Her breaths came out harsh and rapid and she couldn't get words to form over the incessant panic in her mind.

Then Tapio was there, blocking out the others, hands on her shoulders, voice quiet and calm and kind. "Let it out. Whatever you fear, it's okay. You can trust us."

His dark eyes were earnest and encouraging and his hands didn't move even as stone crept underneath them. Brenna licked her chapped lips. "I…Sometimes I think it would have been better if I hadn't been born."

The room stilled and with the first words out, the rest flowed easier. Still, she did not seek out her sister as she whispered, "I'm too ugly, too blunt, too quick to anger."

The dais became a column of light as Tapio put a hand on her face, but instead of covering the mark, his hand cupped the opposite cheek. He smiled gently. Stone shifted back to skin. Brenna closed her eyes, relishing on the warmth on her cheek. Had anyone ever touched her face for any other reason but to hide it?

The wall behind them reopened to Denwes, showing the castle and city against the sea. The dais opened in the middle to reveal a small, jagged stone that pulsed a gentle golden light: the heart piece. Brenna pulled away and stood as Delja picked up the small stone. Brenna pulled out the box holding the Aywornian heart and held it open.

Delja grinned and carefully dropped it inside. Once close enough, the two pieces merged in a flash of light, leaving no seam where it had once been broken. One step closer.

She looked around the group, ragged and slumped as if they fought a great beast rather than simply spilling their greatest secrets. Freja took her hand and squeezed it. Tapio picked up his crutch and rested his hand on her shoulder for a moment before letting his hand drop.

"No matter what brought us here," Tapio said, looking at each of them in turn. "No matter the reason that spurred us to action, we guard each other's backs from here on out. We owe each other that much."

Brenna looked at Einar, getting a momentary glimpse of a boy that was desperate to save his family, desperate to save a life, a boy who failed. She held out a hand. Einar shifted on his feet, fingers twitching at his side. The air shimmered; it felt like she plunged her hand into an icy river and then she was holding a bouquet of holtasoley.

She rolled her eyes and handed them off to Delja, who clapped in delight when they transformed into fireflies. Einar grinned. "Any chance we can meet the queen again? I have some words I'd like to tell her."

"You and me both," Brenna muttered. Some warning would have been nice.

"Let's just count this as a win and head back." Freja shifted so her arm was around her shoulders and Brenna returned the hug. They had made it out. They had two of the five heart pieces. Freja grinned. "We can start the plan for Nolpa next."

XII

Skägget i brevlådan

Caught with your beard in the mailbox

$\mathcal{T}$he road back to the ship was quiet as they each mulled over the truths now laying on them like a thick blanket on a warm night. As the joy of victory faded, the weight of revealing such secrets pressed on them. Tapio's flask grew emptier. Silence stretched into awkward.

"I don't care about the miniature lynx, we're leaving with the tide," Einar said as he threw ropes in a way that probably made sense to him.

"We're not leaving Signe." Brenna scanned the port. It was a risk bringing their mouser and giving her free reign, but it was Signe. They were not leaving her, fate of the world or not.

Brenna glanced at Tapio who seemed to sway opposite of the waves, his eyes glassy, and pursed her lips. "Don't you think you've had enough?"

"Are you saying you wouldn't rather drink than deal with the fallout of what was spoken?"

She did. But the drink would run out eventually. And oddly enough, it was not the others she feared speaking with but her own sister. They didn't keep secrets. At least, that's what they told each other. She used the excuse of looking for Signe to spot Freja on the opposing rail. Perhaps Brenna wasn't the only one avoiding a frank discussion.

"It's not your fault," Brenna said. Tapio grunted in protest and pushed away from her. Sighing, she moved to stop him. "You said we stand with each other now, yes?"

"Yes," he ground out.

"And that includes outside of battle." Brenna did not have the death of her kingdom on her shoulders. She would not belittle his pain by saying she knew what he was going through. But wallowing in that grief and pain was only succumbing to the darkness as well. A different darkness that plagued them.

Tapio huffed and made a dramatic show of capping his flask and tucking it away. "You're a right pain, Princess."

"Not a princess anymore." A statement she'd happily shout from the highest mountain. Not a princess. No longer burdened.

Tapio raised an eyebrow in challenge and pointed toward the gangplank. Tail high in the air, Signe sauntered up to the deck. She sat down and gave a *mmrp*, turning golden eyes to Brenna in haughty permission.

"Oh, are we allowed to leave now?" she said dryly, then called out, "Hear that Einar? You can leave with your precious tide, Queen Signe has allowed it."

"I'm tossing that cat overboard halfway there," Einar said, flicking up the last anchor to the shore with a flash of magic. The boat lurched away from the shore.

"I might let him," Brenna told the cat, who was now preening her long fur, pausing only to offer a baleful look. "Or maybe I'll lock you in with Hrolf. You two can bond or fight for true leader of this insane quest."

Her tail flicked in response as she followed Freja below deck.

The choppy waves and rocking boat caught up with Tapio's inebriation and he pursed his lips. "I'm going to go lay down."

Brenna couldn't imagine that would help, but she nodded and walked over to the stern where Einar was standing at the helm, hands sure as they rested on the ship's wheel. It was an odd picture, as sightless eyes gazed out at an empty horizon.

Einar said he stole the magic to save his brother; he was cursed for it. And for the first time since meeting the obnoxious boy in front of her, Brenna put herself in his shoes. What would she risk if Freja or Arne were dying? What lengths would she have gone if she could save Hilde? She wasn't really fond of magic or the fae, of the consequences that came with such power, but to save her family? Maybe she would have done the same.

And if she failed, left with magic she didn't truly want and the lack of sight, she would have grown bitter and scathing as well. Would she stop caring for those around her? Would she have thrown aside all that Hilde had beaten into her and stopped trying to help?

Maybe.

Brenna prayed she'd never know.

"Paint a picture, it lasts longer."

She rolled her eyes and shifted so she faced the unending sea. "How do you know where we're going? Can you tell the sun's position with your magic?"

"I was blessed by the Norns to instinctively know the way the winds blow and thus, never get lost," Einar said with a wise nod. "It's actually really annoying."

"Uh-huh." Brenna let the blatant lie roll off her.

"Or it could be that I'm following the ley line laid out in the charter." He offered a nonchalant shrug but Brenna took it for the olive branch that it was.

"You've mentioned a charter before, what exactly is it?"

His lip curled as if about to hurl another lie, another insult. But he stopped and took a deep breath, closing his eyes for a moment. "It's said that when the darkness fell, the Lost Isle closed its borders and was thus protected from the stain. The only ones that could travel to the island were those gifted with a blessing from the fae queen. Gifted only to those worthy."

Einar's nose scrunched and he rolled his shoulders, his tone regaining its bite. "Honestly, each ship captain must request a charter from the fae to find their way to and fro. It's just a rock with a magical ley line embedded. Nothing so fanciful, but historians like the romance, don't they?"

"Maybe there's some truth to it," Brenna said as her eyes traced the lines of the waves until they shimmered into indiscernible blue. "Maybe the fabled fae queen did something that later became the charters."

He grunted in response. "You're being hopeful. It's disgusting."

Snorting, she pushed off the rail and stretched, letting the warm sun bathe her and shake off the darkness. "No one's been mauled, maimed or killed on the journey and we're practically halfway done. I think that merits some hope."

"Gross."

"Alright, I'll work on it." She grinned. "How about, I expect one of us will be mauled, maimed, or killed in Nolpa. I hope it's you."

"Better." Silence stretched between them like a winter fox stretching in the rare sun of the season. She took a deep breath to let the new dynamic between them settle.

Einar, of course, ruined it.

"Get out of my space. You're just using me to avoid your sister. I'm appalled and disturbed." He reached into his pocket and pulled a rag out to tie around his eyes, protecting them from the rising sun. "Leave, Thing One. I'm done with you."

Brenna stuck her tongue at him and ducked at the bolt of magic he sent in retaliation. As she made her way down, the stairs to the helm shifted and grew branches, blocking him from conversation.

Brenna made her way below deck and sighed as she let her eyes adjust to the darker interior. Delja waved at her and motioned further down the hall, most likely where Freja hid herself. She signed, "Thanks."

Delja beamed at her before scrambling topside.

Right, nothing for it.

She didn't knock on the door that led to the small bunk space the girls shared. The ship wasn't large enough for separate rooms for everyone. The girls took over the captain's quarters as the largest space and the boys took the crew cabin. A large storage space had to be converted to stables for Hrolf. Brenna was adamant on that as well. Hrolf and Signe were part of their crew and would be treated as such.

The first thing she noticed was Signe glaring at her from the bedpost, fluffy tail twitching, set up high like that made her appear as a gargoyle, a demon of protection. She nodded at the silent reprimand. If Einar was telling her to talk, then the rift between the sisters was bad.

Freja didn't look up at her entrance, sitting in the bed, knees up as she stabbed a needle and thread into the fabric as if it offended her. She was really mad if she was showing her emotions. Countless lessons and years of practice meant Freja could be raging inside yet look serene as a mountain lake in summer to any onlookers.

Brenna sighed and stepped in further, taking the silence as encouragement to continue. She kept going until her legs hit the bed and she crumbled next to her sister, taking a peek at what she was embroidering.

The Aywornian crest. Brenna could just make out the talons clutching a lotus.

Freja must have brought the materials from home. Brenna hadn't seen a vendor selling the distinctive purple, a color she knew intimately as home. She watched the needle punch through the fabric and pull the thread for a few minutes as she tried to form the words.

"I was always jealous of how you could speak your mind," Freja said in the silence, her voice quiet and thoughtful. "As if you didn't have doubts gagging the thoughts before they could form into words."

Brenna leaned against the wall, then shifted until she rested her head on Freja's shoulder, watching the needle wink in the mage light. In. Out. In. Out. "I hated that mother loved you more. That everything I did was in comparison to you. That I was never good enough even when I tried."

"I knew it weighed on you, I just didn't realize how heavily. Bri, I..." The needle stopped flashing as the sound of water crashing against the sides as the boat pushed through the sea filled the air. "I'm thankful every day that mother ate both flowers."

The story of their birth, of the curse mark Brenna bore. After years of not producing a child, of finding no fulfillment in Arne's adoption, their mother turned to fae magic for a solution. The hag she met offered a resolution to her pain: follow her instructions and have the child she most desired, a child that would be utterly perfect in every way.

It was a simple plan: cast water under her bed and eat the beautiful flower and leave the disfigured one. Instead, the queen ate both and gave birth to twins. Brenna was born first, face marred by the stain on her face. Hilde once said that at her birth, the mark resembled the flower the queen ate, a reminder that she made the wrong choice.

Just as well that Freja was born moments later, perfect and loving in every way.

As they grew, they fell into the roles the queen built for them since birth: Freja was the perfect daughter, Brenna was the fateful mistake.

Hating the heavy feeling between them, Brenna huffed and said, "I am a pretty fantastic sister."

Freja grinned at her. "The best."

"Arne's lucky to have such amazing siblings," Brenna said, a wave of homesickness overtaking her for a moment. A home she would never return to, a home that had no Hilde anymore. She hid trembling hands in the folds of her shirt.

"Can you imagine what Hilde would say seeing us in this mess?" Freja asked, her voice dropping to a whisper and still breaking. Brenna wasn't the only one homesick. She wasn't the only one grieving.

Brenna pressed her lips together until she could be sure they wouldn't waver. "She'd probably smack us upside the head for our idiocy."

It had only been a handful of days since that fateful attack and yet it seemed an eternity. Brenna was glad for the busy insanity of this quest as it kept the pain of grief at bay. Talking about her now was like speaking with broken glass in her throat and she wasn't sure she could continue. Had it been any of the others, they would have received her anger in response. But Freja was hurting too. Freja felt the aching loss.

"I keep thinking we'll go back home and it'll be as if nothing has changed." Freja rested her head on Brenna's, letting her embroidery fall into her lap. "We'll tell Arne of all of our adventures and he'll try hiding us in the Sticks with Idunn, plying us with sweet bread and Hilde will work out her worry by beating the rugs a little more harshly than necessary and hover over us with critiques on our posture."

"She would check on us more in the night," Brenna whispered, adding to the fantasy. "And Arne would sneak in and we would pile up on the floor."

How many nights had they spent huddled on the floor, giggling as the embers of a dying fire flickered on the ceiling like stars? She closed her eyes and let the memory overtake the present.

"By morning we'd be covered in soot because you decided to re-enact our adventures." Freja scooted further in the bed so they were stretched out and staring at the dark wood ceiling, pretending it was home. The mage lights did not flicker, but they were dim enough to pretend.

"That's because I'm the best at storytelling."

Freja snorted, but didn't argue. The crash of waves overtook them for a moment, calming the bittersweet words between them. "What will you do? When we defeat the darkness?"

"I'll see the world," Brenna said with a smile. "Anything. Everything. Tatterhood will be known across the five kingdoms, not just Ayworn."

"She won't be able to beat out Bri, the amazing princess that banished the darkness from whence it came," Freja teased, but there was an undercurrent of pain and aching, a familiar argument.

"What will you do?" Brenna asked, not willing to fall into the debate, not willing to let go of Tatterhood with Hilde's death feeling so raw.

"Hmm, I think I'll have my first royal project."

Brenna sat up and looked at her sister in confusion. A royal project was a building that was dedicated by the royal family for a specific purpose. The queen was known for orphanages as her royal projects while the king had built specialty barracks. The people that went through a royal project were given training and care in the expectation that they would serve the kingdom in a meaningful way. Such buildings had fallen to the wayside in recent years. There was too much to do simply to survive, too many people needing help.

"What sort of project?"

Freja smiled, a spark of mischief in her eyes. "A very different sort."

"Well, now you have to tell me." Freja mimed locking her mouth shut and Brenna whined, "Freja, you have to tell me, it's gonna kill me not knowing."

Freja patted her head comfortingly but offered no secrets. Brenna flopped over in her lap, groaning. "The worst sister."

Brenna opened her mouth to try and pry the idea from her when shouts and thumps wafted over the sound of the sea. Frowning, she leaned toward the wall. "What—"

The boat gave a sudden lurch and it was only Freja grabbing her and pulling her back that kept her from ramming into the wall. Brenna leveraged her weight and stood. "Come on!"

Thankfully it was just that one painful sway before the boat settled, but as they scrambled topside, shouts and screams filled the air.

Chaos reigned.

Another larger ship had come up beside them, filled with dozens of people armed to the teeth. Several ropes had been thrown between them, connecting the ships and keeping them close. Tapio was at the rail with a shield and sword, face in grim determination even as his eyes struggled to focus. Delja hid behind some crates, hands over her ears and eyes squeezed shut. Einar was alternating between throwing bolts of magic and keeping the ship from crashing into the other ship.

Brenna took all this in and squared her shoulders. "Freja, get your bow and keep that ship busy."

She didn't wait for confirmation; she ran to Delja, putting a hand on the girl's shoulder. Delja startled, staring at her with wide, fearful eyes. "Delja, I need you to help Einar. We need him to use magic and he can't do that and steer. Can you do that?"

"I..." There was a roar from the enemy as they worked to board them. Her whole body shook but Delja nodded. "Try."

"Good. Stay low and stay safe."

Brenna ran over to Tapio, who was still watching the pirates without action. Growling, she yanked the shield from him. "If you're going to be of no use, then get below deck, you idiot."

She didn't wait to see if he listened. Hefting the shield up on her left arm, Brenna drew her sword and ran to the rail, working to rid them of the ropes. The excitement of battle rushed through her, strengthening her mind and body, helping her to lift the shield as arrows and spears rained on her.

Thwack. Another rope gone.

She dared to look down the rail, half a dozen to go. Brenna skipped the next three and cut the fourth.

Thwack. This time a man accompanied the rope to the sea, his startled yelp and subsequent splash drowned out by his companions' jeers.

166

Light soared over her head and a rope beside her disintegrated. She sent a grin and salute to Einar from the helm. He offered a nod in response. Freja was in position nearby, aiming and loosing arrows into the offending boat. While Brenna doubted she wanted to hit anyone, it was enough to cause chaos and hesitancy from the group.

Thwack. Brenna huffed and whirled to the next one.

And met the sneering face of a pirate.

She reacted instinctively, whacking the guy in the face with the shield, forcing him to drop to the sea. Brenna smirked. "Have a nice fall."

"That was horrendous," Einar said, suddenly next to her. She glanced at the helm, seeing a pale but determined Delja at the wheel. "There are so many better pun opportunities."

Rolling her eyes, she raced to the next rope. *Thwack.*

A boot came down on her sword as she aimed for the next rope. She lifted her shield just in time for the other foot to kick her aside. Brenna let go of her sword to keep her from getting injured.

With a huff, she tossed the shield aside and unsheathed two of her daggers. Rolling her shoulders, she took a defensive stance. "Just try that again."

The pirate cocked her head and hopped off the railing as if at ease with the world. Obviously the leader, the captain of this enemy ship. The captain had dark skin and dark eyes and dark hair in dozens of braids, with colorful beads dotting through. Oddly enough, there were no runes etched in those beads, no blessings of protections, no prayers for success. Her eyes were decorated with gold paint that caught the light. She was dressed in sturdy leather over a cream blouse and brown pants, sharp steel decorating her hips and back.

Magical light shot at the captain and splashed around her as if hitting an unseen barrier. Einar startled. "What—"

The pirate captain focused on him for a moment, a condescending smile in place. "The eye of Berundi grants me protection against the fae and their unnatural ways."

Einar snarled. "It doesn't protect your men."

"It protects enough and you cannot defeat us all." She spread her hands out in faux peace as more of her people boarded their boat. Brenna's knuckles grew white as she held her stance. Freja joined her side, arrow nocked and aimed at the leader.

"We have nothing of value for you," Freja said, ever the diplomat, ever willing to resolve things with words rather than steel. "Let us part in peace."

The captain turned to her. "I too aim to part with you in peace, but you are mistaken when you state you have nothing of value. I have no wish for bloodshed. Offer your charter and we will part in friendship."

"I thought you wanted nothing to do with the fae." Einar pushed a sword out of his face. "It *sword* of seems like a contradiction asking for the fae's blessing."

"We want what all do in these trying times," she said calmly, looking at Brenna for a moment. "Safe passage through this darkness. Would you deny us such hope?"

"And leave us stranded in the process!" Einar snarled.

The charter was their only way to the Isle. Without it, they would be forced to drift in the sea aimless or stuck in Denwes until another charter or passage could be received. If it could be received.

The captain sighed. "If we can reach no agreement, we will take what we need by force. The only injuries are the ones you cause yourself."

Brenna raised her daggers at the implicit threat and felt Freja beside her tense. Her eyes darted from the captain to the ever growing number of her crew boarding the small boat. There was no winning this. Even with Einar's magic, they were outnumbered.

Before anyone else could speak, before anyone could make the first move to break the tenuous truce between them, both boats lurched sickeningly, waves crashing against the boats as if stirred up by a tumultuous storm.

The sun shone brighter in retaliation.

XIII

Det blæser en halv pelican

It's blowing half a pelican

Chaos reigned for several minutes as seasoned and new sailors alike attempted to regain their footing. Delja screamed from the helm, thrown from her position by another vicious tumbling. Brenna sheathed her knives, knowing she was at a higher danger of hurting herself rather than an enemy until the world stopped shifting.

"Get the charter!" The captain shouted. Her men rushed the helm.

Brenna helped Einar up. "I'll get Delja, you stop them."

"With pleasure." He rolled his shoulders and shot a burst of magic over their heads, unaffected by the rolling deck of the ship.

Brenna grabbed the railing for stability and knocked over the two guys nearest to her, using the movement of the ship and their own instability to tip them over. They fell into the sea, the churning water masking their splashes. Her stomach rolled along with the ship and she took a deep breath to calm it.

"Bri!"

Brenna whipped around and ducked as someone swung at her. The sailor joined his companions in the sea. She grabbed Freja and pulled them both toward the helm. "What is happening?"

There was no reason for such violent shifting of the boat. The sky was clear and the wind absent.

"I think it's something in the water!" Freja said. They fell into the staircase, leaning against the wall until the ship stilled enough for movement. "I heard one of the sailors say syrenka."

Brenna wasn't familiar with the word, but she could guess. The fae of the water. The demons of the sea. Her people had their own term for the one that called to sailors and lured them to their deaths. If they could not appease them, they'd be lucky to have a boat left to sail.

"We have to get Delja." Freja clutched a railing to stay upright.

They stumbled up the steps and ignored the pitched battle between Einar and the captain at the helm. Delja was clinging to the rails as water drenched her. The red patchy skin on her arms shifted to blue-green scales as she got wet. With her hair plastered to her, her ears stuck out, pointed tips plain for all to see. She and Brenna's gazes met in another lurch, a webbed hand reaching out for Delja.

"Delja!"

A wave came up and nearly swallowed the entire ship. When the water cleared from Brenna's eyes, Delja was gone.

"No!"

The ship stilled and Brenna whipped around in time to see the captain pull out a sparkling stone from beneath the helm. Einar was trapped in chains that held the same gold paint and patterns that decorated the raiding crew, something that held his magic in check. She rushed up the last few steps to regain the charter, only to be met with a wall of swords.

"Thank you for your cooperation. We wish you the best of luck." The captain saluted, then barked out orders to her men to disembark.

Brenna lunged forward to retaliate, but Freja dragged her to the rail. "Do you see her?"

Delja. The charter was lost, but they could still save each other. Brenna scanned the sea frantically, then began to pull off the heaviest of her gear. "Grab me some rope, she can't be too far."

The last of the pirates were back on their own ship, sneering and mocking from safety. In her periphery, Brenna noted the captain being the last to board. The captain turned to them and gave them one last mocking salute before stepping onto her ship.

In doing so, the world lurched once more.

But unlike the churning of the sea from the mysterious attackers below, this disorientation came from the sudden shift in the sun and disappearance of the raiding ship. All at once, Brenna had the ill sensation of having moved despite the lack of physical movement.

"What…" Brenna blinked at the empty sea around them. "What happened? Where'd the ship go?"

"They took the charter," Einar said, free from his bonds. His voice was flat and empty of its usual bite. "Delja?"

"She just fell. I'm sure we can get to her if we just—"

"Don't bother. She's lost to us now."

Brenna frowned at the shift in his mood, at the utter emptiness he was displaying. "She's not lost."

"The marmennlar would have reclaimed her," he said as he turned back to the helm, ending the discussion as he walked away, but not before throwing a bolt of magic, shifting the ship's wheel into a large pine tree.

She stared after him until he disappeared below deck and then turned to her sister. "Hand me the rope."

"I don't think we should." Freja was watching the water, now calm as it lapped against the wood. She frowned as if seeing something just beyond the surface and shook her head. "I'll go check on Einar. You should check with Tapio. We'll regroup and form a plan."

Brenna stared at the water, tempted to dive in anyway, but sighed and stepped back. Freja usually had a good instinct, especially in all this fae nonsense they found themselves in. Freja squeezed her hand in relief as she declared, "She's not gone. We'll figure out a way to get Delja back."

Freja smiled. "Of course. But first, a plan."

Which meant getting the boys back on track. Brenna had lost sense of where Tapio went after she told him to get below deck. At least it wasn't a large ship. With a salute to her sister, she went below to search.

It did not take long to find Tapio. She followed the sound of shattering glass against wood. She pushed open the door to the boy's room to find him throwing bottles of ale at the walls, eyes dark and glowering as he soaked the room in the musty scent of spilled drink.

"Tapio?" She hovered by the door, unsure what was sparking this fit of rage.

Another bottle met its end.

"Tapio!" She lurched forward before he could grab broken glass. "What is going on?!"

He swayed, shoulders heaving as he sighed. "I was useless. I was so lost in my grief. I've been so lost in drink that I…"

Maybe Brenna had been a little harsh in the heat of battle. All her instructors were quick to point out her flaws, stating that any weakness would be the reason she fell in an attack. And in her attempt to prove them wrong, she grew sharp and pointed. Seeing Tapio on deck as they were being overwhelmed…it had been instinct more than anything. Hide the flaws, protect any weakness.

She hadn't meant to send him into some sort of personal crisis.

"You couldn't have known we would run into trouble," she said, not really sure how to comfort. The annoyed glare he tossed her way proved how effective she was being. She tried a different track. "Alright, fine, you drink way too much. You let it cloud your judgment. And yes, we lost the charter and we lost Delja, but we're going to get them back. "

"I won't touch alcohol again," he swore.

"We need a plan. Freja is wrangling Einar. Come on." She didn't comment on his promise. It was not unusual to promise such things when consequences fell. How many times had she heard soldiers promise the same? Only to find them back at the tavern after a rough shift patrolling too close to the darkness.

So she didn't comment on it. Didn't place expectations. If he wanted to quit, she would support him, but she would be there if he chose to pick it back up as well.

"I smashed all the alcohol," he said, as if it led credence to his promise. That he couldn't back out even if he wanted to.

She smiled and tugged him upstairs. "Stop blaming yourself. Now, come on."

He stumbled after her as they made their way above deck. Freja had managed to get Einar back up but judging by her pursed lips, he was not being cooperative. He was also sprawled out on the deck, eyes staring unblinking at the cloudless sky.

Brenna sighed, the tenuous truce they had built wavering. "Alright, let's take stock of what happened."

Because something had happened beyond being thoroughly trounced and raided. The sun, which had been shifting west in the afternoon, had been on their right side and now it was directly in front of them. The sky had lost the few clouds that lingered. The pirate ship disappeared in the blink of an eye.

"That charter was stolen." Einar's voice was devoid of any emotion and he didn't sit up from his position.

Brenna glared, biting back the urge to snap. Freja put a hand on her arm and said kindly, "And what does that mean?"

"We're lost."

Tapio cleared his throat. "Ships that lose a charter through force are transported to a random place at sea. It ensures the Lost Isle stays, well, lost."

Great. So turning around and heading back to Denwes wasn't an option. They could be near Faldinn for all they knew. Brenna pulled out a knife and twirled it in her hands as she thought through the problem. "Well, we can't just drift. Could we petition the water fae for help? We could ask them to return Delja as well."

"I don't think they'll be forthcoming," Freja said.

"It's worth a try at least."

Einar sat up abruptly, fixing his pale gaze on her, anger breaking through his apathy. "Do you have any clue what you're saying? You're idiotic and naive."

Bristling, Brenna stepped forward, the knife shifting to her palm. "I don't see you coming up with anything! You seem content to resign her to her fate!"

"Because she's lost to us!" He growled and stood, hands glowing in his anger just as surely as her hands gripped her dagger. "Do you know what the marmennlar do to half children? They free the fae from the human. A pretty way of saying they kill them. Just because they're different. Because they share two cultures instead of one. And it's your fault they took her!"

"My fault?!"

"She should have stayed below deck."

"We needed help against the attack."

"And where did that get us?" he demanded, the air around him growing charged, as if a storm swirled around them, waiting to strike.

Freja stepped in to diffuse, putting a hand on each of their chests. She sent a hard glare at Brenna and a softer look at Einar. "This isn't the time or place. Right now, we need a plan. Let's pick a direction to sail. If we come across the borders of the darkness, we will at least know which way to turn."

The darkness, for reasons Brenna did not know, disappeared at the sea. At least from sight. Boats that attempted to cross the invisible barriers dividing the kingdoms were met with watery graves. How the fae circumvented this was unknown. If they ran into the darkness out here in the wide sea, Brenna was not convinced they would have a chance to turn away.

"Fine, whatever." He waved his hand and the tree shifted back to a wheel once more. His shoulders were tight and rigid as he turned. "Just get Scarhead away from me."

It wasn't the worst Brenna had been called, but with the sun beating down mercilessly, with her rage just under the surface, it was the last straw with Einar. Momentary understanding and tenuous trust between them gone in a vapor. With a growl, Brenna shifted forward, only to have a hand catch her arm. Freja shook her head and Tapio pulled her back towards the hatch.

Brenna ripped away from him. "Don't touch me."

She stalked downstairs, suddenly wishing she had more of Tapio's bottles to smash against the wall.

"You need to get over your anger." Freja was leaning against the doorframe, arms crossed.

Brenna twirled her knife and threw it at the wall, finding satisfaction in the way it embedded in the wood. "Don't start. Don't take his side!"

"He can't see you, Bri," she said with a sigh, her tone scolding as if Brenna were a child. "He has no idea what you look like. He was guessing and hoping you'd react just like you did."

"You're still defending him." She ripped the knife out of the wall and took a few steps back to throw it again.

"He didn't kill Hilde." Freja was soft and quiet.

Her focus slipped and the knife clattered to the ground, missing its mark. "…What? Of course he did. It was his raid."

That was the whole point of the life debt, why Einar was in their service to begin with. Brenna stared at her sister in disbelief, confused. Freja pushed off the door and picked up her knife, handing it back to her. "It was a collapsed passage."

"No doubt done by that oafish troll." Brenna didn't want to be talking about this. She didn't want to think about what happened to Hilde. It was too soon. Too raw.

"I asked."

"Asked what?" Her voice didn't waver but she wished she could take back the words. She didn't want to know.

Freja sat on the bed and stared at her hands. "Before we left. I asked what happened. I…I had to know. It was the south end hall that led to the rose gardens."

There were half a dozen halls in the castle that were closed due to the danger of collapse. The hall to the gardens was one of them. It had beautiful glass windows and ornate tapestries that decorated the space and a large sign posted in stark black letters. There weren't enough people to help rebuild the castle. There weren't enough supplies or money.

Freja continued as Brenna stood frozen. "Apparently a couple kids had been playing in it despite being off limits. When the attack happened, they hid there. Hilde got them out."

"Why are you…" She couldn't focus on it, couldn't dwell on the awful images that came so easily, so she switched tactics. "That would get Einar out of his debt. We still have use of him."

Freja's lips pursed in a flat line as she raised an eyebrow, a look too reminiscent to the queen, causing Brenna's rage to flare up again. "He could easily figure it out himself. He's not here because of his debt anymore."

"It's—that's beside the point! It was still his raid that triggered the collapse."

"And it's his magic and his boat and his expertise that has gotten us here thus far!" Unimpressed with her excuses and anger, Freja's voice raised to match hers. "Stop being angry at him for something that's not his fault."

"You can't tell me you're not in the least bit angry about her death! That you don't hate him for losing the only person we had as a mother." She wrapped herself in the pain and hatred and anger like her cloak.

Freja stood, her hands clenched, her perfect court mask slipping to mirror her sister's anger. "No! I'm not angry at him! I don't hate him. You wanna know what I hate? Do you want to know who I blame? Tatterhood!"

For the second time that day, Brenna felt her world shifting and crashing without movement. "W-what?"

"You and Hilde and that cursed cloak! She taught you that that ridiculous ratted cloth meant more than your life. She taught you that kindness meant sacrifice. And in the end, she died for that belief." Her voice cracked as it dropped to a whisper. "Do you ever think what it would do to us if we lost you?

"Freja, I—"

But Freja wasn't done. Her voice rose to a steady, aching tone, never rising to a shout. "No. You don't. And neither did she. She died to save those kids and she taught you how to do the same. You fought a pair of draug single handedly without once thinking to ask for help. You should have died that day. For what? Vengeance for a couple of sheep? You throw away your life for a patched castoff and I'm left alone."

Brenna opened her mouth, but nothing came out. She couldn't renounce Tatterhood, it was the only title that held any worth and it was her last remaining tie to Hilde, to the woman who loved and taught her so much. But neither could she refute Freja's claims. She would have gladly died protecting her people, defending her family. She didn't have to think twice about it. Her sister was right, she didn't think about how her siblings would fare if she went out as Tatterhood and never came back one day.

Taking a deep breath, Freja pulled herself together and moved to the door. "So no, Brenna. I don't blame Einar. I can at least count on him to save his own skin if needed."

Freja walked away without another word.

Stumbling back, Brenna fell on the bed, sinking into the lumpy mattress. She tugged off the cloak, fingers tracing the patched edges, remembering all the times she spent repairing each hole and rip. She didn't like embroidery, didn't have the patience to sit and create artistic beauty, but she loved patching the cloak. She had enough patience to sit and darn and whisper to Hilde what adventures caused the tears.

She yanked off the cloak and threw it in a corner with a huff. She pulled her knees to her chest and let the raging wound left from Hilde's death bleed just a little.

Until someone knocked on the door.

It had to be Tapio. Freja would need time to cool off and Einar was unlikely to seek her out. Resisting the urge to yell, she unfolded herself and yanked the door open to…

To the empty hall.

Perhaps it was a spray off the ocean or a confused fish swimming too close to the surface. Brenna shook her head and turned back to the room, not ready to face everyone. As her eyes fell back to the bed, she froze.

The cloak was folded neatly and cleanly where she had been sitting. Her eyes darted to the corner where she threw it, empty now, then back at the innocuous cloth. The air above it shimmered and in a blink, a holtasoley flower rested on top. An apology from Einar. She sighed and picked up the delicate white flower.

Anger vanished, leaving exhaustion and grief in its wake. Brenna placed the flower and cloak on the nightstand and curled up under the covers.

She did not realize she drifted asleep until she was being thrown from the bed by a violent lurch of the ship. Landing hard on the floor, she threw out her hands to stop from slamming against the wall. She turned her back to the wall with a grunt and pushed herself up to stand. Her hands found the cloak and fastened it automatically around her neck.

She glanced at the windows, showing a violent sea and black sky, and stumbled out to help. Tapio and Freja were dripping wet in the hall, looking as if they fought the storm themselves. "Where's Einar?"

"Keeping the ship from ripping apart," Tapio shouted over the roar of the sea. "Said to stay below deck."

She risked a glance at the hatch leading to the top deck, then looked at Freja. Her sister was resigned, her eyes red from crying. Brenna's shoulders slumped and she nodded. "We should fasten anything loose down here, just in case."

Freja's relief was palpable as they split off into different rooms, bolting down boxes of supplies. Brenna fell to her knees often as the ship rocked. Even in the underbelly of the ship, water made its way in, making the floors slick. Brenna never saw the box sliding from the shelf. No. One moment she was sliding through the room, grabbing anything loose to tie with a rope, unable to hear her own thoughts over the raging storm, a sharp pain in her head, and the world succumbed to darkness.

XIV

Båtlaus mann er bunden til land

Boatless man is tied to the land

*B*renna woke up with her mouth and hair full of sand. Her entire body felt like one big bruise. She could feel her heartbeat in a lump on her head. Groaning, she sat up and took stock of her surroundings. Her pack was next to her, empty save for the box holding the heart pieces. A small mercy.

A mountain range loomed over her with ever white peaks and sprawling dark green wood. At first glance, she would have thought she was home. But the difference between the hills of home and these was the black shadows obscuring half the range. Unless something drastically changed in the few days she had been gone, this was not Ayworn. Ealic was the only other kingdom with coastal mountain ranges.

One piece of the puzzle solved, she looked around once more. Frantically, she called out, "Freja? Tapio? Einar?"

"Do you always have to be so loud?" Einar sat up from further up the beach and shook off the sand. Two other lumpen shapes shook as well, revealing Freja and Tapio.

"Anyone hurt?" A stupid question after the horrific storm and subsequent beach stranding. "Where's the ship?"

The sand around them lacked driftwood and remains of their ship. Nor was the boat drift by the shore. Had they shipwrecked like she thought, the remains of the ship should be scattered along the beach with them. It was just them half buried in the white sand of this natural cove.

"We capsized," Einar croaked, his voice rough from salt water. "Something knocked me out so I don't know what happened."

Hrolf and Signe were on that boat. Brenna closed her eyes for a moment to feel the pang of loss. Would she be striped of everything from her home by the end of this quest? Pain radiated up her legs as she stood, sending her stumbling back to the sand. Gritting her teeth, Brenna stood again. "We should find the nearest town. I think we're in Ealic."

Einar frowned and cocked his head as if listening. "Yeah… we are."

Brenna held out a hand for Freja, who took it gratefully. Hugging her, Freja whispered, "I'm sorry."

Offering a half smile of acceptance, Brenna pulled away and helped Tapio up. He accepted gratefully. "I think I've lost my cane."

"Probably."

Casually, he lifted his hand and brushed her cheek, dusting off the sand. She felt every particle grate against the stained mark.

Blue eyes met dark brown and red flushed on the other side. She pulled away quickly, her breath coming out in short huffs.

Einar was standing already but was hunched over on himself, his face twisted in a grimace. "Town's this way."

They lost Delja. Hrolf and Signe were likely dead or stranded in a boat with no rescue. Brenna wanted to scream until her voice gave out. Heartsore with no healing in sight, she fell silent instead. Her breathing hitched over the pain as she followed Einar.

Thank the Norns for Einar's abilities. She would never be comfortable with magic, but having a magic user keep them from getting lost in the woods was useful. She walked with Tapio in the shifting sand, silently offering her arm or shoulder for stability. Perhaps they could find a sturdy replacement to his crutch in the woods.

Freja came up on Tapio's other side, raised an eyebrow at Brenna, then nodded pointedly at Einar. Brenna sighed. He had apologized for the argument; it was only right that she offer the same. Leaving Tapio in her sister's capable hands, she jogged up to their fearless guide.

"If you're here to be obnoxiously cheerful, you can go back to Sir Limps A Lot."

Well someone woke up on the wrong side of the beach. She pulled her cloak around her tighter, wincing as she felt a patched seam give way. "I was going to apologize, but I'm reconsidering."

"Good." His feet were sure as the land shifted from sandy beach to shaded forest, unerringly finding a game path to follow.

"I'm not a flower kind of girl though," she said, keeping her eyes on the ground, ignoring the way he tensed. "I prefer things with a sharp edge. Also, thanks for keeping us from not dying, I suppose."

She didn't have magic to offer gifts of friendship and reconciliation and grabbing the nearest branch seemed paltry. She looked down at her cloak, ripped and tattered from the most recent brush with death. With careful precision, she tugged a piece off long enough to tie around his head and offered it to him. "In case your eyes need a break or something."

He didn't say anything and Brenna was beginning to regret offering at all. He could have pulled the cloth from his own clothes, probably would prefer it to hers. This was dumb. Her hand began to pull away but he swiped the strip of cloth away. "Yeah, whatever."

Rolling her eyes, she fell back. Freja gave her an unimpressed glare and Brenna retaliated with a gesture of her own. Freja raised an eyebrow, and caught up with Einar herself, determined to smooth out any hurt feelings.

"He doesn't want to talk, I say leave him be." Not that her sister was listening. Brenna glanced over at Tapio, who was watching with amusement. "How are you feeling?"

"Ironically clear headed, given the thrashing we just endured." He smiled and her stomach twisted in knots. "And wishing I had been brave enough to quit the drink sooner."

"You were doing what you needed to survive. There's no shame in that." Brenna didn't want to think about how she would be faring if they had gone home to deal with Hilde's death instead of going on this quest. She was barely handling it as it was. Hilde. Delja. Hrolf. Signe. How many names would join the lost?

"Still, I'm grateful a spunky princess showed up in my corner of the bar to drag me out by my cane."

"Bri," she said quietly.

"What?"

Brenna rolled her shoulders and looked ahead at Freja conversing quietly with Einar. "We've all nearly died half a dozen times. You should just call me Bri."

"Bri," he murmured, testing her name out. A small thrill went through her with the way he said it, so different from the familiar way her family used her name. Could he feel the sparks running through her as he leaned against her for support? "Hmm, no, I think Princess suits you much better."

To show just how much she approved of his quippy remark, she jerked away from him, letting him stumble at the lack of support. He had the audacity to laugh. Her heart had the audacity to flutter at the sound.

But Brenna wasn't a monster, so she found a suitable stick and offered it to him instead of her arm, needing the small amount of space to reclaim her bearings. "Does it hurt? Your leg?"

"No. It's pretty much a dead weight from my knee on." He tested out the offered branch and nodded as it held. "I have to be careful because I don't feel it if I get injured."

"How did it happen?" The words came out in a rush, a question that had been burning in the back of her mind since the day they met, tempered and caged by endless lessons on polite conversation.

"Nope. My turn."

"What?"

Tapio smirked and again she was left feeling as if she were still on the rocking boat, unsteady, uncertain. "You asked a personal question, it's my turn to ask you one. That's how the game works."

She rolled her eyes. She was just satisfying her curiosity but she supposed it was fair enough for him to get a turn. Brenna motioned for him to get it over with.

His smirk shifted into a snort at her antics and she silently berated her nerves. "Why did you pick the name Tatterhood?"

Her toes found a root at that moment and she flailed as she fought to stay upright. She smoothed out her shirt and cleared her throat. "I didn't pick it. It was…Hilde was Tatterhood before me. She would use the cloak to distribute food and medicines to the Sticks. Before that it was her aunt as the royal seamstress, who took any leftover cloth to mend for others unable to afford it."

The cloak had once been a patchwork of fine cloth, burlap, and scraps. As Hilde adapted the role, the cloak too adapted to dark colors meant to hide rather than showcase a seamstress' skills. More repairs were needed once Brenna took the role, adding on the sturdy, plain cloth that appeared more seam than cloth. Her fingers ran along the carefully sewn edge meant to prevent fraying.

"Who's Hilde?"

"I believe it's my turn now."

He scrunched his nose and sighed. "I suppose I set those terms. Are you changing your question?"

Biting her lip, she weighed her options. Asking about his leg was a deeply personal story, one that could merit one of hers in return. With a huff, she batted back the edge of the cloak. "Not unless you want me to."

Tapio fell silent and she didn't push. Had he told the story before now? Beyond the basic explanation of Faldinn falling and all with it, did he ever tell anyone the details of his darkest day. Brenna kept her gaze neutrally forward, but she noticed his fingers twitching as if seeking the familiarity of a flask.

"That's…a story that needs a more apt setting," he finally said, leaning more heavily on the crutch, holding a weight beyond the clothes on his back.

"That's fine," she said, forcing a lightness in her tone. "You'll just owe me one. What's your favorite food?"

They left the dark and prickly conversation behind them, trading favorite foods and colors and nonsensical things that belonged to a brighter and normal world. He did not ask about Hilde. She did not ask about his family. In a different life, in a different time, Brenna could imagine this was a conversation she would have had with him in a ballroom, with arms around each other and music swelling. She would have been wearing a mask, a cover to hide her disfigurement.

When was the last time she had gone so long uncovered, unhidden from the world, from who she was? She brushed a loose strand behind her ear, fingers trailing the mark briefly. Would Tapio, unburdened from the loss of his family, care about the disfigured princess of Ayworn?

"Chatterboxes, we're stopping for the day."

Brenna blinked at Einar's intrusion, surprised to see it so dark out. She flushed at Freja's slight smile, at how close she and Tapio had gotten as they walked. She stepped away and cleared her throat. "We can't make it to town?"

"It'll take us half a day tomorrow to reach it." Einar stretched out on the ground. "I, for one, have no desire to listen to you three attempt to walk through the woods in the dark."

"How can you tell?" Once more, Brenna was left baffled by Einar's strange not-sight.

"Magic." He grinned lopsided, showing sharp teeth.

That was always his answer and Brenna didn't believe it for one minute. "Or…?"

He didn't answer right away, hooking his hands behind his head and tilting back as if to view the forest canopy above. Just as she was about to give up getting an answer, he sighed. "Used to call this home once."

Oh.

Obviously Einar had a home, one that wasn't a tavern with his raiding troupe or the wrteched excuse he called a boat. Brenna left his sour mood alone and went to get wood for a fire. Game was scarce, but they managed a few conies to split amongst them for a meager dinner. No ship, no supplies. Two out of five heart pieces. No money to restock. Delja gone.

Brenna stuffed her cloak into a ball and used it as a pillow, laying back with a groan. She stared up at the shadows cast by the flickering fire, picking out the stars in the gaps of the trees. She frowned as a glow of green built across the sky.

"What is that?" What else were they going to endure on this journey? She sat up, hand slipping to her knife.

Einar tossed a bone in the fire, forcing it to flare up. "Weird lights in the sky?"

"Yes, what—"

"It's the revontulet. Fox fires." Einar leaned back on his hands, eyes closing as if he could sense the ethereal light now dancing over them.

"What are fox fires?" Freja asked as Brenna got up and began to climb a nearby tree, eager to get a better look.

He waved his hand at the sky. "Those are fox fires. You don't have them in Ayworn?"

Brenna missed the scathing look Freja tossed at him, instead wholly focused on breaking through the canopy. She gasped. Dancing across the night were streaks of green light, slowly shifting like smoke in the wind. It was like nothing she had ever seen and it stole her breath away.

"Perhaps we once had them to the north, but if so, the stories have been lost," Freja said from below, her voice carrying through the branches. "Why do you call them fox fires?"

Brenna watched the sky display in wonder and awe. Below, Einar found his voice, markedly more solemn and quieter than before. "My father claimed the first fox looked out on the tundra, frozen and desolate, and ran. It ran and ran and ran until its feet and tail grew sparks and created the first flame. The snow and fire mingled and instead of smoke, it let out light to guide weary travelers to the warmth.

"He said that since the darkness, the fox still works to protect its people, offering light and warmth on the coldest nights." There was a pause and some shuffling. Brenna's tree shook and Tapio's head appeared. He grinned and joined her to watch. "It's a bunch of romantic nonsense. Meant to make you feel better."

"I like it," Freja said. "Revontulet. It's a sign of hope."

"Gross." Einar gagged.

An unfelt wind shifted the colors, forcing the green to dance across the clear night sky, obscuring the stars in its brilliance. Beside her, Tapio's breath caught.

"It's beautiful," Brenna whispered.

"My people," Tapio said, slow and quiet. "call it revontulet as well, but it means spell fire in our tongue. We believe the lights to be those who came before us, approaching the land to guide and warn. I never witnessed them before, but my mother said she saw them once as a little girl, just after her grandmother passed. She often attempted to paint the experience as a record, but she was never happy with the result. I didn't understand until now."

No. This was not something that could be captured by human hands.

Conversation ebbed and the noises of the night grew. The fire below dwindled to embers as the fire in the sky sparked. Somewhere deep in the underbrush, a fox called for its mate. Brenna stayed up late into the night to watch, even as Tapio whispered his goodnights and those below fell into slumber. She stayed until her eyelids drooped and she leaned dangerously from the high branches.

Even as she climbed down and laid in the underbrush, she picked out the ethereal light between the canopy and wondered if this omen was for good or ill.

~~*~*~*

"Up, Bri, up."

Brenna opened a crusty eye and quickly shut it against the dawning light. She turned and mumbled, "Later."

Freja grabbed her makeshift pillow and yanked. "We're not sleeping the day away in the woods. Einar says we can make it to town by lunch if you don't hold us up."

"Me?" She sat up and glared, only to see her sister smugly grinning at successfully getting her up. Brenna scowled. "If anyone holds us up, it's him. He's setting the pace."

Einar was slouched to her left, the strip of cloth she offered yesterday tied around his eyes. "I'll be sure to go faster then."

"Take it back, Bri, before he starts running," Tapio groaned from her right, still laying down with an arm flung across his face. Apparently the only morning person of the group was Freja. Figures. She was also the most demanding person in the group. If Einar wasn't around, she'd definitely top as the most annoying as well.

The most demanding, morning person handed out the leftovers of dinner. "Eat up. We're not stopping until we reach civilization."

"How civilized can it be?" Brenna grumbled as she hunched over her meager breakfast. "Einar grew up here after all."

A rabbit bone hit her on the cheek. Einar bared his teeth in a facsimile of a smile at her glare. Freja smacked her hand before she could retaliate. "Do you know if the heart piece will be close to this town, Einar?"

Einar shrugged. "Given that I am not royal and thought they were a myth until you two crashed into my life, I couldn't say. It is the capital though, so if I were a gambling man, I'd bet it's close."

"You are a gambling man," Brenna said as she finished her meal. "You gamble with our lives constantly."

"Lies and slander."

With Freja's nagging insistence, the group shuffled forward to the unknown destination Einar claimed was a town. Aches and pains from being shipwrecked and a night of sleeping with roots and stones left everyone grumbling under their breath and in no mood for conversation. They stopped twice at streams for water and rest before continuing through the woods. The trees never lessened. A road never appeared.

Near midday Brenna reached the limit of her patience. She stopped under the dappled light of the trees and crossed her arms. The brush was so thick that the trail they had been following had disappeared. Nothing but trees and birdsong surrounded them. "You have no clue where we're going do you? If this supposed town was close we would have seen evidence of it by now."

Einar stalked over to her, getting into her face. Without a word, he shoved her backwards through the thick brush. She yelped as she fought branches and leaves, falling onto a paved road.

A road. Thank the Norns. A road!

Einar was already a ways down the road as he called over his shoulder, "Well? You coming or what?"

Freja and Tapio looked down at her, heads poking out from the underbrush. Her sister, the traitor, shrugged. "You were asking for it."

Tapio helped her up at least. "If you go after both of them, just let me know so I can get out of the way."

"This is why you're my favorite." Realizing her tease could have deeper meaning, but not wanting to take it back, Brenna scrambled to catch up with Einar rather than face Tapio.

Einar did not stop at the first inn they saw, which was probably wise given how much the men leered at them, but neither did he stop at the second. Or the third. And he did not make for the castle, shown only by one lonely tower and ratty flag. Instead he dodged pedestrians and questions as he wound through to the city proper. Dirty streets and crowded corners greeted them. People watched with gleaming eyes and flashing knives.

Brenna thumbed a knife as the roads became alleys and the people gained a hungry glint to their eyes. It reminded her of the Sticks, desperate people all crammed into the last refuge from the darkness. But unlike the Sticks of home, these tall buildings were made of stone, permanent fixtures of people living on top of each other. Somehow it made it all the more devastating.

Einar made a sharp left to one such building, climbing up four sets of stairs before stopping by a plain door with a star etched into the wood.

"What is going on, Einar?" Freja asked as he shifted from one foot to the other, making no attempt to knock or continue.

Einar took a deep breath. With one hand he pulled off the cloth around his eyes and slipped it in his pocket. With the other, he flattened his pale hair. "Right. Thing One, fix the rat nest you call hair."

"Hey!"

He continued, "Lame-o, your leg is bad, not your back. Stop slouching."

"I'm not—"

"Copycat, I'm sure you've missed a speck of dust somewhere. Fix it."

Freja looked down at herself in alarm, hands fluttering to find one thing out of place. Einar straightened his shoulders and pushed the door open.

A dozen eyes belonging to kids from five to fifteen turned to them in eerie unison. Brenna blinked. What?

"Einar's home!"

XV

Without justice, courage is weak

$\mathcal{A}$t the proclamation, the tension in the air popped and the kids converged on them, dragging them in, pelting them with questions, rifling through their pockets. Brenna smacked a few roaming hands and pinned the unrepentant child with her best impression of Queen Beret's glare number six. The urchin had the gall to offer a cheeky grin as another tried swiping the knife at her boot.

Einar stepped aside, saved from prying hands, and watched in great amusement.

"What is happening?" Brenna asked, bewildered.

"Isn't it obvious?" Freja asked, looking at the kids and smiling at the younger ones. "They're Einar's family."

"How is that obvious?" Brenna glanced at Tapio, who seemed just as lost as her.

Freja raised an eyebrow with a look that told her she was being particularly dense. "They look exactly alike."

What? Brenna looked between the kids and Einar and wondered if Freja hit her head at some point. While Einar had no color to him, this family exploded with color. All the kids sported dark hair, tanned skin, and jeweled tone eyes, as if mocking their pale brother. But, she supposed, they all shared the same almond shape to their eyes, the same pointed nose and sharp chin, the same mischievous smirk that set her on edge.

Einar would have looked like them before he stole the magic and lost his sight. The realization jolted through her like lightning.

"What did you bring us? I want a new dolly!" A young girl pouted at him.

"Sorry Ragnheiður," Einar said, crouching to the young girl's level. "I don't have anything today. What happened to the doll I just got you?"

"Floki ate it!" She pointed an accusing finger at a dog snoring in the corner. She pouted, then turned green eyes to the group. "Is the pretty one your girlfriend?"

Einar smiled and shook his head; he didn't meet Brenna's gaze, his eyes never quite focusing, but there was no doubt that he was facing Brenna instead of Freja. "No, she's got heart eyes for the cripple. Personally, I think she could do better. He smells really bad."

A blush crept up her neck to her cheeks.

"Einar!"

Oh thank goodness. An adult among the mess. A plump woman came out with a babe on her hip and several other kids trailing after her. Her dark hair was going gray and her eyes seemed to shift colors like the sea. She put her free hand on her hip in disapproval as she stared at her oldest. "What'd I tell ya about outing young couples?"

Einar straightened and grinned, crossing his arms. "To make sure you're present when I do it."

A beat of silence. Brenna glanced between them, waiting for his mother to berate or scold. Instead, she broke out in a huge grin. "That's my Einar! Welcome home!"

The baby was thrust to the nearest person, which happened to be Brenna, as the mother rushed to hug Einar. Brenna held out the child at arm's length. She liked kids. But not before they started talking. Was this a girl or boy? She couldn't tell. In retaliation, the baby gurgled and Brenna was sure it was about to throw up all over her.

"Freja," she hissed. "Take it."

Her sister shook her head in fond amusement and took the baby, cooing and rocking the child until it let out a delighted laugh. "Oh, you're the sweetest little thing."

Tapio yelped as one of the kids kicked out the stick posing as his crutch. He pursed his lips and knocked them with it to get them to back up. The kids giggled and started a game of jumping over his cane without getting hit.

Einar's mother wiped a smudge of dirt from his cheek as she pulled back, studying her son then each of them in turn. "I don't see a bag with ya. Where're the supplies?"

"Our ship was waylaid," he said lightly, as if they hadn't crashed on the shore after being raided by pirates and tossed about in a storm. "I'll bring more next time, promise. We just need a place to sleep before the next raid."

"Of course, honey. Of course. You can have the attic." She turned towards them, her amiable nature dropping to suspicious. "Friends of yours?"

"Yes, ma."

The suspicion cleared as she grinned, wide and bright. "They'll bunk with you, but I'm expecting extra rations next time to make up for it. And they eat last."

Einar's personality was starting to make an alarming amount of sense as the kids pressed against them and the mother took back her youngest. Freja smiled. "We won't press your hospitality long. We simply—"

"Need to plan the next raid," Einar finished, grabbing Freja's hand and pulling her towards the stairs. Tapio and Brenna followed. "Got an idea that'll bring in more than I've ever done alone!"

"Well, good. I didn't teach ya to be a bump on the log." Einar's mother shooed them away and Einar pushed them up the stairs and into an attic space. Boxes and bundles were shoved along the walls and Brenna had to crouch as the ceiling was too low to straighten. A lone window provided the only light, showing a breathtaking view of the dirty alley.

He closed the door behind him and held up a hand for silence. His head cocked to the side and he said loudly, "Now, the plan is to use Ketill as bait."

Footsteps clattered down the stairs. He waited a moment then nodded. "All clear. No one listening."

"Just how many siblings do you have?" Brenna asked as she sat on a lump of discarded cloth.

"Doesn't matter. Hallbera won't let you stay more than one night. Don't get comfortable."

Brenna shared an uneasy look with the others. "Which one was Hallbera?"

"My mother," he said, in a tone that implied it should have been obvious. Freja leaned into her sister, a delicate frown marring her features. "The castle closes to the public every day by midmorning. That said, the king is a fat lard uninterested in anything considered noble or righteous."

"He won't make an exception for visiting monarchs?" Freja asked.

He shook his head. "If he thinks you have something of value, he'll take it."

That could be an issue. They had been fortunate in Denwes that the queen had been willing to share the location of the heart piece. Brenna pulled her pack off and checked the box holding the heart pieces, no longer feeling safe enough to keep it out of sight. Seeing her intentions, Tapio handed her a supple pouch meant to be worn about the neck. She smiled gratefully and moved the glowing stone to the pouch and stuffed it under her shirt. Better.

"You don't have any clue about where the heart piece could be?" Tapio asked, stretching his leg out on the bare wooden floor.

Einar shrugged. "I could list a dozen places I would hide it, but no. If it was in the treasury, it would've been bartered off by now. The archives might have a clue."

The ground rattled beneath them followed by a chorus of curses. Einar sighed. "Just stay up here. I'll bring up some food later."

The door opened before he could move and one of the teenagers stuck his head in. If Brenna had to guess, he was only a year or two younger than her. "Stefan blew up the nursery again. And Ragnheiður wants a story."

"I'm coming."

The teen grinned, then looked over at Freja and winked. "Hey, how you doin'? You're single, yeah?"

"Don't." Einar shoved him through the door.

Brenna slumped and sighed. Freja shook her head and looked around, uncertain about where she should sit in the cramped space. She finally settled on a crate that creaked under her. "Well, that was interesting."

Snorting, Brenna closed her eyes. Had she been asked what Einar's family or home looked like, she would have given a very different answer than what they just witnessed. While he admitted to having an older brother, one he failed to save that cost him his sight and gifted him with magic, he never once mentioned others. No wonder he had to raid other people, with so many other kids needing to be fed and clothed in his own home.

The afternoon passed slowly and quietly, with random noises coming from below. To pass the time, Brenna listed all the things she was going to berate Einar over once he returned. The longer they waited without food and without word, the longer her list became.

But when he finally returned, the sun falling rapidly behind the horizon, with his face pinched and his eyes pained, Brenna forgot her list and took the food he offered without complaint. They all settled in for a long night. Einar sat up against the door, eyes wide and unblinking. Brenna tossed and turned even as Freja's breaths grew even and shallow beside her.

They trudged out of the finally silent house just before dawn. Brenna tightened the cloak around her at the chilly hour and even Freja's eyes drooped in sleepy half-awareness. Einar rolled his shoulders and took a deep breath. "So the archives are built into the castle wall. I got a buddy who should let us in."

"And we just poke around hoping to find something?" Brenna asked, the loss and rough travel days catching up with her, coloring her tone.

Einar tensed ahead of them but kept walking. "I don't see you coming up with anything better."

The sounds of discord forced Freja to wake up and she put a hand on Brenna's arm. "I'm sure it'll be a fruitful time. If nothing else, this can provide us an opportunity to know more about your home."

It was not a fruitful time.

The archives was a vague name for a dusty, crumbling hole that held some scrolls and a few books. Einar's buddy was an archivist, dedicated to preserving Ealic history as the country succumbed around him. He did not know what a heart piece was, much less where it would be hidden, and admitted that most of the sacred tomes he protected were incomplete and illegible. The darkness had not only stolen land and people, it had stolen culture and language. He let them search the shelves, but he had nothing else to offer.

In addition, Einar was the only one of the group who understood the Ealic language and he could not read.

By the end of the day, Brenna rested her head on a desk as Freja wandered dusty shelves and Tapio tapped out a pattern with his crutch.

Freja stopped in the aisle and took in everyone's dead eyes and bored expressions. "We should call it a day. Start fresh tomorrow."

"We're not going back to my house." Einar's tone offered no room for argument, which meant Brenna had to at least try.

"Afraid we'll meet your dad?"

He flung a spark of light at her and it zapped her elbow. She yelped and rubbed the spot. "We'd be in serious trouble if you met him, considering he's in jail."

"Perhaps we should try our luck with the king," Freja suggested for the eighth time. "It can't hurt to simply ask."

"Be my guest," Einar crossed his arms and leaned against the wall. "Say hello to dear old dad as they toss you in a cell."

Tapio ignored the bickering as he began to draw diagrams in the dirt. "It has to be somewhere near or connected to the castle. If the current monarch was not given access, it would be in a guarded place, like the Denwish piece."

"Great." Brenna had no desire to turn into stone. Again.

"There's nothing like that here," Einar argued. "Even the prison's a joke. My dad is only there because he doesn't want to come home. I've broken out multiple times."

Their pointless conversation was interrupted by a series of short, high-pitched barks. Curious, Brenna stuck her head out of the archives.

A small arctic fox, its fur just beginning to pale as winter approached, sat in the middle of the road and watched her with dark, glittering eyes. A shiver ran down her spine as it raised its snout and let out a series of barks again.

Tapio and Freja joined her after the second call, but even with the approach of several humans, the small animal remained where it was sitting. Brenna frowned and looked back at Einar, who hadn't moved from his spot, still sulking. "Uh, there's a fox out here?"

"Yes, and?"

"I think it's waiting for you." That was ridiculous. She felt ridiculous saying it, but nevertheless, it felt true.

"They're basically rats," Einar said, waving a hand in dismissal. "Just scare it off."

"Perhaps it intends to lead us," Freja suggested, her eyes growing distant as she stared at the fox. She blinked and smiled. "Isn't the arctic fox the animal totem of Ealic?"

"Only because we hate it so much." Einar scowled. "Ugh, fine, I'll get rid of it."

He stepped out as the fox was barking again. As he did so, the fox stood and ran down the street, stopping just a few feet away before looking back. A clear call. Einar stopped in retaliation. "I am not chasing down a puffball."

"We can go back to your house instead if you prefer," Tapio said with a smirk.

Einar's scowl deepened until his face became a giant wrinkle. "Snow rat, it is."

Sensing his cooperation, the fox once again trotted off, tail high in the air as it bounded down the narrow street. By accident or design, they ran into no other pedestrians as the day waned.

The fox followed the castle wall as the city sloped downward. Brenna caught Tapio's arm a few times as the incline grew too steep for sure footing. He acknowledged her help with pursed lips and a sharp nod.

The fox stopped outside a small hole in the wall. It looked like it had once been a sewer outlet, meant to keep the castle clean by dirtying the city surrounding it, but instead of cutting straight through the wall, this hole went down. Brenna peered down but saw no evidence of the ground below. She took a deep breath, smelling nothing but the dirt and stone around them. She put her hand in and felt as if her hand dipped in an icy sea. Shuddering, she pulled back.

Freja traced etchings on the surrounding stones. "There are runes here. Protection. Hiding. Worth?"

The fox gave one last yip before diving into the unknown. There was no sound of it landing. Einar shook his head. "Nope. You found its home, now let's find a bed to crash. I bet I can get us into one of the inns."

Three collective eyes rolls met his statement. Tapio eased to the ground, letting his feet hang in the hole. "I'll go first and yell if there's something besides that fox waiting for us."

He slipped down without waiting for approval. Again, no other sound floated up from the void. Freja frowned. "I'll go. The heart piece is close."

Brenna didn't ask how she knew that, if she could somehow feel power radiating from the underground. She held her breath and waited until her twin disappeared in the depths. "Freja? Did you make it?"

There was no answering call.

"Right, let's go." Brenna sat on the ground and hesitantly let her feet dangle.

"There is no way you are getting me in that rancid hole." Einar crossed his arms. "It reeks of decay and death, and I can't even sense a bottom. I am not dying because of a fox."

She offered a smile that was too wide and bright. "I wouldn't even think of asking you to do such a thing. You can wait here until we get back."

He relaxed as she readied to jump. At the last minute, she reached out and grabbed his ankle, dragging him into the pit with her. She didn't need to know Ealic to know when someone was cursing her out. She had just enough time in the fall to wonder if they would be falling for the rest of time before the ground caught up with them. They fell in a heap of thankfully unbroken bones.

"I hate you so much," Einar groaned.

"Bri? Einar?" That was Freja. Also not dead. Brenna was counting this as a win.

Brenna sat up and rubbed her eyes, looking around for her sister. She blinked. Rubbed her eyes again. Nothing. She saw nothing. She touched her eyes, yes, they were open. "Freja?"

"Yes, I'm here. So is Tapio." There was a grunt in response, somewhere to her left. "Can either of you see?"

Oh, good, it wasn't just her. "Nothing. Einar?"

He didn't respond, so she nudged him with her foot, oddly thankful they fell together so she knew he was still there instead of a disembodied voice like her sister. He cursed again, but his voice was shakier than it had been on the way down.

"Einar?"

"I...I can't see."

"Well, duh," Brenna teased. "But how about that magic?"

"I can't!" Okay, he was definitely panicking. "My magic helps me be aware of my surroundings so I get a...fuzzy idea of the world. I'm aware of shapes and objects and movement. If I wanted, I could follow a wind to its source. I could pick out a bug in the walls. But somehow my magic's gone!"

That was a problem. As was the increasing frequency of his harsh breathing. Brenna reached out and patted the air until she found what she hoped was his arm. She squeezed gently. "Okay, deep breaths. It's probably a protection for the heart piece."

"Effective," Tapio said from the void. "We're essentially trapped in never ending darkness. At least this darkness holds no creatures to devour us."

If she knew where he was, Brenna would have smacked him. She could feel Einar tensing beneath her hand. "Shut up, Tapio. There's a way out of this, right Freja?"

"I..."

"Nevermind." She knew that tone. That was never a good tone coming from Freja. Brenna took a deep breath. "Look, Einar, you're our only hope at getting out of this."

"What?"

"The fox led you here, not us." And for the moment, she pushed away the negative thoughts of a trap aside. "And let's face it, magic or not, you're the only one with any experience navigating blind."

Einar scoffed, but didn't remark on the accuracy of her joke.

"Come on. Don't make me go all sappy to motivate you." No response. "Einar." Still nothing. She bit her lip. "Fine, you're asking for it. When I was fourteen, my father told me I would never be married and he refused to look for prospects. He thought he was being kind, telling me that I failed once again. I was so bad at being a daughter, I couldn't even secure a marriage alliance.

"Hilde found me later. I…I was in a bad spot, thinking about how pointless it was that I was around, how everyone would be better off if I hadn't been born. I wanted the pain to end." Freja's breath hitched somewhere near her, but she pressed on. "That's when Hilde taught me about Tatterhood, about someone who did good, even when the world grew darker, especially. She pulled this cloak on my shoulders and told me to make it my own.

"Nothing had really changed. My parents still hated me. I served no purpose in their world and had no right to their court. The world was still falling into darkness. But I had changed. On days it was too much, I threw myself into that cloak, that identity, and I made someone else's day brighter. You can do this, Einar. We're more than what people see in us. You're more than your magic."

A beat of silence, only broken up by harsh breathing and ruffled clothes. Einar shifted into a sitting position. "That was vomit inducing."

Brenna gave him a light kick. "Just get us out of here, you nitwit."

"Fine, fine." More shuffling. The arm under her hand moved so it was his hand instead and he pulled her up to stand. "Everyone grab a hand. I don't have all night. Up. Up."

Tightening her grip on Einar, Brenna waved her hand around until she found someone else, Freja judging by the slender fingers. Freja whispered. "I've got Tapio."

"Good." Einar paused, testing out a step, waiting for everyone to shuffle forward with him. "Onward, I suppose. Maybe we'll trip over the cursed rock and be put out of our misery."

A yip resounded through the void. The fox was back.

"Was that left or right?"

"Left. Definitely left."

"No, it was behind us, we should turn back."

"Everyone quiet," Einar hissed. Brenna clenched her jaw, keeping the biting retort behind her teeth. A series of barks pierced through the black void. He took a deep breath, then began to pull. "Don't let go."

He led without faltering as the fox continued to call out in random intervals. The ground beneath them was smooth, so keeping their feet under them was an easy feat. Brenna closed her eyes, unwilling to look out and strain to see nothing.

No one spoke. Freja's grip on her hand grew tighter as they went along and Tapio grew more reluctant to move forward, becoming a deadweight in their chain. Brenna couldn't imagine the horrors he was reliving. But they continued with Einar's guidance, pulling each other along in the vain hope that perhaps there was an end to their journey.

Fur brushed along her leg and she yelped, nearly letting go of her tethers in an effort to get away from whatever touched her. Einar stopped.

"Einar?"

He knelt down, letting go of her hand as he spoke softly, in a language she did not know. Brenna held onto Freja tighter in response.

He took a deep breath, held it, then exhaled slowly. Around him the world exploded into light.

Brenna blinked back the stars in her eyes and looked around the room they found themselves in. It was oddly similar to the Denwish cave, minus the statues of thieves past. A few bones cluttered in corners, too small for anything humanoid, but it was remarkably clear of sinister decor. The fox sat on a pedestal, tail swinging gently, eyes meeting Einar's.

In his hands, he held a gently glowing stone. He held the ragged piece out for Brenna to take and she placed it with the others in the pouch around her neck. As he straightened, a ladder unrolled from the ceiling and a hatch opened up. The way out.

"Well that was obnoxious," Einar said as he turned to them, looking no worse for wear. "What are you all staring at? Let's get out of this pit."

XVI

Att lägga lök på laxen

To put onion on the salmon

Despite disappearing in a sewage hole in the castle wall, deep into the city, they came out in the bustling streets of the docks. Sailors yelled. Children played. Seagulls terrorized. Sight and sound clashed with the quiet and once dark void they were emerging from. Brenna welcomed the chaos, welcomed the vibrant life, and breathed in the salt air.

"I never want to venture underground again," Brenna said, then frowned as she took in the bright morning sun off the horizon. "Wasn't it nightfall?"

"Astute observation," Einar drawled. "Next you'll be telling me we're near the ocean."

Freja took her hand and leaned against her for a moment, relishing in the fact that they survived once more. They had three of five heart pieces. They were that much closer to finally being rid of the stain on their kingdoms. Tapio took several breaths, eyes darting at every reminder that they were no longer in the dark.

Pulling back, Freja surveyed the dock. "We should find passage with a boat to the Isle."

"So being obvious runs in the family then?" Einar asked sarcastically, then cocked his head as if listening. A smile built slowly on his face, but it caught halfway, as if he were unsure if he should be happy or not. Before Brenna could remark how dumb he looked, he bolted.

"Einar!"

But he wasn't listening. He was dodging between people, quickly lost in the crowd. Brenna groaned. "Do we have to follow?"

Freja smiled and tugged her forward. "Only two more heart pieces and you'll be rid of him forever."

It couldn't come too soon. Brenna reached back and grabbed Tapio's free hand to drag him along with them. He was closed off, no doubt still dealing with whatever memories resurfaced from their time in the dark. She wouldn't push, but she wasn't leaving him behind either.

If this is how he dealt with temporary darkness, not even a fraction of the darkness they would encounter on Faldinn, how would he handle leading them in his kingdom? And did Brenna have it in her to ask that of him? It had been one thing to ask a stranger in a pub for help, not knowing his pain, not knowing what they faced. It was entirely something else to ask Tapio to endure his worst nightmares once again.

She would ask Freja's advice later. Her sister would have wisdom for her; she was sure of it.

They wove through the crowd, only keeping sight of Einar by the brightness of his hair in the early light. He was heading for the end of the docks where a lonely ship was moored. This ship, unlike the others filled with bustling crews, seemed abandoned. Instead of warm cream sails and shining wood construction, this ship looked as if it had been dipped in an inkpot: black sails, black wood, black ropes.

Brenna shuddered at the sight, unsure why it gave her such a horrible premonition. Then she saw the ugly, carved helm. The very familiar, ugly helm. It was their ship!

Einar was at the edge of the dock, talking and gesturing wildly with a young girl. Brenna squinted as they got close, then broke into a grin. "Delja!"

Brenna sprinted forward and hugged her. "We were so worried! Einar said you were dead."

"Did not," Einar grumbled as Delja patted his arm in consolation. Despite Einar's warnings, Delja didn't appear injured. She was different though. She stood straighter, confident. Blue-green scales adorned her skin where red, dry patches once marred her. Her hair no longer hid the point to her ears.

"Not dead," Delja said with a smile. "Family found me. There was…misunderstanding."

Delja looked fondly out on the water and Brenna followed her line of sight. Was that something peering just out of the water or a just wave? She took a step away from the water just in case as Freja hugged Delja. "What happened?"

Delja was more centered and more ethereal than before. There was no missing the pointed ears now poking through her shiny black hair or the slight glow to her eyes. She was not fully human and Brenna couldn't mistake it now.

Lifting her hands, Delja signed, "I thought they hadn't wanted me, but they had been searching for me since my mother's passing. When they sensed me on the boat, they thought I was captive. The pirate that attacked us is known for her attacks on their people. On my people. So they pulled me to safety.

I explained everything. I told them about you all and they promised to help. The darkness has split their communities under the sea just as on land and has cut them off from trade. They helped me find the boat, but you were not on it."

"We hit a storm," Brenna explained, looking at the boat with even more apprehension. "What happened with the ship? It should have been smashed by that storm."

Delja shrugged. "I think it passed through the darkness. Signe and Hrolf were upset at being abandoned."

"They're okay?!" Brenna didn't wait for a response, scrambling up the plank and then below deck. Hrolf huffed at her, nipping at her clothes when she got close enough. Signe yowled as Brenna held her close. "Oh, I thought you were lost. Did you protect the boat for us, Signe?"

Her yowl settled into a rumbling growl so Brenna set her down to hug Hrolf instead. He was skittish under her touch and she murmured soft promises of apples and good brushes until he calmed. He pressed his snout into her chest and she closed her eyes. They were safe. They were here. She didn't lose them.

"Having a moment?"

She threw a glare behind her. "Go away, Einar."

He pushed off the wall. "Delja's not done with her story and she won't finish until you come back so get over yourself and come back."

She sighed and patted Hrolf's nose. "I'll be back. Promise."

Following Einar back up top, she blinked at the others sitting on the deck. Einar sat close to Delja, a protective arm wrapping around her, ready to bolt if her family decided to change their mind. Freja swatted at him; she was sitting behind Delja and was braiding her hair in a typical royal style of home. Tapio was on his back, sprawled out and soaking in the sun.

Brenna walked over and nudged Tapio's leg to make room for her. He cracked an eye open and threw her a mock glare.

"Sorry for interrupting, Delja," Brenna said, mainly because she wanted to throw a smug look at Einar. She knew her manners, unlike some people.

Delja was not one for grudges or polite conversation. She beamed at her and pulled out a small bundle of cloth, cupping it in her hands. "Something for you. From Nolpa."

Frowning, Brenna reached out and took the bundle, slowly unwrapping it. Her eyes bugged out as a small stone was revealed. "You…you got the heart?"

"Family helped. To apologize for any hard feelings about taking me away." She leaned back against Freja's hands with a content sigh. "They did not know you were friends."

"How did you get it?"

Sorrow passed over her face for a moment and etched itself in Delja's smile. "Gave up my humanity. I can't be on land more than a day now. Talking hurts more. Still. Worth the price."

"This is…" It felt surreal. Just one piece left and they would be free. Brenna stole a glance at Tapio, who had tensed beside her. His face was passive and closed off, eyes on the far horizon. The next stop was Faldinn.

Brenna reached out to comfort him, but he pulled back, dragging himself up and hobbling towards the rail, leaning heavily on his crutch. Delja frowned. "Was that wrong?"

Brenna shook her head and sighed. "It's really good. We're very close to finishing now. It's…I can barely comprehend it."

"We'll need a charter to get to the Isle still," Einar reminded them. "I appreciate having my ship back as it's a pain carving out the smuggle holds, but it's basically driftwood without a charter."

Delja grinned, sharp teeth and squinting eyes that belonged better on Einar than her. "Or syrena to guide you. The Isle belongs to the fae and the fae belong to the Isle."

"You can get us there?"

She shook her head. "No, but family can."

Delja stood and dragged Freja and Einar up, pulling them to the bow of the ship to show them her family. Brenna hung back and joined Tapio on the side. She said nothing. Simply stood by his side and offered her support as she leaned against the railing, squinting at the sun reflecting off the waves. He didn't speak as he gazed out towards the horizon.

The ship started with a lurch, an unnatural cast off by unseen helpers below.

Brenna waited until the dock slowly disappeared. Tapio sighed and gripped the wood until his knuckles grew pale and ashy. "It wasn't all at once."

Turning, Brenna leaned back against the railing, her back to the sea. "What?"

"When the darkness finally overtook the entirety of Faldinn, it wasn't like everyone dropped dead. It was a mad scramble for the coast, for escape." His voice was hoarse and tight. "We got separated quickly. I didn't know my family's fate until I got to the Isle."

And now he was facing that pain and heartache, returning to his greatest nightmare. Brenna had no love lost for her parents, but had her home faced the same as Faldinn, would she have the strength to return? To return to the place she lost it all? A shudder ran through her. She couldn't even imagine going back to the hall where Hilde fell.

"I'm so sorry," she said, the words feeling inadequate. "Tapio, I—"

"Hey, losers, stop moping and get over here. Delja wants to play a game."

She turned and glared at Einar, briefly wishing for the ability to turn him into a toad or some other less irritating creature. Though he probably could be just as annoying with webbed feet as he was now. Less talkative at least.

Tapio pushed off the rail and offered a smile that didn't quite mask his grief. "He's going to be insufferable around Delja now."

"Going to be?" she asked wryly. There was no 'going to'. The only thing 'going' would be Brenna's last vestiges of patience. She put a hand on his arm to keep him from heading over, determined to say her piece, to not let the conversation end so sadly. "You're not alone. Not anymore."

Not ever if she had her way. If Ayworn was lost to her, then Brenna would make Faldinn her home. She could help rebuild there. She could find out who she was outside her parents' sneers and derisive comments. She could find out what this spark between them meant.

If he wanted that as well.

His smile lost some tension and he shifted his arm so that he was escorting her as if in court. "I'm forever grateful. Let's see if we can get his incessant yipping to stop."

Einar had somehow procured cards, but without the ability to see what was on them, he was shunted to the side while the four of them played. He provided commentary that was wildly inaccurate and completely over the top.

The time passed quickly and happily, their little crew whole once more. According to their underwater helpers, they would not arrive to the Isle until the next morning. As the sun fell below the sea, Einar dragged Delja to a quiet corner and Freja retired with her embroidery, still tucked safe in their room.

Brenna lingered on deck, fingers tracing patterns in the now dark wood. She would miss this; miss the quiet moments, miss the camaraderie, miss the bond. With their adventure nearing an end, everything she was avoiding was rapidly approaching. Freja would have to go home, wedded to some noble to secure advantageous alliances for Ayworn. Einar would no doubt return to his raiding ways, Delja to follow. Or perhaps she would return to the sea, where her newfound family waited.

They would scatter in the winds, reuniting only by chance or fate.

With such bittersweet thoughts, it was no wonder Brenna had such an awful time sleeping. It was nearly daybreak by the time she gave up on the notion of sleep and she took the opportunity to watch the sunrise on the horizon.

The Isle loomed in the distance, a cluster of trees and land. Unlike their first voyage that masked the island until they were docked, she had a chance to watch their approach, to see the place that held the hub of chaos and magic on its shores.

It looked so innocent from far off.

Brenna yelped as the boat lurched to a stop, hitting her knee on unforgiving wood. "What the—"

She peered over the edge, where several water fae had popped up and were chirping at her in the bells and whistles of fae language. Shaking her head, she called out to them, "I don't understand. I'll get Delja. Just—no, hey wait!"

They disappeared below the surface and she cursed. She ran for the hatch and nearly crashed into the person she was searching for. Delja squeaked in surprise, ducking out of the way. "What happened?"

"I don't know." Brenna grabbed her hand and pulled her to the edge of the boat. "They just left. I didn't understand what they were saying."

Delja leaned over the edge, peering into the depths, following shapes that Brenna's human eyes could not catch. "They're leaving. They didn't say goodbye."

Brenna wrapped an arm around Delja's shoulder. "Maybe that's what they were trying to tell me. I'm sorry I wasn't faster."

"But why?"

A cold trickle went down her back, like snow melting down her spine. Einar and his magic. She growled, ready to smack his pointy face. He was just climbing up deck, Tapio and Freja flanking him, disrupted by the sudden halt to their journey. But they weren't looking at her.

There was a tree on the boat.

A tree with shiny green leaves and twisting branches and gnarled roots that somehow merged with the wood of the deck. And because that was not weird enough, the large trunk, which easily spanned over a meter, had been shaped and molded into a seat, complete with armrests. No, not a seat. A throne.

And it was occupied.

A man appearing to be her father's age was seated, a crown of ivy and holly twisted in his hair, bright red berries replacing jewels. His hair was light, prematurely gray, and his eyes dark, framed by long lashes and tanned skin. Though he was sitting, he was still tall, regal, imposing. Pointed ears stuck out of his hair and his eyes produced an inner glow.

Delja fell to her knees in respect, bowing her head so low that her nose nearly touched the deck. Einar, too, bowed at the waist, all trace of humor gone. Tapio and Freja's bows were not as low, a mark of royalty meeting royalty. Respect, but not subjugation.

Brenna felt the call to bow, to give in, to defer to authority like a pressure on the back of her mind, but she had been ignoring that call her whole life. She would not obey it now. Her eyes dropped to the floor for a brief moment, the only allowance she offered, as she moved to stand at Freja's side. She was not subtle as her hand went to a knife.

Her sister tensed at the rebellious act of will, but the fae king stood and held his hands out for peace. "Calm yourself. I do not come in strife."

Brenna did not relax.

Freja kept her stance gentle, unassuming. "We were not expecting an audience with the king of the fae. Forgive our appearance."

"I considered sending a guard to meet your bold assumption," he said, his voice rumbling like thunderclouds, his robes, dark green, whispering secrets of the forest as they grazed the floor. "But I wished to hear your explanation myself."

They all exchanged uneasy glances, all but Delja, who remained on her knees. Freja's shoulders straightened, as if wearing a fine gown instead of grubby travel clothes. "I'm afraid we don't understand. Have we violated your laws in some way?"

He met her gaze and grinned, offering sharp teeth in response. Brenna resisted the urge to step between them. "You come to my kingdom without charter on a ship that drips of the black stain and dare presume you may dock?"

Well, yes.

"Our ship crossed the darkness after an unfortunate storm, one that caused us to be land bound. We have only just recovered it." Freja spread her hands in surrender and peace. "As for our charter, it was stolen. When the fae of the water offered us safe passage to your kingdom, we did not stop to consider this unwelcome."

A pause. Bated breath. Stifling air. The king sank into the throne, breaking the spell as Einar shuddered behind her, then scrambled to Delja and wrapped an arm around her. The king relaxed in his throne as he said, "I ask for the names of those so arrogant to come to my home uninvited."

Freja's eyes narrowed in response, her words careful. "You may not have our names, but we are known as Princesses Freja and Brenna of Ayworn, Prince Tapio of Faldinn, Sir Einar and Lady Delja. We meant no offense in our arrival."

"These are dangerous times and you carry dangerous cargo." He broke Freja's gaze and looked at Brenna, then at the pouch around her neck, safely hidden under her tunic. Brenna raised a knife, he raised an eyebrow.

"Brenna," Freja commanded sharply, reminiscent of their mother that had her instinctively dropping her blade. "What may we call you, sir?"

His eyes sparked with unknown delight. "King Óðr, Princess Freja."

She bowed her head in respect. "King Óðr, how may we correct this grievance on you and your people and show that we mean no harm?"

"You ask so openly, naively," he said, a slow smile stretching over sharp teeth. "Perhaps I will claim your lives as mine for all of eternity."

Brenna's breath hitched. Her body naturally slipped into a more defensive stance, knees bent, muscles loose, ready to move, to strike. Their options were limited. No help would come from the sea or land. Was this better or worse than being raided by pirates?

In the face of an explicit threat, Freja remained calm. "But you won't. Our actions do not demand forfeit."

Why did she get to say things like that but everytime Brenna snapped back she got reprimanded? Brenna looked warily at King Óðr, releasing her breath when it seemed he wasn't upset. "You have a sharp mind."

Freja did not smile, that would be too obvious, but her sister caught the slight crinkle around her eyes, the way her chest puffed at the comment. "We ask for safe passage to and from your kingdom, as a charter grants, to fulfill our mission. What price would you place on this?"

"You run a fool's errand," he said as he leaned forward, resting his chin on steepled fingers. "I cannot allow this ship to dock. It presents too close to an ill omen."

Fair enough. Brenna had no desire to be on this clearly cursed ship either. Needs must and all that. This didn't bother Freja. "Supplies then."

"Arrogant," he said with a grin. It was presumptuous. They had nothing to barter but scant supplies and money. And what king would need their coin? He had them desperate and desolate and he knew it. "I am not a humble delivery child. The price will be high."

Freja would not barter anything of true value. She was able to trick the few fae they came across with clever wordplay, but it would not be so here. The king was on guard and they were backed into a corner. Brenna's eyes darted along the ship, looking for anything that could be traded, anything they didn't absolutely need.

Nothing. Worthless. Needed. Her hand went to the clasp on her neck that kept her cloak on her shoulders. Would it be enough?

"You demand too much." In her musings, she missed what the king said, only Freja's reaction. Oh, how she wished they could get five minutes to discuss this privately. Nothing for it.

"Freja." Brenna's voice was quiet, wavering. She slipped the dagger in its sheath and undid her cloak, passing it to her. "For supplies."

Brenna felt exposed and cold without the familiar weight on her shoulders, but she did not take it back. Her sister's eyes widened at her offering, mind whirling, shaking her head minutely in surprise. Brenna pushed it into her hands. Tapio stepped up beside her, putting a hand on her shoulder in commiseration, in support.

"A ratty piece of cloth? Is this your best offer?" The fae king sneered, derisive and scolding.

Freja thumbed the frayed edges, gripping the cloth tightly, and did not look up as she spoke, cold and clear, "Two things: Supplies for our journey and a charter, modified to moor us here when we return. In exchange…" She wet her lips and looked up. "In exchange we offer the cloak of the one who raised us. We offer the story and legacy of Tatterhood."

XVII

Der er ugler i mosen

There are owls in the bog

$\mathcal{B}$renna could not look at the cloak, fearing she would snatch it back with second thoughts, nor could she look at her sister, knowing the sympathy and concern she would find there. The king tilted his head, curious at the shift among her friends. Tapio squeezed her shoulder, an anchor in the swirling mess of emotions raging through her.

"To know if it is a good bargain, I must know the value of what you offer."

Brenna knew he would ask. She knew what she was offering. Not just words, but her title, her last remaining tie to Ayworn, her legacy. And what the fae took, they did not give back. She would not be Tatterhood after this. She would only be Brenna.

Freja opened her mouth to speak, but Brenna stepped forward. This was her story. This was her right. She looked at her friends then met the fae king's gaze. All the hatred and anger and rage swirled within her, seeking a worthy target. She hated this man. She hated what he represented. She hated what he was taking from her.

"Tatterhood is a heroine to her people, a light in the encroaching darkness. She is passed down through the generations, growing and adapting to the needs of Ayworn. She began as a seamstress, clothing the needy. And then she was a baker, feeding the masses." Her voice faltered at the thought of Hilde, of losing her connection with her.

Freja took her hand, intertwining their fingers and smiling sadly. "And then she was their defender, protecting any who asked."

Tapio stepped up to her side again. "She does what she must to save lives and she doesn't quit on someone, even at the cost of her own comfort, even if she has to drag them kicking and screaming."

"She is a friend," Delja said, beaming at her, dragging Einar forward, completing the line. "Learning to communicate when words are hard. Inspiring when days are hard."

Brenna closed her eyes, focusing on keeping upright. Her lips trembled. Breathing became ragged and stuttered. Their words hit like arrows to her heart, piercing and aching. She would not cry.

"She's a pain in the—ack!" Delja stomped on Einar's foot and he scowled. "She's stubborn. Once she sees a wrong, she will make it right, no matter what it takes."

Brenna took a deep breath, pushing back the wave of heartbreak. She would not fall in front of the fae. She would not break where he could manipulate them. She raised her chin and met his gaze once more.

Dark, glimmering eyes studied her, calculating, no doubt working this in his favor. Kinder people would say he was thoughtful as he digested the information. Brenna was not so kind. Slowly, he stood and stepped forward. "I will restock your ship twice in exchange for this."

"Five times," Freja bargained, no room for argument in her voice as she held the cloak tighter. "And a charter as well."

"The charter is a separate issue." He shook his head. "Five times and forgiveness for any and all slights against the fae, both in the past and future."

That was not a paltry offer. Freja glanced at Brenna and she nodded. It would have to be enough. They would have to bargain for the charter with something else. Freja took a deep breath and let go, stepping forward to offer the cloak. Tatterhood's cloak.

Brenna's cloak.

"We have a deal, King Óðr."

The moment the cloth touched the king's hands, it disappeared. Brenna's legs suddenly gave out. Tapio caught her, holding her close to his chest, keeping her upright. She felt when the king took the cloak, felt it as if he grasped her heart and pulled. There was an aching hole within her that she feared would never fade. And as the chasm took her, one thought drifted through her. Hilde was gone. She was gone. And Brenna no longer had ties to her, except a few knives and sparse stories. She was gone and Brenna destroyed her legacy.

But they weren't finished. She couldn't fall to pieces yet.

"The deal is met. If you can recover your original charter, I will modify it without charge." King Óðr snapped his fingers and his tree throne disappeared. "The ones who stole it do not belong among my people."

Freja frowned. "We are willing to try, but we would need to get to the Isle for such a task."

"Your crew agrees to recover the charter?" he asked, meeting everyone's gaze in turn and getting a series of nods in return. "Humans are foolhardy. Very well. I will arrange for your transportation. Be prepared at dusk."

And then he was gone. Their audience with the fae king was over.

Brenna fell to her knees and sobbed.

Warm hands pulled at her, gentle as her body shook. Soft voices drifted over her, comfort on deaf ears. They guided her below deck, plied her with blankets and soft surfaces. Freja huddled close, sharing her grief, sharing the burden. Time became fluid and nonexistent, marked only by the swaying of the ship. The gentle hush of the waves lured her to comfort in her grief.

"Perhaps the king will offer information."

"Yeah, he seemed really chatty before."

Voices drifted over and gained meaning. Had Brenna fallen asleep? She wasn't sure, but her eyes were dry and her heart empty. She blinked as she registered everyone crammed onto one bed below deck. When had they carried her down?

"Einar and I can get the charter back, you girls stay here."

That spurred her to sit up, forcing everyone to look at her. Brenna rolled her shoulders and cleared her throat. "Only way you're keeping me here is if you tie me up and stuff me in the pantry."

Tapio scowled as Einar raised an eyebrow. "You were catatonic all day and you expect us to think you're up for this?"

Brenna knew he couldn't see her glare, but it didn't stop her from trying to burn a hole in his face. "I don't care what you think, you're not leaving me on this ship."

"Bri, maybe—"

To prove her point, she brushed them all away and stood. Freja squawked and made a grab for her, but Brenna wasn't having it. She twisted away from their grasp and headed for the ladder. "If you want, feel free to wait here while I get it."

She appreciated their concern and if the circumstances were different, maybe she would have wallowed in bed while the world turned. She felt raw and jagged, as if she were made of bleeding glass shards instead of flesh and bone. But they didn't have time to bleed. They didn't have time to grieve.

She had her cry; she would deal with the rest later.

The sun was rapidly setting on the sea and the ship bobbed gently in the waves. She took a deep breath, focusing on the heat from the last rays, the movement beneath her feet, the salt in the air. Tapio approached, his cane thumping irregularly. He cleared his throat, a piece of cloth in his free hand.

"Not as much history, but figured you'd want something." He held out his own dark gray cloak.

Thankfully, her hands did not shake as she took his cloak and pulled it over her shoulders. The weight was familiar and she managed a small smile. "Thanks."

"We're all in this together." Tapio shrugged. "So let's get the charter back and finish this once and for all."

"You realize," Einar drawled as he joined them, Delja and Freja after him, "that I won't be able to use magic against that lowlife, right? If she has her entire squadron with her, we're going to end up with the same outcome."

Brenna frowned. "What about magic on us? Would she be able to see through magic that could conceal us?"

He opened his mouth, then closed it. If they could hide through magic, then they wouldn't need to fight. Brenna grinned and her tone turned cajoling. "I mean, we do have someone on our crew that is notorious for stealing. He should be able to steal one measly, little charter."

"I know what you're doing and it's not going to work. It's too risky. And I'm not sutpid enough to do it." Einar crossed his arms and stuck his nose in the air.

"So you're saying you can't do it?" Tapio asked, smirking at his outraged look.

"That's—you—" he growled. Delja smiled and held his arm, turning as she signed something at him. His lips pursed in response. "You should all be ashamed of yourselves. Fine! Whatever. Let's go steal a charter."

Brenna snorted, then pulled the pouch holding the heart from her neck. "Can you put this in one of your smuggle holds?"

It would be safer here on the ship than on an island filled to the brim with sneaky hands and slippery people. Even tucked under her shirt felt too vulnerable. She didn't want to have it out of her sight, but it would be better than risk having it stolen. Einar frowned and flicked his wrist. The pouch disappeared to places unknown. She resisted the urge to demand it back. No cloak. No heart. Her skin itched with loss.

Before any other plans could be made, the world around them shimmered and dissolved.

When the world righted itself, they were no longer on the ship, surrounded by the sea, but in a thicket. Brenna leaned against a tree and groaned as her stomach rioted against the strange movement.

"Why are we in the woods?" Tapio asked, shifting to get a better footing amongst the roots and leaves.

"I'm going out on a limb and say it's because the charter is around here," Einar said, his voice dry. He was the only one who looked unruffled from the travel as he stretched. "Now, let's work out how to hide everyone. Starting with you, Double Trouble."

"What?" Brenna took a step back, shoulders tense. "Why me first?"

"Because I've been waiting for you to disappear since the first day we met. Now hold still." Einar raised his hands and muttered under his breath. His hands glowed for a moment and Brenna squeezed her eyes shut. A cold, sticky sensation traveled from her head to her toes.

She shuddered. "Did it work?"

"Not in the slightest." Freja grinned as she watched.

Einar growled. This time it was a feeling of warm and wet that made Brenna want to jump in the nearest body of water. She scowled. "Warn me before you do that!"

"We can still see her," Tapio pointed out oh so helpfully.

Brenna yelped at the shock of magic running through her once more. "Do you even know what you're doing?"

"You asked a blind man to hide you," he snapped. "Forgive me if I'm finding it difficult to know how to make you unseen."

"If you can't do it, just say so!" Brenna hissed as magic ran over her again, cold again. Freja shook her head in sympathy. They could still see her.

"Magic is instinct. Difficult to direct and explain." Delja stepped up to Einar before he could snap at them again. She put a hand on his arm and smiled gently. "You were not born blind. Must focus on the sight you once knew, not sight as you know now."

Einar calmed at her touch and nodded. He closed his eyes, still for a breath. Two. When he opened his eyes to try again, they glowed a faint green, a mockery of what they once were. Brenna braced herself. This time the magic clung to her skin instead of passing over her and traveled along her skin like a thousand spiders.

Not a pleasant feeling.

Freja looked at the spot she was standing, her gaze sliding over her as if searching for her. Brenna looked down at her hands, grateful she could at least see herself. She stepped to the side, closer to Einar. "About time."

Einar rolled his eyes. "I can still sense you, but you four won't be able to see each other, so get close and grab a hand before I do this."

Brenna took Tapio's hand, making him jump. "Well, that's terrifying. Thanks for the heart attack, Bri."

She grinned and used her other hand to crawl up her sister's arm. Freja flailed to get the unseen bug off her. "Bri! That's not funny."

"It's a little funny." Brenna took her hand and squeezed it gently. Delja held onto Einar and reached out for Freja. One by one, they each disappeared from view. Brenna held tighter to Tapio and Freja, focusing on the feeling of their hands in hers, Freja's small tapered fingers, a copy of her own, and Tapio's large calloused hands, bearing marks of a warrior.

"Right." Einar's disembodied voice sounded from the left. "I built a safeguard into the spell. If you get separated and need to lift the spell, just say your name. Like so: Einar Bjornson."

He shimmered back into view, gave a little bow and then waved his hand to disappear once more. "Do me a favor and don't get lost. I'm not your babysitter."

"Which way is town?" Freja asked. "If we do get lost or separated, we should all agree to meet at Middle Court Tavern."

"Town is due south. We're not that far actually."

Brenna regarded the trees carefully. They did not feel close to town. The trees crowded just as well as the press of bodies in town, with shrub and bush disguising trails. She grew up riding and exploring the forest paths near the castle so she knew the way of the woods. She knew the dangers and risks of traveling too far afield. She knew the way the trees felt cool in the summer and promised secrets in the dark.

But this forest did not feel like home. It was sweltering and oppressive in the setting sun. The magic in the air was nearly visible, scintillating in the air like suspended water droplets. Brenna knew without a doubt that these trees whispered to each other, that they led strangers with ill intent astray. People that wandered in these woods were more likely to meet disastrous ends with vicious glee from the forest.

She almost wished to be in Middle Court Tavern instead.

Almost.

"So which way is the charter?" Brenna asked, ready to be out of the trees, longing for their ship, cursed or not.

"How am I supposed to know?" Einar's disembodied voice called out in front of her.

She resisted the urge to smack her forehead, settling instead for a growl. "You can't sense it or something?"

"The magic in the air is like syrup. Trying to pinpoint a specific strand, which has the exact same properties since, you know, the charter is meant to direct you back here, would be like finding a piece of dirt in the sand." Einar tugged them along in a random direction without warning. "So if you have any other brilliant ideas, please say so."

"Search for no magic?" Delja asked. "They are hiding, yes?"

Brenna cursed as she ran into Freja as they came to a stop. This was going to get old fast. Before she could snap at their leader, he said, "Delja, you are truly a genius and the only one pulling their weight around here."

Brenna didn't need to see to know that the girl was now blushing head to toe from the compliment.

They fell silent as Einar pulled them forward with new confidence. The leaves shifted in the slightest wind, snickering at the stumbling humans beneath their shade. Roots lifted, tickling and enticing toes to trip and ankles to roll. The heat pressed and suffocated.

Voices filtered through the trees as they slowed to a halt. They had found the camp.

Holding hands was not going to work if they wanted to sneak into the encampment and steal the charter. Brenna frowned and whispered, "I'm going to get a closer look. Stay here."

"Einar goes with you," Freja whispered back.

It was not the time or place to argue about the need for backup. And if Brenna had her choice on back up, Einar was not her first, second, or third choice. Unfortunately, he was the only one able to know where everyone was and the only one that had a chance at getting them out in a hurry, so she kept her tongue in check and reluctantly let go of her sister and Tapio. Einar made no noise as she moved forward so she continued in the confidence that he would follow.

In another life, Brenna would have been trained and given to the kingdom's spymaster. She knew it was why her father agreed to her training in the barracks, to allowing her a sword and dagger. He permitted her freedom knowing he would have use for it later. He told her she would one day work missions for the crown, to finally be of use to him.

She played the dutiful daughter and agreed that she would work hard to make him proud, all while soaking in the skills to better help her people, to be Tatterhood.

But now she was banished and cloak free.

The skills remained though and she used them now to get close to the camp, wary of sticks looking to alert her presence.

Being invisible did not make her silent. She settled at the base of a tree, grateful for the slight elevation that allowed her to look over the small camp.

There were six people gathered around a fire. All six held the gold markings of their cult. All six held weapons with the familiarity of warriors. There was a single tent set up in the small clearing and several bedrolls tucked up by rocks and trees, waiting for true nightfall. The captain spoke quietly with her people, passing out jerky and tack.

The captain must have left the bulk of her crew on the ship to avoid suspicion. What were they planning out here in the woods?

It didn't matter. They were here to get the charter and nothing more. Brenna looked around the clearing again. They must keep their packs in the tent as there were no personal belongings strewn about them. Why carry the charter out here instead of leaving it with the ship as per the norm?

Brenna slowly signed the word for tent to warn Einar what she was doing before slinking around. She had no way of knowing if he understood or if he simply followed. Maybe he wasn't even there and she was making a fool of herself. Well, at least no one would know.

As she crept to the tent, conversation washed over her. Complaints about the fae's riches, about their power over nature. They weren't exactly wrong. She carefully pulled back a section of the tent, relieved to find no one there, then pulled it open further.

Something, someone, crashed near her. Brenna glared at the offending noise as six heads snapped toward them. She had just enough time to drop to the ground as a knife sailed past her.

The captain stood, curved sword in hand. "Who goes there? Show yourself!"

Silence. Not even the trees breathed. The captain nodded to a man to her right and he loosed several arrows in quick succession. Brenna heard Einar hiss as he dodged, the bushes flailing in response.

The man nocked another arrow and Brenna reacted. "Wait!"

She and Einar were close enough to mask that there were two people. Only one of them had to take the fall. This was a bad idea. Freja was going to kill her. She signed 'trust' to Einar and stood straight. The captain fixed her glare in her general direction. "Reveal yourself or succumb to our sword."

"My name's Brenna Eriksdóttir." She took a deep breath as the weapons focused on her once she shimmered into view. "And I was hoping to join you."

XVIII

Å ha en finger med i spillet

To have a finger included in the game

Brenna forced herself to remain calm under the captain's scrutiny. This was not a good plan. They just needed the charter. But she was not letting Einar get stabbed on her watch. She would never hear the end of it. And really, the charter was not lying around waiting to be snatched. This crew needed it for something. So it only made sense to offer herself up to get inside information, to offer them more time to get what they needed.

At least she didn't have the heart on her.

The captain remained unmoved by her plea to join them, but Brenna wasn't dead yet. "Brenna Eriksdóttir, you have no idea what you stumbled on."

Brenna raised an eyebrow and did her best to keep her panic unseen. "You're working to destroy the fae and their influence, right? To cure our world of this darkness by striking at its source?"

The captain had a great poker face, not so much as twitching at her statement. She flicked her braids behind her shoulder. "Why the change of heart?"

"I only came to this place because someone stole magic and cursed my sister," Brenna said, slowly, letting the truth bleed through her words. Lies spilled out easily, a large part of her agreeing with what they're doing. "We managed to lift the curse and heard of a way to defeat the darkness. It was all a fae lie. We barely managed to escape by the skin of our teeth. I sent my sister home and bartered my way here to offer my services."

"That's a nice story."

Brenna took a deep breath. "The fae need to be destroyed. They tricked my mother, played on her desperation for a child and ensured my birth would be a curse to her. They ensured my birth would be a stain and burden as surely as the darkness is on our land. I want to see them all dead. If you cannot help me in this quest, then I'll do it myself."

It was terrifyingly simple to place the blame for all the wrongdoings of her life at the feet of the fae. Brenna still stewed in bitterness at her parents for their treatment, but the root cause of it all had been magic. No magic, no magic flowers that allowed the queen to give birth. No magic, no magicians wreaking havoc and causing corridors to collapse, snuffing out life like a candle. No magic, no magical darkness spreading through the lands like an unending shadow.

No magic, no problem.

The captain narrowed her eyes and stepped up to her. She was shorter than Brenna by a head, but her presence made up for her lack of physical height. She reached out and put a hand on Brenna's mark on her cheek. It took all within her not to flinch at the touch.

"I see the rage in you," she said. "You have been marked for death by the fae, but we will offer life."

"I ask for my chance for revenge." Was that pushing it too far?

"And you shall have it. First, introductions. I am Yrsa." She grinned and introduced the rest of her crew. The names washed over Brenna, meaningless as she thought of the million ways this would go wrong. Seeing their captain's acceptance, the crew relaxed and lowered their weapons. "We all share the same pain you carry. And I swear to you, the fae will rue the day they left their Isle to terrorize us."

Fun. The crew let out a cheer at her declaration. Yrsa pulled her into the circle and chatter broke out once more. Brenna accepted the stew pushed into her hands with a tight smile. Her eyes darted towards the tent.

"I would offer you the marks of my crew, but I do not know how it would interact with the mark you already bear." Yrsa's eyes traced the red blotch on Brenna's cheek. Brenna touched it self-consciously and looked away.

"I was told it could not be removed." Not by magic. Not by healing. Perhaps by the fae king, but at what cost?

Humming, Yrsa leaned back. "You are the missing piece."

Brenna startled and looked at Yrsa, feeling the weight of her dark gaze. "Missing piece?"

Yrsa smiled bitterly, the gold paint adorned her eyes, making them bright even in the fading light. "My crew, my family, we have all been affected by the fae, by their abnormalities, but you were born in it. You have a connection to defeat them from within."

"I…I hope to do so," she said, careful with what she promised. She would rid the world of the darkness, and while she hated the fae, she would defeat this curse without mass loss of life. The world had seen enough of that. "How did you learn those protections? You mentioned Berundi? I am unfamiliar with this practice."

Yrsa fished out a necklace with a trapezoid pendant of bright gold, a dark emerald in the middle. "The eye of Berundi, a gift on my darkest day. My family has long followed Berundi and her edicts. We were ostracized for it, ridiculed, but I was taught how to protect myself from unwholesome magicks from a very young age."

Tucking the medallion back in her shirt, Yrsa sighed. "It did not save my family. When the darkness consumed my people, there was not enough power to protect us all. My father channeled it all to me and I fled by the skin of my teeth."

"You're from Faldinn," Brenna said, the realization jolting through her and causing the stew to spill on her hands.

Yrsa closed her eyes and gave a short nod. "One of the few left. Or perhaps the only. I have not met other survivors in my travels."

Brenna opened her mouth, then closed it. She thought of the lonely prince, wallowing in drink and grief, believing to be the last. How many others were scattered amongst the lands and unable to reach out? Perhaps they were not as alone as they thought.

But she couldn't tell this girl. She couldn't offer comfort. She bowed her head and murmured, "I am sorry for your loss."

"The loss has made me stronger."

That didn't sit right. Yrsa was not stronger for her loss. She was bitter and snarling, a wounded dog lashing out at scoffers and helpers alike. She was strong, but loss did not hone it. Loss made her strength tattered and unfocused.

Brenna did not want to think how closely she resembled this manic captain. Thankfully, she didn't have to as Yrsa brought out exactly what she needed. The charter. A lodestone that reflected the flickering firelight. Yrsa grinned at her and held it out. "A sample of what we are up against. The key to their destruction."

"I don't understand," Brenna said, hesitantly taking the stone, resisting the urge to bolt. "How does this play into it?"

"A charter is a manifestation of their power." Yrsa leaned forward, eager to explain. "When the darkness fell, it is said the fae queen fell as well. The fae will tell you she died to save their Isle, my father told me the truth. The fae king sacrificed her to spread the darkness. The charter holds her power. If we bring this power to her resting place deep beneath this island, the curse will turn on the fae and the darkness contained to these shores."

That didn't sound true. Some of her doubt must have registered on her face because Yrsa reached out and closed Brenna's hands over the charter. "Can you not feel its taint?"

Brenna frowned and closed her eyes, focusing on the warm stone in her hands. It was easy to identify the magic emanating from it. There was a cloying sense of wrongness that resonated deep in her bones. Brenna got the same feeling from the Isle, from the fae they had met, from Einar's magic. But was that it? Did all magic feel the same?

Her breathing slowed as she sat there, the stone rough on her skin. In a second, in an eternity, the magic shifted.

Brenna gasped.

Delja said all magic was born from instinct and Brenna felt emotion rolling off the charter; the instinct to flee, the instinct to find home. Memories of getting lost in the woods and desperately seeking home filled her. Memories of seeking comfort on bad days, curled up on the floor with Arne and Freja as Hilde sang softly over them. This stone was created to encourage travelers to find safety and warmth and rest.

In a world torn apart by shadows, that place was the Isle.

For Brenna, her comfort, her safe place, her home belonged in her family. Once she realized this, she saw Freja, crouched in a bush, whispering quietly to unseen friends as night fell. Images flashed in her mind, traveling along the waves, until she saw Arne, sitting by Idunn, new lines etched on his face, worried and stressed.

Brenna dropped the charter and the images disappeared. Her voice was flat as she spoke, "That's horrifying."

"Which is why we must succeed," Yrsa said with a solemn nod. "We owe it to all we have lost, to all who remain."

"You said the darkness would return to this island," Brenna said, numbness making her feel oddly detached despite the danger. "How do you plan on getting out before this place is consumed?"

"I won't lie to you, Brenna, we may not make it out before the shadows converge." Yrsa put a hand on her arm in faux comfort. "But our sacrifice would be a noble end if I ever knew one."

On any other day, Brenna would take that chance. If she had lost Arne and Freja, if she had never met Einar and Delja and

Tapio, then her desire to burn this island and everyone who stood for it would have consumed her. The rage was there, all it needed was a spark.

But Brenna did have her family. She had her friends. She had a mission to end this madness without bloodshed. She held onto the charter, feeling the magic pulsing out a call for home and safety like a heartbeat.

"Yrsa, I'm sorry." Brenna stood slowly, holding the charter against her chest. "We may have the same goals, but our methods wildly contradict."

And then she bolted.

Hoping that Einar was near enough, Brenna focused on the magic of the charter, leading her to Freja, and ran. An arrow whizzed past her, another skimming the edge of her cloak, leaving a trail of frayed threads. She dodged between trees for cover.

"Einar!" Brenna hissed, in case he didn't understand that now was the time to act.

"I'm working on it." Einar called somewhere to her left, muffled by the crashing of the angry pirates she just left.

"Work faster," she demanded. Her breath came out in harsh gasps as she moved forward, weaving between trees and bushes to minimize herself as a target.

"If you would just stop moving—"

An arrow embedded itself in the tree nearest her. It caught the edge of her borrowed cloak and Brenna ripped the clothing free. "Not an option."

If becoming invisible was not an option then running towards the others was not a good plan. They wouldn't be able to help her escape. With that in mind, Brenna changed course, veering south toward town. If she could make it to town, then she could lose her pursuers. Right?

"Get the others!" Brenna called out to Einar, not pausing to talk it through or argue about her decision.

It was truly dark now and without the glow of the fire, Brenna moved blind. Miraculously, she didn't trip. The roots that reached for her earlier now behaved and lay flat with the ground. Branches shifted to make room for her, clearing the way to town, putting more distance between her and Yrsa.

Judging by the cursing behind her, Yrsa and her crew were not having as easy of a time.

Note to self: don't anger the magical forest.

Brenna scrambled behind a large boulder to catch her breath, resting her back against the rough surface. She waited for the sounds of murderous rage. Noise in the underbrush quieted; maybe they had given up. Waiting around to find out wasn't an option. Pushing off the rock, she quieted her breathing and headed for the flickering lights of town through the branches.

The hair on the back of her neck raised and Brenna turned just in time to see the glint of metal in the moonlight. She felt the bite of the blade a moment later, a cut to her under arm, probably meant for her ribs but she had twisted before the dagger could meet its mark.

Brenna hissed and jumped back. Yrsa glared at her. "The charter, Brenna. Give it freely or die holding it."

Brenna moved until her back was at a tree, counting the crew. Two flanking Yrsa. Another in the trees, arrow notched.

246

One approaching from the right. There was one missing. She pressed her injured arm to her side in a vain attempt to staunch the bleeding. "You don't have to do this. I know the pain, the ache, you feel, but destroying this place will only cause more hurt. You condemn every human that fled here in refuge."

"They abandoned their homes and trusted in magic." Yrsa raised her head, beads in her hair clicking softly with the movement. "Their fate is out of my hands."

Brenna slipped the charter in her pocket and pulled a dagger, widening her stance and bracing for the first attack. She was still missing one person. "Yrsa, please. You can join me and we'll get rid of the darkness together."

Silence stretched between them, marked only by the growing stain on Brenna's sleeve. Yrsa faltered, then grew cold. "Goodbye, Brenna Eriksdóttir."

Brenna tensed as the missing crew member made themselves known. Oddly, they fell to the ground as if tackled. Her eyes met Yrsa's in equal confusion. Then Yrsa fell to the ground with a cry.

"My name is Freja Eriksdóttir and you will not harm my sister." Freja shimmered into view in front of Brenna, bow drawn, looking the picture of avenging doom. In that moment, Brenna swore Freja's eyes glowed.

Yrsa stood slowly as her people retreated from unseen attackers. She looked past Freja to Brenna, dark hatred rolling off her like water. She signaled a retreat to her crew and ran for cover under the trees.

Freja waited until noise from the underbrush silenced before turning to Brenna. "Are you hurt?"

"Yes, but not now." They were too vulnerable in the woods. Freja could play nurse once they were back on their ship. Whispers surrounded them as their friends rejoined them in the visible world. "How do we get back to our ship?"

The words left her mouth and the forest dissolved around them. Brenna blamed the blood loss for falling into a graceless heap. Her world swam even as it grew solid. The ornate tree throne took its spot on deck, now ordained with glittering jewels that captured the beauty of the stars. Empty for now.

"Bri!" Freja kneeled by her and she offered up her injured arm. Adrenaline flagging, Brenna's arm burned. The ever growing stain made her dizzy. Tapio knelt on her other side, wrapping an arm around her shoulders to keep her up. Freja carefully cut back the soiled cloth around the injury, her hands trembling slightly. "It doesn't look too deep. Einar, do you know healing magic?"

"I'm not sure you want me—" Einar hedged. Brenna rested her head on Tapio's shoulder.

"Yes or no?" Freja's voice cut short and sharp like her embroidery needles.

Delja put a hand on his shoulder and nodded encouragingly, and he sighed. "Give me some room. Magical healing is not gentle so don't mind the screaming."

"I'm not going to scream," Brenna said, rolling her eyes. Honestly, how weak did he think she was?

"Who said you'd be the one screaming?" he asked as he settled in Freja's spot. He did not touch her arm, his hands hovering just above the still bleeding wound. His eyes slipped closed, his brow furrowed, and his hands glowed green.

Brenna was not prepared for the sharp pain as the glow touched her skin, but she did not scream. She pressed her face in Tapio's tunic as every muscle in her body locked. The magic burned hot and cold at the same time, radiating down her arm to her fingers and up her shoulder. She gritted her teeth as her breaths came out in a hiss. Tapio's grip on her shoulders tightened, expecting her to flinch.

Einar knit her skin back together until all that was left was an angry red scar. Once finished, he slumped back, sitting on his feet. "Well, the bleeding's stopped and she's not dead. That's better than the last time I healed someone."

"The last time you healed someone they died?" Tapio asked, his voice coming out in a rough growl.

Einar waved him off. "Relax, obviously it didn't happen this time."

Delja moved around him to hold a cup of water to Brenna. She smiled in thanks, testing out her newly healed arm. Weakness lingered, an ache already fading as the new scar settled on her body. She lifted the cup carefully and huffed.

"At least it wasn't a poisoned blade," Brenna said. Yrsa seemed like the type of person to carry poison tipped blades and arrows. She set down the cup and pulled out the charter. "And I got the charter."

"Congratulations."

Five heads snapped to the throne. King Óðr joined them with darker hair and smoother skin, younger in the night. Delja recoiled as she knelt, Einar at her side in an instant, and Freja stood, eyes blazing once more with a cold fury. No longer willing to be diplomatic in the face of her injured family, she stepped towards him as an incensed equal.

"You knew." Freja spat. Her voice was cold and measured, eyes a dark blue like a storm on the sea. "You knew she was in danger. You knew she had the charter and yet you did not pull us out until it was nearly too late."

King Óðr met her ire passively, lounging on his throne in disinterest. "I did."

XIX

Is í magen

Ice in one's stomach

"She could have been killed." A tremor ran through Freja's frame, too faint for anyone but Brenna to notice. Unable to be seen as vulnerable in the fae king's presence, Brenna slowly stood and touched her sister's arm.

Sure, it could have been bad, but she was here and she was fine. New scar notwithstanding. Freja looked at her, pain and fear shining through for a split second before being locked away.

"Yet here she stands," King Óðr offered a lazy wave.

"You harmed my blood kin, a member of the royal family of Ayworn," Freja said, her words clipped as her eyes narrowed. "And I demand restitution for such careless action."

That got his attention. King Óðr sat up straighter, then rested his chin on his fist, wholly focused on Freja and her demands. A shudder ran down Brenna's spine and she grabbed her sister's

251

hand as an anchor. The king spoke coldly, "That is a bold claim. There will be disastrous consequences for unfound claims."

In the Aywornian royal court, demanding restitution called out someone's honor. A duel could be called, but only in the direst of circumstances. For a people who valued honor and bravery above all else, demanding restitution was not lightly done. Brenna only witnessed it happen once in her life. An elder noble called out an entire line for defiling his daughter. The king pronounced the claim valid.

The entire family had been cast from the court, forever shamed and banned from noble benefits and responsibilities.

Adding magic to an already serious claim only grew the list of possible outcomes. Freja called out the fae king and magic would preside over in judgment. Magic would have no mercy or grace should Freja be in the wrong.

Brenna leaned in and whispered, "Are you sure?"

Freja raised her chin in response, needing no crown to mark her regal heritage as she stared down King Óðr. "I stand by my demand. We are not your pawns to use as you see fit and you will pay for the damage done."

King Óðr raised an eyebrow. "Very well. May magic judge your claim and find truth. What are your demands, should the fault be mine?"

"Protections for the trials we face in Faldinn," Freja said, her voice clear. Protection for failing to protect was fair, though Brenna doubted what he would truly offer.

"A fair request," he said with a nod. "But should your claim be false, your payment will be your life tied to mine."

Brenna wanted to argue, to deny the request, but her mouth stopped functioning. Magic filled the air like syrup and pulled Freja away from her. That forced a cry from Brenna, but her feet grew rooted to the spot.

Freja and King Óðr faced each other in a swirling storm of magic. Colored light surrounded them, making wind visible as it wrapped around them. Still sensitive to whatever she did with the charter, Brenna could feel the testing, the intent to discover truth, like a brand on her skin. She turned away from the magical onslaught.

And then it was done.

Brenna rushed to her sister, planting herself at her side, ready to snatch her away should the fae king be granted his request. He would not have her, magical claim or not.

Amused, King Óðr studied her for a moment, then returned to his throne. "Well done, Princess Freja of Ayworn. You have accomplished what few humans have dreamt of; a free gift from the fae."

"I demanded my due. It was not free." Freja held her hand, squeezing just as tightly.

"The protections I can offer will not save you from the darkness," he said. "Not even my magic can keep the shadows completely at bay. The magic I can place on you will allow you to see in the darkness, however limited. To offset this limitation, because I feel generous to you, I will answer one question fully without barter."

Freja's mouth dropped open with a small 'oh'. She blinked and worked to hide her shock. "That's…"

"Choose your question carefully."

Freja glanced at Brenna, eyes wide, mind whirling at the limitless possibilities. What to ask? The obvious answer would be about the darkness, but they already confirmed reuniting the heart would defeat the darkness. He would not have information about Faldinn, not more than Tapio. Brenna had no idea what the best question to ask would be.

But Freja did. Her overwhelming shock hardened into strong determination. She nodded at Brenna and turned back to the king. "What are fae marks?"

What?

King Óðr smirked, the left side of his face ticking up as his dark eyes glittered, and focused on Brenna for an uncomfortable minute. She resisted the urge to hide her face. "All children born through a fae deal carry a mark, visible or not. Before the darkness, this ensured that we could identify them should we need to steal them back."

What a horrifying thought. Cold settled in her gut and spread through her body. King Óðr continued, never breaking his gaze. "You would have been snatched immediately, had times been different, and taught how to dance with the stars."

What?

What did that even mean? Dance with the stars? Snatched by the fae? Brenna could have been free from the queen's scorn and the king's disappointment. But without Arne and Freja and Hilde. Without Tatterhood. The good taken with the bad.

"You cannot have her." It was Freja's turn to hold her like a lifeline. "Can the marks be removed?"

254

"It is not a matter of can but will. No, I will not remove the mark." He held up his hand to stop her protest. "Nothing you say or give will change my mind."

Fair enough. Brenna never thought she had an option of removing the mark and the idea of being free of it unsettled something within her. This whole conversation unsettled her and she wanted it done.

"Is it dangerous?"

"The mark itself? No. It does nothing but indicate a magical birth. Among the fae, it is a grievous crime to injure one that is marked. Unfortunately, the humans have no such care." King Óðr leaned back on his throne, his voice growing dark. Brenna shuddered. He took a breath and grinned wolfishly. "Of course, those marked often have a propensity for magic and mischief. In my experience, humans have very little tolerance for such acts."

The charter in her pocket pulsed. *Home*, it told her, *safety*, *Freja*. Brenna put a hand in her pocket and held it tightly. She took a deep breath, then another. She didn't want to hear this, didn't want the confirmation of how different she truly was. It was too much.

"Freja," she whispered, unable to get her voice to cooperate. "That's enough."

Freja looked at her, bewildered. "But—"

"I don't want to know." It didn't matter what the mark on her face was. It didn't. It didn't. They had a quest and a kingdom to save and she wanted everyone to stop looking at her with pity. "We have to go."

"Bri…"

King Óðr watched her too closely, as if he knew her thoughts and secrets. She wanted him gone. Brenna turned to Einar. "Set a course for Faldinn. It's time we end this."

Einar didn't get a chance to agree or argue as King Óðr stood, the throne vanishing behind him, commanding their attention once more. He straightened his coat and dusted lint from his sleeve. "One more parting gift: you will not succeed at Faldinn."

Anger replaced her fear. King Óðr no longer represented everything she worried about herself or everything wrong with her world. No. Now he was just another person in a long line who told her what she could or could not do. She wasn't having it.

So she met his gaze with fury and spite and said, "Watch me."

Amusement glittered in dark eyes, and he tilted his head in acknowledgement before disappearing without a sound. She muttered a curse in the whisper he left behind.

"So…Faldinn?" Einar said as the silence stretched.

"No." Freja's voice carried over the small ship. "No. We should rest tonight. It's…it's been a trying day."

No one could argue with that. Two meetings with the fae king, camping out in the woods, Brenna got stabbed; she deserved a little rest. Especially with the looming threat of Faldinn as their next step. But she felt restless, unsettled, antsy. The mark on her face, which never bothered her except when people stared, seemed to burn and writhe under the skin.

Brenna shoved the charter into Einar's hands, ignoring the ache of loss. She didn't want magic. She didn't want to feel it pulse and resonate with her. It didn't resonate with her. Nope. Not at all. It didn't matter what the fae king said, she was nothing like the fae.

She huffed and stalked off to the bow of the ship, glaring at the speck of island bathed in moonlight.

Delja slid up next to her, quiet, unassuming. She stared at the waves and, no doubt, saw the riches below. Hidden cities in the depths, sparkling for the water fae, calling to her as the charter called to Brenna.

"I don't have magic," Brenna said to the ocean, a silent plea and demand. "It's just a stupid mark on my face."

Delja tilted her head as she looked over at her, dark hair that gained a blue tint in the night falling over her shoulder. "You're human. But humans can have magic."

Brenna's scowl deepened. "I don't want it."

"No," Delja said with a sigh. She stretched out her hands, showing her arms covered in splotches of blue-green scales, the same places that used to be red and bleeding on land. Then, she turned and signed silently, "It's hard. Being both and neither. I am human. And I am fae. And because of that, I travel both worlds. Fae family didn't understand my human needs. Mother didn't understand fae needs. I thought that made me less."

"No, Delja, of course not. You're not…I mean, I'm not saying…"

She smiled and waved off her concern before continuing to sign. "It's hard being both and neither. But being both lets me meet new friends and new family. Being neither lets me define me, be new. Your mark and Freja's mark are not defining. They just are."

"Wait, Freja's mark?" Brenna frowned, looking back at her sister talking quietly with the boys. "She doesn't have a mark."

"Marks are not always visible to humans, but she was part of the deal as you were. She is marked too."

Hadn't the king said as much? Brenna resisted the urge to bang her head on the railing. She was so caught up in her own misery that she overlooked Freja, as usual. Sweet, diplomatic Freja, who could twist words with the fae and come out victorious. Hardheaded enough to match with the fae king and make a deal with him with her soul intact.

Magic that Brenna knew belonged to the court, but never once considered worth her time.

"I'm an idiot," Brenna said. Delja's hands moved at frantic speed to assure her but Brenna put her hand on hers with a smile. She was an idiot. It happened from time to time. "Thank you, Delja. I'll work on seeing it that way."

"But—"

Brenna smiled. "I'm okay. Promise. Or, at least, will be okay. I want to talk to Freja about it."

Delja determined that was a good idea, nodding and letting her go on her way. Brenna walked back to Freja and pulled her below deck to their room. The pouch with the not-quite-complete heart rested suspiciously on her pillow. She didn't take it, unwilling to know how it would feel now that she was more sensitive to the magic around her.

"I was an idiot. I'm sorry," Brenna said, sitting with her sister on the bed.

Freja's eyes narrowed for a moment before she smiled. "I know. It's okay. I went a little overboard."

"You guessed about the mark."

The room fell quiet as Freja ruminated over her words. Brenna didn't mind. She laid back and pretended she didn't see shapes in the now black wood ceiling. If she closed her eyes, she could imagine they were at home, in their resplendent room decked with satin and lace, polished marble, and scented perfume.

"Something about the Isle made sense," Freja said quietly, jostling Brenna as she laid next to her. "Like it was an answer to a call I never knew about. I feel alive on the island. Like I spent my entire life sleeping. But you were agitated by the magic, you hate magic."

Brenna hummed out a sigh. "When I was with Yrsa, she gave me the charter and told me it was tainted. Said they had to destroy magic to rid ourselves of the darkness. And I sat there, holding the charter, holding the dumb stone that somehow makes it possible to get to the Isle that no one knows how to explain and I just… I do hate what magic has done to our people, to our world. Magic created the darkness. But in that moment? Magic showed me home. It showed me you and Arne, and I sat there in that feeling of safety and warmth and…that's not so bad."

Brenna would never practice magic like Einar, no matter her capabilities. It did not sit right with her. She was enough.

"Honestly I wanted to be rid of the mark so we could return home without worrying about it," Freja said. "At least it isn't harmful."

"At least I'm not stuck looking like a dead fish like Einar," she teased, hoping to lighten the mood.

Freja shot her a stink eye, then rolled her eyes. "That's something to discuss. Are we really going to drag him to Faldinn?"

"No," she grumbled. "We'll give him a choice in the morning."

Freja hummed in agreement and closed her eyes, the day weighing on them both. It was now late into the night. Brenna listened as her sister's breathing evened out, as Delja crept in and curled into Freja's other side. She tried to sleep, tried to let the creaking wood and gentle water lull her unconscious, but she was too ruffled.

Slowly, Brenna sat up, careful not to disturb Freja and Delja, and grabbed the small leather pouch. With a deep breath, she slid out the heart.

It was near completion, the biggest piece cutting a ragged edge to the center. It pulsed with an inner glow, shifting from blue and purple to green and gold. There was also an etching on the jewel, incomplete and incomprehensible without the final piece. Brenna carefully traced the indent and closed her eyes.

Desperation. Fear. Hope. Those feelings all swirled like the colors inside. She couldn't quite make out purpose, like she could with the charter, but she could sense the tangled web of emotions.

Her father told them that each kingdom had been given a piece for safekeeping, generations ago when the darkness first fell. Safekeeping from what, he didn't say. It was part of their history, he said in a near whisper, their legacy. Each kingdom had values they lifted above all else; Ayworn and honor, Faldinn and strength, Ealic and cunning, Nolpa and family, Denwes and trust. And each kingdom took the piece most attuned to those values.

She was only twelve when he showed them the small ragged stone and she thought then how small and insignificant it looked. Nothing like a heart piece. If not for its glow, the piece would have blended with the rubble that surrounded the castle as their home slowly fell apart. But even as a child, she felt the ache, the brokenness that emanated from it.

She didn't understand then.

She wasn't sure she understood now.

With a sigh, she put the stone back in the case and settled in for a restless night.

The morning dawned muggy and gray, a suitable match to their voyage, and Brenna was the last one to scramble on deck, crusty eyed and sore. Their motley crew sat in a loose circle on deck, quiet and thoughtful as they ate. She rubbed her eyes and joined the circle, accepting breakfast from Freja.

"So," Einar said, breaking the tense silence. "Last piece."

"Yes," Freja sighed. "And…Bri and I have something to say before we leave."

Oh, so they were doing this now. Brenna straightened and took a deep breath, then nodded to her sister to continue.

Freja looked around the circle with a fond smile, before settling on Einar. "I consider your debt to me fulfilled."

The oath broke with a snap in the air, and Einar sat so ramrod straight that he would make Brenna's etiquette teachers drool. He blinked. "What?"

"We know what we're about to face," Brenna said, looking down at the bowl of fresh fruit, courtesy of the fae king's restock. "No one should come along unless they want to. Freja and I can handle it alone."

Brenna looked up at Tapio, ignoring his stricken look, and repeated firmly, "No one."

It would be hard without a local guide, but Brenna couldn't… she couldn't force Tapio to come with them. If something happened—a high likelihood—she couldn't bear the guilt of being the one to drag him back. She would rather stumble and fail alone than succeed and bear the weight of their deaths.

"You can't do that!" Einar stood quickly, hands clenched at his sides. "That's just not right!"

Brenna blinked at him, confused by the sudden anger. "You've been asking to end the debt since the second it was made. We're just doing what you've been begging for."

"Uh, yeah, to get the glory all for yourself." He crossed his arms, fists stuffed under. "I was going to be an unwilling martyr. How dare you take that from me!"

Einar stormed off in a huff before she could apologize or refute his claim. Freja shrugged helplessly when Brenna looked over for answers. Delja shook her head and smiled. "Einar does not like emotion."

Okay. It wasn't worth Brenna's time to figure out the convoluted mess that was Einar. Instead, she turned to Tapio, her heart fluttering as she waited for him to beg a way ashore. He stared at his leg, his brow furrowed, his voice gruff. "You don't think I can do it."

"What? No, that wasn't—"

"Don't." He grabbed his cane and slowly stood. "I'm not some invalid begging for scraps. I know my duty."

And then he was gone too. His cane thumped a little harder than necessary as he walked to the bow of the ship. Brenna slumped. "What just happened?"

Delja rolled her eyes and signed, "Boys."

The boat lurched away from the Isle with a vindictive turn, Einar's scowl bearing down on them. They were on their way to Faldinn whether they were ready or not. Freja patted her knee and tilted her head to Tapio.

Brenna put down her breakfast—it tasted like dust anyways—and followed after him. Tapio was leaning over the railing, face twisted in bitterness and anger, knuckles turning white as he gripped his cane over the waves. He looked up at her approach then decisively turned his chin away.

Brenna shifted from one foot to another, words caught in her throat.

Signe padded over, weaving between their legs with her tail high, demanding pets and praise. Some of the tension dropped from his shoulders at her touch, and he reached down to scratch her chin as was her due.

"I don't think you're an invalid," she said in a rush, the words coming out all at once. His less-than-impressed glare told her how effective her statement was. "I don't. I…I think you're an amazing representation of your kingdom, of your people."

"A crippled drunk who belongs in a tavern instead of a quest?"

"No!" She ran her hands through her hair, tugging on the ends with a huff. "I wanted to give you a choice."

"I don't need you saving me, even if it's from myself." He stopped petting Signe, who gave a *mrrp* in protest before sitting at his feet, tail flicking in annoyance.

That had not been her intention. Brenna wanted him to know it was okay if he couldn't face the darkness again. She wanted him to have an out if it was too much. She had never truly faced the dark stain that plagued their world, which worked in her favor in this quest. Fear curled in her gut at the thought of what they would face, but it was vague and formless, without a face or name to strengthen it.

Tapio did not have such mercy.

Brenna joined him at the railing, offering a scritch to Signe in appeasement. "I'm sorry. I don't think you're incapable. I don't see you that way."

"No?" He huffed, not looking at her but not moving away.

"No." She stared out at the waves, saying lightly, "I figured since you were off drink you could finally see how insane my sister and I were and were ready to run for the hills."

The last of the tension dropped off as he let out a soft chuckle. His body shifted and turned, sliding down to sit on the deck. He rested his back against the rails and Signe took the opportunity for a free lap. "Perhaps I share the insanity. I did join you on a cat's insistence."

"As you should," she said, reaching over and petting the cat. "Signe doesn't take kindly to disobedience."

He looked up and smiled at her, and she took care to memorize the way his lips curved and his eyes crinkled, at the buried light in his dark eyes and fuzzy braids hanging and offering shade to his face. They would face Faldinn together and she swore he would smile at her again.

XX

Eteenpäin sanoi mummo lumessa

Forward, said granny in the snow

*T*he approach to Faldinn and the encroaching darkness was subtle. Unlike the Isle, which could appear without notice and smack unsuspecting travelers in the face, Brenna could not pinpoint the moment they entered under the shadow. Like a low fog, the shift gradually overtook them until she wondered when they left the sun behind. Apparently, when a kingdom fell, the darkness spread out against the ocean, reaching like stormclouds towards the Isle.

With the sun's disappearance, as colors faded to gray, came an overwhelming sense of dread and fear. That was most noticeable through Delja. She started their voyage by filling the air with songs she learned from her family, songs meant to lure and entice, meant to call from the depths. It thoroughly distracted Einar in a way that would have been amusing had the circumstances been different.

Her song tapered off as the darkness grew.

Dark, murky water swirled around them, providing the only sounds in the absence of Delja's song. No one spoke. In the absence of light, the temperature dropped. Brenna's breath came out in gray puffs as she tugged her borrowed cloak tighter. At least they could still see.

Einar remained at the ship's wheel to steer but everyone else huddled in the bow, eyes straining for some indication of land or life.

"Why did you join us?" Brenna asked Delja, desperate for some distraction from the growing doubt in the waning light.

"Mother loved the sea." Delja sighed, her voice taking on a lyrical quality as she peered over the water. "Made trips weekly to find lost sailors after storms. Father was a lost one she couldn't save."

Delja hugged her knees as she spoke, unable to sign clearly in the dark, but growing confidence in her voice. "I was twelve, she went out after a bad storm. The dark border moved in the night, broke a lot of ships. She…she didn't know the border shifted. Got too close."

Brenna put a hand on her arm as Delja stuttered to a halt. Her fingers felt soft skin shift to smooth scales. "I'm sorry."

"I wanted to avenge her," she whispered as Freja put an arm around her. "But I didn't know."

"Know what?"

She sniffed, trembling. "I have cousins, half fae too. But they are more fae, less human. They said…Mother took me out to meet them, but ship brought us too close to the border. Father saved me, but darkness did something to me. Maybe…Maybe I didn't use to hurt so much."

"Oh Delja," Freja murmured as she pulled her into a proper hug. Delja turned into her and cried.

A shudder ran through Brenna. The darkness changed Delja, took her parents from her, crippled Tapio, produced heinous creatures like the draug. And they hoped to come out unscathed?

The ship came to a stuttering halt to a dock Brenna could have sworn hadn't been there moments before. Perhaps her sight was not as clear as she hoped. The shadows twisted and taunted with the lack of light.

"We should lash together before we leave the ship," Freja said, her voice quiet in the gloom. "We don't want to get separated."

Brenna fumbled around to find rope, then helped tie the rope around everyone's waist. They would need to keep their hands free in case of attacks. Tapio in front to lead, Delja in the middle for protection. She finished the knot on Tapio and said, "The knots should come free if we need to run."

Brenna looked up but his face was too obscured in shadow to make out details. He put a hand on her shoulder. "Thank you."

Einar appeared, holding torches of green flame. They did little to provide light, the shadows somehow absorbing the luminescence, but Brenna took comfort in them anyway. He handed one to Tapio in the front then tied himself to the back.

"Wait!" Brenna quickly untied herself. "We need Hrolf."

"I am not leading your mangy goat through this darkness," Einar said, his scowl made known in his tone. "What would we need him for anyways?"

Brenna glared at him, sticking her tongue out. "A quick getaway."

"That's not gonna help all of us."

No, but if needed, it could help one. It could ensure whoever had the heart piece could get out. Should the worst happen, Hrolf could be what saved them all. But Brenna didn't say this as she went below deck, careful to lead him out. Hrolf shook his head, rearing up slightly. "Shh, shh. It's okay, Hrolf. Easy now. Easy."

Hooves clomped on the wood, the noise sharp in the quiet tension. Hrolf stamped, then tensed, huffing, unwilling to venture into such a strange world. She stroked his nose and carefully tied a blindfold around his eyes. He relaxed under her touch and let her lead him to the others.

Einar let out a dramatic sigh, then offered the length of rope. Brenna smiled gratefully and tied the rope to his halter. She patted his neck once more. "Remember, he bites."

"I might bite back," Einar mumbled.

Brenna retook her place in line between Tapio and Delja, securing herself before checking her knives and sword. Behind her, Freja strung her bow.

"My father hid the stone in a beach cove not far from here," Tapio said as he led them off the boat and down the dock. "He said the Norns gave him a vision that it was needed here instead of the castle."

"Convenient." Einar jerked away from Hrolf as the horse butted against him.

"I couldn't find it when I fled," he continued. "I tried, but… it was not this calm that day."

They passed through the empty port, Hrolf's hooves and Tapio's cane offering a soothing rhythm that echoed down empty streets. No building remained untouched from the catastrophe. In some places, only rubble remained to indicate where a house or store once stood. In others, the building looked fine until Brenna noticed the collapsed roof, the entire inside caved in. While there were no bodies to litter the streets, she could not help feeling as if they were walking through a crypt, the dead watching silently, counting their numbers, marking their steps.

"What happened that day?" Brenna asked. What horrors could they expect to run into?

Tapio veered left, following the road that ran along the beach, away from the well-ordered and empty port. "The darkness descended like a storm. The black border that had slowly fenced us in had suddenly swallowed us whole. Fires wouldn't start. Unholy creatures terrorized anyone caught outside. For some… some simply fell where they stood in the first moment of darkness and did not rise."

Brenna fought the draug seemingly an age ago and barely escaped by the skin of her teeth. A shudder ran down her spine.

"And if you come across black sludge, do not touch it. It will destroy whatever it touches."

A broken shingle crashed near them and Delja screamed, jerking their line left. Brenna shifted to the balls of her feet, sword in hand, but nothing made itself known. Just a broken town continuing to degrade.

"Sorry," Delja whispered, her hands over her mouth, looking impossibly small in the gray shadow.

Einar offered Delja the flame, which illuminated her face but not her tunic, making her look like a floating head. She took it gratefully, signing her thanks with one hand.

A faint fluttering was masked by harsh breathing.

Talons tore into Brenna's shoulder.

Delja screamed and dropped her torch.

Brenna swiped up with her sword, the edge slicing through air, hissing at the burn of an open wound. "Run!"

But running while connected by rope was akin to an uncoordinated dog sled with no main lead. Tapio ran forward, Delja sidestepped right, Hrolf tugged back to retreat. The knots, as designed, wrenched free and Brenna grabbed it in a last minute panic. "Don't lose the rope."

Don't lose each other.

Brenna wrapped the rope around her wrist and followed Tapio's lead. Whatever flying creature attacking them had friends and blended with the dark. Einar's flashes of magic showed silver talons and maroon beaks with black wings longer than she was tall. When her blade made contact, they let out a screech that vibrated her bones. The rope on her arm burned as she let Tapio drag her to places unknown.

In the flashes, she saw Freja covering Delja, unable to use her bow without letting go of the rope. Einar's face twisting into snarls and curses as he flung magic like stones. Tapio looking back, mouth in a grim line as he led them.

Brenna shifted her sword to her other hand and grabbed a dagger, throwing it during a flash, hitting her mark as one beast dove for her sister. She let out a breath of relief as it flew away.

The ground beneath them transitioned from paved stone to shifting sand, and Brenna switched her sword again, cautious with the unsteady footing.

"Duck!" Tapio commanded as he pulled them forward. Brenna obeyed on instinct, her hair brushing a low stone ceiling as she did so. He stopped abruptly and she crashed into him. Delja, Freja, and Einar were quick to join them, mashing into each other in the back of a cave.

Hrolf whinnied. No. She wasn't losing him.

Brenna unwound the rope and darted back out. Grabbing his reins, she barked, "Hrolf, down."

He bowed his head and then went to his knees. He just barely fit in the entrance and could not stand, but at least he was safe. Brenna hugged his neck, breathing hard and shaking. "Shhh. Easy, boy, easy."

"Can you seal the entrance, Einar?" Tapio asked.

Einar responded with a wave of his hand. Green magic shimmered over a narrow cave entrance before fading from view. The flying creatures thrashed on the beach, occasionally crashing into the entrance.

Once satisfied Hrolf would not try to stand and injure himself, Brenna crawled over to Freja and hugged her tightly, words and fear caught in her throat like unswallowed food. Her breaths came out in gasps as the adrenaline slowly trickled out. Freja held back just as tightly. Delja joined them, tears soaking their tunics, and she pulled in the boys, who completed the tangle of shaking limbs and frantic heartbeats.

They stayed in the hug until the crashing dwindled.

"Does anyone need healing?" Freja mumbled from the middle of the pile.

Who didn't need healing?

"You'll have to make do with bandages," Einar said, pulling back first. "I'm not some vast pool of magic to beckon at your command. And don't even try the whole life debt on me. I'm a free man, thank you very much."

Brenna touched her shoulder and winced. The cuts weren't too deep, but they stung and burned in a way that suggested poison or worse. She flexed her hand, frowning at how stiff she moved.

Bandages were passed around and Tapio helped wrap her shoulder while Freja helped the cuts on Einar's arms. Tapio's fingers were calloused but gentle as he pulled back the torn fabric to show the gouges underneath. The blood looked black in the shadows, unnatural and diseased.

"I'm sorry," he said gruffly.

"I'm not," Brenna responded, holding his gaze, hoping he read her kindness in the near black darkness. "Besides, what's one more scar for the fate of the world?"

"Speak for yourself," Einar snarled. Delja patted his back comfortingly.

Brenna rolled her eyes, having no energy to snark back at him. "How close are we to the heart piece?"

"I'm not sure," Tapio said, leaning back once he was finished with her bandage. He settled against the rough cave wall and took stock of his own injuries, prodding at his lame leg. "The beach is dotted with these caves. My father hid it in one and marked it with our family crest."

"Great," Einar drawled. "Beach combing while dodging talons of death. My favorite hobby."

"Oh, go stuff it," Brenna said. "You can go back to the boat if you're going to complain the whole way."

Einar hissed as Freja pulled the bandage tight on his arm, his retort dying on his tongue. Freja leaned against Brenna. "Let's wait before venturing out again. If we're quick, we can use the caves as shelter."

Crash.

Rock and dust rained down on them with the winged evil's attack. Everyone huddled closer together as Hrolf nickered softly. Delja coughed, hoarse and raw.

"What will you do, Tapio?" Brenna asked, desperate to fill the silence with more than her worst fears. "When the darkness is gone, will you rebuild? Reclaim your throne?"

Tapio shifted next to her, stretching out his legs as much as allowed in the tight space. He pressed against her, shairng his warmth. "My people don't follow lineage lines for the throne. Our reigning monarchs must overcome the trials."

"What?" Brenna and Freja's family traced their lineage to the founding of Ayworn. There had been a few rebellions throughout their history, but they remained in power. Their father pressed on them the responsibility of this legacy, the honor and duty to ensure it continued.

She didn't know there was any other option for a royal.

"My father and his father were both king, but before that it was another family," he explained. "Our people honor the victors of the trials. My brothers had planned on competing for the throne, but I didn't really want to be king. I'm not…I don't know what would be best now."

"Your people will need someone to lead," Brenna pressed gently.

"I have no people."

Brenna scowled, resisting the urge to smack him for his defeatist attitude. "You don't know who escaped. That pirate captain, Yrsa, she was Faldinnian. Once the darkness is gone, people will come out of hiding. They'll come home."

Brenna had no doubt that once the lands were free and safe, people would flock to their old homes, to the places they once knew, to reacquaint themselves with the forgotten. Those unable to face the memories of all they lost would seek a new place to put roots down. All the people that did not belong on the Lost Isle would find a new home.

"What would you do?" Tapio asked instead of responding.

Brenna shrugged. "I'd see the world. Everything I couldn't see before, I would look upon it and etch it into my soul."

"Sap," Einar coughed. She nudged him sharply with her foot in retaliation. "You two are going about this the wrong way. Exhausting travels and boring leadership."

"Then what would you do?"

"Go back to my nefarious, devious ways, of course."

Brenna rolled her eyes as Freja sighed. "Come on, Einar. You can be honest with us."

Silence stretched between them like a cat, her needle like claws pricking as she arched. Einar huffed a few times, shifting position in the sand. Delja reached out and put a hand on his shoulder.

"My brother wanted to be a healer. I guess that'd be okay."

"You've got a horrible bedside manner," Brenna said, squawking as a handful of sand hit her face. "Hey!"

Delja was signing, but in the shadows, her hands were just darker shadows shifting around. Einar thankfully took up as translator once more. "Delja says she would learn to sail properly and live on the water."

"I would have to go home," Freja said with a sigh. "But I'll take the long route home. Start in Denwes and travel east."

One last adventure for the two sisters, crossing borders and lands long since impassable, finding roads that forgot the touch of travel. It sounded like a dream. Brenna leaned into her sister and closed her eyes.

"I think they're gone," Einar whispered, dreams popping from the air like soap bubbles.

"I'll check." Tapio shifted in the dark.

"Don't be ridiculous," Brenna said, shoving him back. "I want another whack at those vile creatures."

He needed to find the last heart piece. Brenna did her duty and got the Ayworn piece, now all she had to do was keep everyone else alive until the darkness lifted. Unfortunately, Freja shared her stubbornness and made her way to the entrance first, bow close to her body, then stretched out as the opening gave way to gray beach and choppy waves.

When nothing sounded but their own harsh breathing, Tapio carefully made his way out. The rope was retied, this time with knots that would not give, and Hrolf was led out. Brenna ran her hands down his back and flank, grateful to find no injuries.

"Almost done," she whispered to him, to herself, before returning to her place in line.

"There's the next cave," Einar said, as he conjured a green flame about twenty yards away. The loose sand made it difficult to move quickly and the flame marker faltered as if battered by an unfelt wind. She couldn't see any evidence of a cave, only a flickering green dot amongst the sea of gray and black.

They made it halfway when the screeching started.

Tapio lurched forward, yanking them to avoid another attack. Brenna gripped her sword. Freja drew her bow. Magic sizzled behind her.

Like a cloud, the birds descended, sharp and deadly.

XXI

Å gjøre noen en bjørnetjeneste

Do someone a bearfavor

*T*he air filled with harsh breathing, muttered curses, and swinging steel. The shadow birds halted any attempts to move toward the cave as they sought weak points with their sharp claws and beaks. Brenna kept her injured arm close and her sword moving. Delja ducked behind her. Tapio held his ground. Arrows whizzed past her.

"Tapio, you have to keep moving!" Brenna shouted over the ear-piercing shrieks. If they couldn't get to cover, they would all be bird food soon.

The rope tugged her forward in response.

A large protective dome of green light grew over them, only to shatter at Einar's shout. Brenna looked back, cutting down a creature that aimed for Delja.

"They have Einar!"

But Brenna couldn't see him. The only evidence that he wasn't right behind Freja was the rope being pulled upward. Freja was quickly leaving the ground from the tug of the rope. She twisted and pulled at it, before abandoning the idea and drawing back her bowstring.

Thwack.

Thump.

Einar groaned, now on the ground. Freja quickly pulled him onto Hrolf and Brenna dragged Delja forward. They needed cover. Now.

The green flame Einar marked the cave with disappeared when he was pulled into the air, but thankfully Tapio found the entrance anyway. He yanked on the rope, forcing everyone into the relative safety of the cave. Brenna guarded the entrance until Hrolf cantered in with a moaning Einar on his back.

"Help me get him down," Freja snapped.

The birds didn't attack the entrance, a small mercy, so Brenna stepped up with Delja to maneuver Einar onto a flat surface. In the dark, in the shadows, he appeared dead. Then she blinked and he was merely bleeding out. In another blink, his body contorted at odd angles. She shook her head and kneeled.

"How bad is it?"

As if anyone could tell in this cursed darkness. Freja's hands roamed his body until Einar smacked her away. "Ge'off. 'M fine."

"You're hardly fine. Now hold still," Freja growled in response, continuing her assessment. "Broken leg, cuts don't seem too deep, no punctures."

He would live. But he couldn't continue.

"Right, okay, new plan." Brenna paced the entrance, her sword drawing lines in the gray sand. "Freja, you take Einar on Hrolf to the boat, get below deck, fortify if you need to."

"Absolutely not!" Freja hissed, standing up. She crossed her arms. "I am not leaving you to get yourself killed in some noble act to save the world."

"Einar needs to get somewhere safe and he can't go alone!" Delja wasn't an option. She was more a danger to herself with a sword or bow. Tapio needed to find the heart and Brenna wasn't leaving him.

"He can stay here," she countered.

"He can talk for himself—"

"Shut up, Einar," Brenna snapped. "Those birds could make it through the entrance. This isn't defensible."

"I'm not leaving you!"

"You're being ridiculous!"

"Stop!" They turned to Delja, who still knelt by Einar, holding his hand. Her voice mimicked sandpaper as she spoke, "The ocean is close. I can carry him to the ship from the water, protect him in the water."

"Are you sure?" Brenna asked, before Freja could object.

"Yes. We make it to the water, we'll be okay."

Brenna took a deep breath, then another, before speaking to her sister, "They need someone to get them to the water, Freja. And Hrolf can only carry two."

Brenna didn't want to separate, to let her sister out of the limited sight she had now, but this was logical, this was right. Freja didn't answer, instead dropping back to the ground to splint

Einar's leg. He grunted at her ministrations but remarkably kept his mouth shut.

Once properly bandaged and triaged, Einar sat up with Delja's help. Freja stood in front of Brenna, her mouth in a thin line. She rushed forward and pulled her into a tight hug, her arms a vice around her neck. "Die and I'll torment you for all eternity."

"Same," Brenna whispered back, before stepping next to Tapio. "We'll offer a distraction while you three get to the water."

They cut and retied the rope, now in two groups. Delja supported Einar while Freja took the back, her bow notched and ready. Brenna held onto Hrolf's halter as her sister's form twisted and disappeared in the shadows.

"I'm going to make noise and draw attention," she told Tapio as she secured the reins to the rope. "Just drag me and keep moving, got it?"

"Got it. Make sure you get them more than they get you." His voice was low and serious and she didn't want to know how keenly he watched her, how his brow furrowed in worry as their group dwindled in the face of this fathomless void.

With a deep breath, she followed Tapio out and banged the flat of her sword on the rocks. "C'mon, you filthy mongrels born from the depths of Helheim! Is that the worst you've got?"

She couldn't see the ocean; she didn't know where the sand shifted from loose to compact. She could hear waves crashing, she could smell the salt air, but she had no clue how long her sister and friends had to trek before they arrived safely. When claws pricked and scraped against her skin, when feathers caressed her cheek in mock gentleness, Brenna continued to yell and spew profanities.

Her sword sung through the air, jarring her arm as it hit its target. The rope around her waist burned as Tapio kept her moving. She fought. She swore. She moved.

The cave they fell into did not have the heart piece. They didn't speak, merely caught their breath and waited for the screeching to lower before rushing off to do it again.

And again.

And again.

Brenna's skin and clothes were a web of thin cuts. Her hair was wild and would have obscured her vision if she could see. Her lungs burned. Her heart hammered. The desolate oppression of shadow and gray made her want to scream and run until her legs gave out. The birds kept coming and the caves were unending and she had to keep moving.

At the tenth cave, which was more an indent than a hole, Tapio whooped. "Here! It's here! My father etched the family crest into the rock."

"Great," Brenna gritted out, unable to muster excitement when her whole body ached. "Get the cursed piece so we can get out of here."

It was calm at the moment, but that could change without notice. Her sword was slick in her hand and she wasn't sure if it was sweat or blood that caused the feeling. She wasn't sure she wanted to know. Her body burned and ached in equal measure even as adrenaline kept her moving.

Tapio ran his hands down the rock before finding a rune, which glowed blue at his touch. The blue light was clean and breathtaking and fought back some of the despair that settled on

Brenna's heart. It remained glowing, offering hope and peace and comfort. That is, until she realized what the rune was for: sacrifice.

"What do you have to do to get it?" she asked, feeling as if they were balancing on a knife's edge, so close to failure or success.

"It's…" he sighed. "Surrender your hand and receive the last hope."

Brenna didn't really like the idea of putting her hand anywhere, especially the hole that opened up in the rock looking for volunteers. Before she could voice her concerns, he stuck his right hand into the void.

With a yelp, Tapio's arm disappeared further into the rock. She cried out and dropped her sword to grab his arm and get him free. After a moment of struggle, he was free and they fell back to the sand. He curled around his arm, his hand clenched in a fist, a small glowing stone leaking light through his fingers.

Tapio released a breath through clenched teeth. "Let's go."

"You have it," she breathed. She leaned forward then sucked in a breath as she watched his fingers grow black under the light. She scrambled to tear off a piece of cloth from her cloak. "Here, let me—"

"I got it," he snapped, pulling back. "I'm not going to be of any other use, so move."

The black was on his wrist now. "But if it's causing the damage—"

"It's not." Tapio stood, his hand cradled against his chest.

"Okay, but—"

"For once in your life can you not argue? Move!" He limped over to Hrolf and mounted. When had he lost his cane?

Brenna pursed her lips and picked up her sword again before mounting behind him. Hrolf danced anxiously, his feet shifting and sinking in the loose sand. With great reluctance, she sheathed her sword and reached around Tapio to grab the reins, not trusting him to not fall off or to lead with any accuracy. Pressed up against him, she could feel how tense he was as he hunched over the saddle.

They just had to make it to the ship in one piece. They could do this.

"Alright, Hrolf, time to show us how fast you can move." Hrolf threw back his head and shook his mane, insulted at the uncertainty in her voice. She flicked the reins as a screech let out to their left.

Hrolf wasted no time, shooting off in the hopeful direction of the ship. Brenna and Tapio bent low over the saddle and held on tight as talons reached for them. She felt more than saw as they transitioned from sand to cobblestone. Hrolf's hooves rang out, echoing down the empty streets.

Hrolf skidded to a halt and reared back as a house suddenly came into view. Brenna slipped down the saddle, panic racing through her. Before she fell, Hrolf landed back on all fours and danced in a circle to get through his nerves. She tapped her heels to get him moving again, gritting her teeth as the buildings once more blurred to gray.

How they made it to the ship, Brenna wasn't sure. But when the ground beneath them shifted from ringing stone to hollow wood, she nearly wept in relief. Hrolf slowed to a trot, leading them down to his stall, thoroughly done with the adventure.

She slid to the ground and leaned against the firm side of the stall for a moment before helping Tapio from the saddle. They collapsed on the floor, sitting side-by-side, shaking in rhythm.

She rested her head on his shoulder and didn't move until she could no longer hear her heart racing in her ears. She took a deep breath. Then two more. Once grounded and less panicked, Brenna shifted back, her eyes seeking out the gentle light in his hands.

"Please let me help," she whispered.

Tapio's shoulders dropped and his head hung forward, like a marionette with its strings cut. He sounded as if he had been screaming as he croaked, "Okay."

With shaking hands, Brenna tugged on his right arm, guiding it away from his chest and into her lap. The heart piece pulsed between them. Instead of prolonging a potentially painful experience, she hooked her fingers under his and pried open his hand in one swift movement. He didn't flinch, even as his hand refused to relax. She took the heart piece and watched as his fingers curled back into a fist.

"I'm sorry," she said, staring at his hand.

"I'm not." His undamaged left hand touched her chin and drew her face up. "If this group has taught me anything, it is that we bear our burdens easier with others. Now, let's end this once and for all."

He got his right foot under him and pulled away so he could stand on his own, his right arm tucking back into his chest. She stood and patted Hrolf on the neck. "Good job, boy. I'll make sure you get all the oats and apples and sugarcubes."

He nuzzled her hair, nipping at her shoulder before shoving her away. Brenna followed Tapio out, leaning close for comfort and a silent offer for support. After a few moments of limping through the cargo hold, he put a hand on her shoulder.

She smiled in response.

Her relief in safety and success slowly trickled back into panic as they looked for the others. Had they made it to the ship okay? Had there been worse dangers lurking in the ocean? Had she doomed her sister and friends to a fate worse than death?

"—it went as you expected, of course." Freja's voice carried out from the girls' room. Brenna's knees nearly buckled, and Tapio shifted so he was holding her.

"What a brat," Einar drawled.

Brenna shoved the door open. Einar was sprawled out on the bed, another splint on his arm, his hair wet and messy. Delja curled into his side, eyes closed as she gripped his shirt. Freja paused in the bandages she was wrapping to look up at them.

She let out a shuddering breath even as she smiled. "Yeah, Bri was a bit of a brat growing up."

Brenna's lips twitched upwards even as her vision clouded with tears. "Tapio and I face impossible odds and you lot are just lazing about gossiping about me?"

"Pretty much."

She collapsed on the bed into her sister's waiting arms, relishing in Freja's bony shoulder digging into her cheek and her pointy fingers digging into her clothes. They were okay. They made it.

"We got it," Brenna said, her voice hoarse from unshed tears. "We got it."

"About time," Einar shifted in the bed, cradling Delja with his uninjured arm. "Did you stop for souvenirs or something on your way back?"

"Keep complaining and you won't get yours," she shot back, near giddy at his retorts, at this normalcy after so much pain and fear.

"Does that mean I get to keep his share?" Tapio asked, sitting on the floor, leaning his head back on the wall.

"Sounds fair to me." Brenna shifted so she could see everyone else without letting go of Freja. If she had her choice, she'd never let go of Freja ever again.

Then Freja sighed and pulled out the worn leather pouch, pushing it into Brenna's hands. "End this and we can discuss wages and compensation later."

If Brenna thought her hands shook when prying out the heart piece from Tapio's fist, it was nothing compared to how they trembled getting the shining jewel out. The moment the heart was free from its confines, it bathed the room in varying hues, fighting back the darkness even temporarily.

Holding her breath, she brought the final piece to the ragged edge, closing her eyes as it glowed bright. Magic pulsed out, rustling their clothes, agitating their aches. The hint of a song tempted at the edge of of her mind, something like a lullaby. Hope and love and home filled her heart so much that it burned

And then it faded.

Brenna opened her eyes.

"No!"

You will not succeed at Faldinn.

King Óðr's words haunted her as she stared in dismay at the gently glowing stone, the world around them still dark and gray and shadow-filled.

"It should have worked," Brenna said, her voice cracking. "Why didn't it work? Five kingdoms. Five pieces. The darkness should be gone!"

"Bri, maybe…"

"Don't." Brenna knew that tone. She hated that tone. That was Freja appealing to her rational mind. That was Freja being kind as she delivered bad news.

Brenna couldn't give up. Brenna couldn't accept that this was the best it could be. Brenna couldn't linger on as the world around them suffocated in the dark, until everyone suffered the same as Faldinn.

The sun would shine again. She would accept nothing less.

Brenna jerked from Freja's comforting touch and gripped the stone until her knuckles turned white. There was something she was missing. Something left to be done still. One more sacrifice she could make, if only she could figure out what it wanted.

Something.

Brenna traced the near complete etching on the stone. There was a sizeable, jagged divot in the middle, one last missing piece, but the image around it was taking shape. Taking familiar shape. Her world tilted and blurred. She was drawing this shape before she knew her letters.

Her fingers traced the rounded outer edge of the flower petals, murmuring, "Honor, duty, family, devotion, pride."

"What? Bri, you're talking nonsense."

"It's the Aywornian crest!" Brenna shoved the jewel at Freja, desperate for confirmation.

Freja took in the wild look in her eye and smartly didn't question her as she took the stone and studied it. She let out a small 'oh' as she fell back on the bed. Numbly she pulled out her embroidery, a near complete picture of what was etched in stone. Her fingers traced where the petals combined, the missing piece on the stone.

Their father said the flower on their crest symbolized the attributes a good king exhibited. A good king, like the flower, branched out in five main areas. The heart of the flower, where the petals joined, was the heart of the people, protected and guarded and cherished.

And it was missing from the stone.

"I know where it is," Freja whispered. "The final piece. The last sacrifice. I know what we have to do."

"What do we have to do? There are no other kingdoms."

She looked up at Brenna and smiled sadly. "Five kingdoms, yes. We're the sister kingdoms, connected by land. We surround the same sea, we each guarded our own piece. But there is one place that lost its name when the darkness fell, that has become the last refuge for people fleeing the darkness."

Realization dawned slow and painful. "No. Please, no."

"It makes sense," Einar said slowly. "No one speaks of their queen, lost when the darkness spread."

"They used to travel broadly," Tapio chipped in reluctantly. "If you listen, they will still mourn and grieve the old ways where they could dance among the kingdoms freely."

"But it's an Aywornian crest," Brenna reasoned foolishly. "There must be something we missed from home."

But she knew the rumors. The fae queen had once been human. The fae queen had fled her humanity to dance among the stars, those of kinder hearts said. Those with darkness infecting their hearts hissed that the fae stole her, broke her, molded her. Whatever the truth, it was clear where they had to go next.

It was time to meet the fae king in his court.

XXII

Det er aldri så galt at det ikke er godt for noe

It's never so bad that it's not good for something

$\mathcal{R}$e turning to the light was just as gradual as the descent into the darkness. Color returned slowly. The sea gained blue in the waves, breaking out from the gray. Brenna's clothes returned to worn out brown, torn and ripped from talons of nameless beasts, stained from sweat and blood. The scrap of fabric holding the Aywornian crest stood out in purple and gold and white.

But even as they fled to the light, not all things were put back to rights. Tapio's arm remained black as tar up to his elbow, matching his leg. Einar did not heal miraculously, did not have enough magical power to do much more than sit up in bed, yelling cranky insults at anyone close enough to listen.

Delja steered the ship to safety, her face set in unusually grim determination. At Einar's request, Freja stayed with Delja, keeping her company and offering her the sailing advice he gave her.

Brenna leaned over the railing, watching as the world regained color and life and sound. Gray clouds stretched out over them like spindly fingers eager to drag them back.

In her hands she cupped the near complete heart, colors shifting to make her palms purple and blue and red. The stone was warm, warmer than it should be, and heavy, as if eager to drop to the ocean, forgotten. Her fingers traced the etched crest over and over and over again.

Questions swirled in her mind, pulsing in time with the light of the stone. Why an Aywornian crest? Why was it broken? Who was the fae queen?

None of her histories told her how the darkness came to be nor why the heart piece was given to them. When her father told the royal siblings about the heart piece, he told them it was a closely guarded secret of their family, that it was their duty to protect it, that it kept the darkness at bay as long as it was safe.

But that did not save Faldinn.

So why?

Was the fae queen once royal blood, an ancestor long forgotten or perhaps omitted from history?

Brenna slid to the deck, shifting her skirts to a more comfortable position even as the myriad of shallow cuts and pricks and bruises protested movement. She leaned against the side and stared at the stone. Could she pick out answers like she felt the purpose of the charter? King Óðr claimed she had magic. Was it enough to discover the truth?

She closed her eyes and focused as she had with the charter. Desperation and fear filled her as she held onto the heart. But there was more, layer upon layer of emotion and intent until they resembled tangled and knotted yarn. Brenna had some experience with that, namely every time the queen forced her to knit. Her hands never behaved for delicate work so she had enough practice undoing knots and mess.

Brenna took it one thread at a time.

Desperation was the strongest emotion emanating from the heart so she started there, pulling and clinging to it as it wove with fear and hope and love.

"This is a human creation, a human problem, we will do nothing." Brenna almost dropped the heart as the ghostly voice swirled around her, a vague figure filling her mind's eye, bathed in silver light. She could not see features, but felt magic and authority and age. The fae king?

"You would condemn my people? Condemn me? Or have you forgotten who I am, my love?" This figure was female, the queen perhaps, and held love and warmth and home, like the charter. "They are dying and we could help."

"At what cost?"

Letting go of the desperate thread, Brenna latched onto fear, so similar to desperation in feel. The silver figures shifted and reformed a dozen times as she followed along the string, slowly untangling it from the rest of the emotions.

"We have to act now! There's no more time left." The fae queen once more, her voice higher and shriller, her form shimmering and shaking.

"No, I forbid it."

"I love you."

The figures faded like fog in the sun as the ship hit a rough patch of the sea and Brenna's hold on the magic faltered. She blinked at the bright blue sky, at the sun gleaming off the black wood of the ship.

Delja laughed at some story Freja was telling her, pulling Brenna back to reality. She dropped the heart back in the pouch, a sudden chill running along her spine.

Brenna was not trying that again.

Venturing below deck to shake the need for more information, she found Tapio in his room attempting to tie a sling one handed. She cleared her throat in the doorway, offering a shy smile. "Need a hand?"

Norns smite her now. What a stupid thing to say. Thankfully, Tapio offered a rueful smile and shrugged. "Probably."

She stepped in and gently tugged the cloth from him, wrapping it around his right arm and then tying it up behind his neck. Her hand rested lightly on his injured arm. "Do you feel anything with it?"

He shook his head. "There's an ache, but I think that's in my head. Happened with my leg too, in the beginning. Like my body's trying to remember how it works."

"Magic can't heal it?"

"Sometimes things don't get fixed," he said, tilting her chin up. "Sometimes you do the best with what you've got."

He would have to live with an arm and leg that never worked, a constant reminder of what he lost, of what he sacrificed. Like the mark on her face, he couldn't wish it away for a better life. Rough fingers traced the blotchy red skin on her cheek, leaving burning skin in their wake. And when she met his gaze, she was not reminded of the darkness they fled, lifeless and cold, but rather the night sky, full of hidden depths and promises.

Brenna leaned closer, her voice breathless. "I've been rethinking what I want to do once we're done here."

"Oh?" Tapio leaned over, his forehead nearly touching hers, his fingers stilled on her cheek.

"Might be nice to land somewhere I can rebuild." Her lips pulled up in a small smile. "Somewhere I can have a clean slate, discover who I am outside my legacy."

He hummed, a sound that resonated in her bones. She had kissed others before, often servants and stable boys, people she knew her mother wouldn't approve of, a silent act of rebellion in the face of the weight of the crown on her head. She knew the heat before a kiss, the tension of a burgeoning relationship. There had been flares since meeting Tapio—he was handsome, powerful, kind—but other things took priority.

She leaned in.

"Stop fooling around and attend to me!" Einar shouted from the next room, thoroughly ruining the mood. "I'm dying!"

Brenna groaned and let her forehead thump on Tapio's chest. "I'm gonna throw him overboard."

Laughter rumbled in his chest and it was the best sound she had ever heard, like thunder before a spring storm. She pulled back and her lips twisted into a tired smile. "I expect to continue this conversation after I murder our friend."

"With pleasure, Princess."

She scrunched her nose at the title. "Or maybe not."

Tapio snorted and took her hand, kissing it as a lord of the court would. Except no court lord ever sent a thrill down her spine at his touch. He raised an eyebrow. "If you're going to badger me into the kingship at Faldinn, I'm going to drag you with me."

"A battle of wills it is then."

He shook his head with a grin, leading her out in the hall as if escorting her off the dance hall. She turned left to go back up and he turned right to Einar's increasing demands. Brenna looked back and bit her lip as Tapio winked at her before disappearing in the room.

Princess didn't sound so bad when he said it.

"What are you smiling about?" Freja asked when Brenna joined the girls at the steering wheel.

She shrugged and looked out at the shimmering horizon. "Just happy to be almost done."

"Securing that last piece will not be easy," Freja said with a frown. She pulled out some bandages and started fussing at Brenna, replacing and straightening the gauze. "King Óðr withheld the knowledge, and his demands…I don't know what else we could offer at this point."

Brenna gave up Tatterhood, gave up her home and lineage: she had nothing left but her life to offer in exchange for peace. If it came down to it, she was willing to offer all she had, but Freja would protest vehemently. And Arne…they didn't really assume their goodbye would be their last. Perhaps the fae king would be merciful and allow her final words.

"Ow!" She yelped as Freja pulled a bandage tight. "What was that for?"

"You're thinking about giving yourself up. If you try that, I will stab you," Freja promised. Her hands shook as she tied off the bandage around Brenna's arm.

"I know. You'll talk him into giving it up for a promise of straw bales or something equally meaningless." Brenna smiled and took her sister's hands. "It's going to be okay."

"We're here," Delja said quietly.

The Lost Isle shimmered in view, falling into dusky hues as the sun began its descent. Unlike last time, their ship did not stutter to a halt far from the dock. Delja carefully guided them right to shore, where the loud chaos of the port greeted them. Several dockhands did a double take at their black boat, then quickly scampered away.

Three arguments, five curses, and twelve threats later, they deboarded. Einar sat sitting secure on Hrolf with Freja behind him and Brenna and Tapio flanking them. Signe led the group, with Delja following dutifully behind, stealing worried glances back at Einar.

News traveled fast as the rumor of their cursed ship spread. People gawked, but kept a wide berth. Brenna kept a hand on her sword hilt in comfort, uneasy at the tension running through the crowd, waiting for the wave to break. They passed into the fae circle of town as a bell tolled.

"Dusk," Tapio murmured.

The fae ruled the night. Maybe they should have waited for morning.

But Signe did not falter, leading them to Middle Court Tavern and stopping to demand they open the door for her grand entrance, as if she were leading this motley crew. Delja looked back and Brenna nodded. They were here, might as well get it over with. Freja dismounted and, with Brenna's help, carried Einar inside. Tapio limped stiffly beside them.

For a moment, Brenna was sure they came to the wrong place.

The tables were cleared, opening the floor to show off the polished wood. The mage lights dimmed to resemble stars among the dark, marble walls, setting off sparkling gemstones flecked in the stone. Fae men and women floated and crowded the once empty tavern. One woman had hair like flower petals and teeth like a shark's. Another had black fur covering head to toe. The ones closest to them grinned and gleamed possessively.

Brenna held on tighter to Einar, who in turn held onto Freja. Tapio guarded their backs while Delja politely excused them as they moved forward.

The fae shifted and danced to a high, ethereal tune that filled the space. The wall that once held a bar now held the tree throne, the bottles of mead, wine and ale still shelved behind it. The tree reached for the ceiling and spread throughout the room, holding more mage lights in its branches.

Sitting in the throne was the fae they first met in the Tavern, the impossibly handsome one that was young and enticing and alluring. The bartender that saw more than he should.

White, hot embarrassment flooded through her like anger as Brenna hissed at Einar, "The bartender is King Óðr?"

"Did you expect him to be someone else?" he asked with undisguised glee. "You should know better than to trust the face of the fae."

Which meant…every bartender they met, he never offered his name. Oh Norns, they met the king back at the beginning. He had been watching him from the beginning. Freja faltered. "Why didn't you tell us?"

"It was funny."

It took everything within her not to drop him here. She twisted and glared at Tapio. "Did you know?"

He winced. "Einar made me swear not to tell."

King Óðr cleared his throat, demanding their attention, looking impossibly young and attractive. "Did you succeed in Faldinn?"

"You know very well we didn't, you manipulative, arrogant, selfish—*mmpf!*" Brenna jerked away as Einar slapped a hand over her mouth.

Freja quickly stepped forward, leaving her with Einar. "Please forgive my sister. It's been a long and arduous journey."

"Was it?" King Óðr settled in the chair like a pompous child king. "Perhaps you should find a place to rest then."

"We're not leaving until we restore the heart," Freja said, lifting her chin, her gaze flinty. Her words hushed the crowd as if she had spoken an oath. Perhaps there was an ancient decree that demanded truth in the fae king's court. "I believe you have the final piece we need, King Óðr. Release it so we may restore our lands."

"You are a child demanding the stars. I am not cowed by such demands." The fae around them withdrew, sensing an anger that Brenna could not detect. Her whole body vibrated as she resisted the urge to punch him, king or not.

298

Which is why Freja was doing the talking, not her. "We are all here because we lost someone to this darkness, we have survived because we had faith and hope of a world without division and fear. Can we not make a deal for the last piece? Can you not help us achieve this?"

"You do not know what you ask." He shifted to dismiss them and Freja grew hard, blue eyes turning to ice and storms.

"And who's fault is that?" Her voice was even and quiet, but carried through the room regardless. "This darkness has robbed us of culture, history, memory. We do not live as long as your people and yet we pressed on. We sought to end this plague."

He stood and, with a wave of his hand, fae cleared the room, disappearing without a sound. Dark eyes glittered with rage and pain and grief, emotions Brenna knew intimately. "You humans brought on this darkness. You wish for knowledge, allow me to educate you then."

Brenna jolted as a seat of vines and branches morphed under Einar, giving him a place to rest. Signe padded over to Freja, staring down King Óðr fearlessly. Delja kept her head bowed low and moved to Einar's side. Tapio put a hand on Brenna's shoulder.

King Óðr took a deep breath. He held out his hand as black lines of sand grew and formed in the air, shaping like a malformed flower with a missing petal. Brenna frowned at the familiar shape and pulled out the heart. For a moment, the cracks that once broke it in five pieces glowed, the exact shape that the king made, before fading back into one nearly whole piece.

"Yes, Brenna of Ayworn," he said quietly, looking at the heart in her hands as if it haunted him. "It is no coincidence that the black tendrils separating your worlds share the same cracks in her heart. It was, after all, the breaking of that stone that caused the shadows to leak in."

Brenna stared at the heart, studying the Aywornian crest, remembering the snippets of conversation she heard from it. "I don't understand."

"That is what I'm trying to correct," he said with a drawl. "The darkness as you know it found its beginning in a single person, in a woman that wished to free the world of magic, to enslave the fae, to protect her people from what she viewed as abnormal, unusual, disfigured."

The last word hung in the air as he closed his hand in a fist, collecting the sand, then opening it to reform it into a woman, proud and regal. The black sand did not offer fine details, but in Brenna's mind, she imagined her mother seeking to rid the world of anything that did not fit in her view of perfection.

Even if it meant her own daughter.

"She discovered an ancient rite that would accomplish her goals," he said somberly, the figurine raising her hands in prayer. The sand around her hands shifted gold, falling to the ground with a sizzle and smoke. "In her arrogance, she forgot that magic is too embedded in the world to simply remove it. Human lineage is littered with fae deals and dalliances. Our worlds are not separate."

Another figure built from the sand, this one in gold, also female. She fell to her knees and begged her dark counterpart to stop. King Óðr stared at the golden figure in longing and despair, and Brenna knew this was his queen and that he loved her even after so much grieving.

His voice did not betray that emotion though as he continued, "Her sister, my queen, tried to reason with her as children around them died. Her sister sought to redeem the little girl she once knew. When that did not work, my queen performed a counter ritual, one steeped in her blood and magic, one that would stop the spread of her malice."

The dark figure melted and the black sand swirled as the gold surrounded her. The gold brightened and the lonely figure fell. in her place, a small orb of golden sand surrounded and encased the black.

"And yet, your people," he spat the word, dark eyes latching on to each human in the room, as if they personally killed his love, "were not satisfied. You demanded her heart. Demanded her sacrifice. Demanded more. Her heart broke and each kingdom stole their due. In their ignorance and fear, the shadows slipped out and have chewed away at the humans with every passing century."

The sand fell away, clearing from the air. A shudder ran down Brenna's spine. The stone in her hands pulse with love and grief and desperation; emotions of a dying woman intent on saving her world, her people, fae and human alike.

King Óðr returned to his throne, slouching into it like a snake ready to strike. "And now you show up and demand the last of my queen. You request, oh so humbly, for her heart of hearts. Your greed drove you to death and you expect the fae to save you, even as you scorn them."

Freja looked back at her, horror etched in her eyes as she pushed back tears. She bit her lip and took a deep breath, composing herself as she faced the throne. "King Óðr, please accept my deepest condolences and utmost apologies, as paltry as they may be."

She turned back to Brenna and took her hand, meeting her gaze and nodding as she slowly gripped the heart. Brenna hesitated, then relaxed. Freja cupped the stone with reverence, with awe in the wake of what they just learned, then stepped forward and knelt before the throne, offering it out. "This is too little and too late, but please let us return this where it belongs."

XXIII

Familie er ikke en viktig ting. Det er alt

Family is not an important thing. It's everything

$\mathcal{B}$renna lost all the air in her lungs as she stared at her sister kneeling before the fae king, offering the one thing they lost so much retrieving. She lost her home for that stone. She had new scars and new nightmares and new fears all in the name of collecting those broken pieces, all in the name of saving the world. Words caught in her throat and choked her. Tapio's hand on her shoulder tightened, pushing caution.

"And what do you demand in return?" King Óðr asked, his eyes narrowing as he focused in on Freja.

"We ask for nothing to return such a priceless gift," Freja said, her hand shaking, the only outward sign of her distress.

Brenna wanted to fling herself at her sister, to hold her and pull her away from the hunger in the fae king's eyes. She wished they never left their crumbling home and faced such dangers. The king stood slowly and fell to one knee as he took the heart. His eyes softened as he cradled it.

"And so my queen returns home," he murmured. He stood and held a hand out for Freja to take. She slowly took it and stood, uncertain, unbalanced. "I cannot defeat the darkness. I cannot heal the last break."

No.

Had Tapio not been holding Brenna's shoulder, she would have collapsed on the spot. Their last hope ripped through her like those winged evils on Faldinn, pulling her heart from her chest. This was it. They would all be consumed slowly. They were all doomed to watch their loved ones perish under the darkness.

Freja's brow furrowed, thoughtful and quiet. "Are there any that can?"

Brenna sucked in a quiet gasp as King Óðr gave an amused smile. "You are more perceptive than most. There is but one who can heal this rift."

"If you wish, please tell us," Freja begged, carrying the same desperation as the heart, as each person in their ragtag group. Please let there be a way to save each other, to save their homes. "We have traveled so far, given so much. If there is someone we must fetch, we will find a way to do so."

Brenna would cross a thousand seas, defeat a hundred evils, convince dozens of leaders, if it meant a last shred of hope, if it meant there was a way out of this desolate fate. The king studied Freja, then at the group that surrounded him, then stared perplexed at the cat at Freja's feet. Signe's tail twitched and she mewed.

The king waved his hand and a second throne appeared by his, this one more delicate in appearance, but no less prominent, meant for an equal force to guide and love his people in ways he could not, meant for a queen to rule. His gaze settled on Freja as he spoke carefully, "Only a fae queen can mend that which was broken."

No.

Absolutely not.

When they were twelve, Freja had received her first proposal. A minor baron with very little prestige had assumed being the first to ask for her hand would provide him leverage that his wealth and reputation would not. Their parents took great pleasure in reading it out at the dinner table, ripping apart each argument while praising their daughter for enticing prospects even as she blossomed from girl to womanhood. Freja, as the only suitable princess, was an asset and treasure to any family that wanted royal connections.

It was the first and only time Freja had allowed herself to cry and rage over her fate, in the dead of night as her sister and brother held her tightly. Brenna swore then and there that any man would go through her before they got to her sister, parental agreement or not.

Brenna never thought to factor in the fae. Or the fate of the world. How embarrassing.

"Oh," Freja breathed, staring at the empty throne. "I see."

No, no, no, no, no. Brenna broke free of Tapio's grasp and stumbled to Freja's side, taking her wrist hard enough to bruise, hissing out, "Absolutely not."

Freja did not acknowledge her, only offering an apologetic smile as she spoke with King Óðr, "May we have a moment to discuss this?"

He looked like he wanted to refuse—they were after all asking him to vacate his own throne room—but something in Freja's eye had him hesitate. With a nod, he vanished without a sound. She took a breath and turned to Brenna, her shoulders tense even as her eyes softened.

"You cannot be contemplating this," Brenna said, her voice cracking. She hated herself for that weakness. "Not when you just lectured me on sacrificing myself."

"Marriage is not death," she admonished, the familiar argument falling on deaf ears. "Bri, he's not going to kill me."

"You cannot tie yourself to him. They are liars and thieves. Freja, please, you cannot. You…We'll find a different way." Please. After all they endured, all they survived, Brenna could not be separated from her sister.

Freja sighed and cupped her cheek. "This is the only way. The fae are incapable of lying and the king is just as eager to save his people as we are."

Brenna shook her head, wild red locks cascading down her shoulders. She wasn't hearing this. She wasn't entertaining the idea of her sister, her Freja, marrying this man. "There's always a way."

"Bri." Her name fell out soft, yet unyielding. Two stubborn forces clashing. Brenna's knees finally gave out and she sank to the floor, Freja falling with her. She wanted to scream and rage and beg Freja not to do this. She wanted to right words to convince even her stubborn sister that Brenna was right to refuse this. "Would there be any man you deemed good enough for me to marry?"

"Yes. Someone decent," she muttered in her arms, hiding her face in the delicate lace of Freja's bodice. How she managed to keep it intact during all their travels, she would never know. Perhaps it was her own brand of magic; the ability to always look court ready. "Arne can't be the only decent royal."

"I am not marrying my brother." Her tone took on the quality of scolding a child.

Brenna, in turn, grew more petulant. "You aren't blood related."

"That is the grossest thing you've ever said to me and I need you to stop." Freja pulled back, somehow producing a clean handkerchief and wiped Brenna's face. "This is a sacrifice I can make so easily, one I have known was coming for many years. Trust me to do it."

Brenna leaned back and sat on her heels. Her voice came out in a whisper. "I can't lose you."

"Trust me," Freja said again, as if she wasn't asking Brenna to hand her her heart.

Brenna took a deep breath. Then another. It took all her strength to nod her consent. Someone pressed against her back and she looked up to see Tapio offering his hand. One last deep breath and she took his offer, standing and wiping away any evidence of her breakdown. She adjusted her borrowed cloak and straightened her shoulders. Sniffing once, she hid clenched fists under the fabric of the cloak, her nails biting into her skin.

Sensing her readiness, Freja called out, "King Óðr?"

He rematerialized in the same spot, his hands clasped behind his back, his face stoic, his voice flat. "You have reached your conclusion?"

"What are your terms?" Freja asked. Brenna reached out and clasped her hand.

His eyebrow ticked up a notch. "Are you the one offering yourself as my bride?"

"I'm the one who will accept or deny your proposal," she said, her voice hard. "I am not offering anything. I am listening to your terms and making an informed choice."

King Óðr grinned, sharp and deadly. "Your duties and responsibilities as queen would be quite numerous, do you wish me to list them out individually?"

Brenna shifted as Freja scowled. "You are being needlessly pedantic. What are the terms of marriage? You require a queen to rule your people fully, we require a queen to provide safety to our people. What needs must be met to merge these two roles?"

Evidently done with their game, or perhaps through thinking over his demands, the king swept back to the throne and sat, steepling his fingers as he regarded them. Silence stretched to uncomfortable before he finally broke it. "You will not leave this island for the first year and you will not enter the human kingdoms for the first ten."

"But my family may visit?"

"With permission," he purred. Brenna held on tighter.

"No monetary payment?" Freja asked. The lords of the court had steep costs attached to their sons, which meant little to the royal family, but would require their parents to be involved.

He waved off her question. "My people do not thrive on your paltry coins. I have no need for it."

"Right." Freja took a deep breath. "Okay, travel restrictions. Is that all?"

He leaned forward. "My people are not accustomed to marriage for politics and advantageous arrangements. I loved my previous queen so I married her. Should I find you deceitful, harmful, or in any way unfit, I will cast you out for all eternity. I may see you executed should the crime be grievous enough."

"I understand." To Freja's credit, her voice did not shake in the wrath of the fae king's threat.

"So you agree to my terms?"

Brenna's fingers trembled, beating out a staccato against her sister's hand, her heart thrumming in her throat. Freja squeezed her hand. "I do, but I have terms of my own."

He relaxed once more. "Proceed then."

"This wedding takes place this evening so that we may prevent further damage and deaths. We fix the heart immediately after." Freja raised her chin as he frowned. "And my brother is retrieved to witness the union."

Silence stretched as her words echoed through the empty room. Brenna held her breath. Part of her wanting to say no, to deny this was happening before the king could accept. She closed her eyes and waited for the sword to fall.

"Fortune smiles on you as it is a full moon tonight," the king said, standing as he made his decision. "I will prepare the hall. You will find anything you and your companions need in the antechamber beyond."

Brenna did not feel fortunate as she helped Einar into the room indicated. Delja gasped as they entered, making a beeline for the sparkling dresses hanging on the right side of the room. Two partitions set up for changing took up the far corners.

A fairly normal looking fae stood to the side where half a dozen chairs were set, looking as if she had been expecting them for years. While humanoid in appearance, this fae had eyes that shifted from purple to gold to green with hair to match.

She stepped forward as they entered and bowed. "My name is Bergfue of shore and wind. My king has sent me to tend to your injuries."

"Thank you," Freja said, introducing the group as Brenna took a step away from the fae. "The boys will need the most tending."

"If it pleases you, ma'am, my king was explicit that I tend the fae-marked first." Her tone said she would not be budged on this.

Weird. Brenna scrunched her nose but allowed her sister to drag her toward the fae whose eyes shifted to yellow and hair to black. Thankfully the fae was quick and silent as she worked. There was a sting to her healing, but nothing like the burning, painful, scream-inducing healing of Einar's magic. The fae left no cut or bruise alone, having an uncanny ability to detect when Brenna lied about being fine.

Then Delja ushered them into baths hidden behind the partition. The first bath since leaving home. Her body melted in the warm water, the herbs a near perfect blend of what Hilde would set for them. The comforting scents of home. The warm water and herbal scent washed away some numbness around Brenna's heart.

The robes provided were soft and plush and she wondered if she could get away wearing it to the wedding. Brenna sighed in contentment, then pushed Freja in a chair to do her hair. Picking up a comb, she marveled as the hair dried when she pulled it through. "Magic drying comb. Well, the perks of this marriage are growing on me."

Her forced lightness didn't even make Freja smile. Her head down as she stared at her hands in her lap. Brenna paused and looked at her in the mirror. "Freja?"

"Is it odd that I am more terrified now than at any point on this cursed trip of ours?" she asked, her breath shaky. "How silly is that? We almost died, multiple times. This…this is simple."

Simple, but no less easy for it. Brenna continued combing as words failed her. She knew if she pushed, she could get Freja to call this off, to change her mind and pretend there was another way to save the world. She sighed and set the comb down.

"Wait here," she said, squeezing Freja's shoulder in comfort before heading to the main room. "Einar, can you get my bags from the ship?"

"I'm not your magic genie to make demands," he huffed, looking healthy as Delja sat in his lap.

Brenna shrugged. "Fine, I'll ask the fae to do it if you can't."

Predictably, he squawked and the bags were there five seconds later. She grinned as Tapio snorted. "Thanks, Einar."

A few minutes of rummaging found what she needed: an old cracked rune and a plain wooden box. She returned to Freja and pressed the rune in her hands. "Until Arne can come and be our lucky rune."

Freja let out a breathless laugh as she traced the rune, the one that belonged to a brother they never knew. Brenna looked down at the box, at the trinkets Hilde left her, items she pretended didn't weigh on her. She pursed her lips and flipped open the lid.

Despite working for the palace, Hilde was not rolling in riches. Her job secured her a safe place to sleep and steady meals. Any coin she had left over was spent on the less fortunate. If she wanted to provide gifts to the girls or to Arne, she would have it commissioned to the palace, allowing the royals masquerading as parents to pretend they cared enough to pay for gifts.

Nestled in the box was a letter, something Brenna could not read, an ornate dagger, something that should have been presented in ceremony upon promotion, and several pieces of jewelry.

The jewelry, a necklace and two bracelets, did not shine or gleam. The necklace was a simple braided cord of dark leather with a silver eagle woven into it. The bracelets, hammered bronze, had runes clumsily etched inside: family, honor, pride. The value of the jewelry was not in their price, but their symbol. These were heirloom pieces, meant to pass down from mother to daughter.

A lump caught in her throat as Brenna took the necklace. She moved back behind Freja and tied the leather around her neck. "And so you may carry me and Hilde with you. I'm not losing you. And you're not losing me. And if he tries anything you don't want, you tell me and I'll stab him, fae king or not."

Freja choked on the surprised laugh that bubbled up. She wiped at her cheeks as Brenna went back to her hair, working it into a traditional bridal style, two small braids on the side, with the rest of her hair free. Had their mother been around, she would have demanded a more elaborate style, but she wasn't and Brenna thought Freja looked best in the simple.

The dress was simple as well, white linen and silk that flowed a bit magically so that it floated more than dragged. The simplicity made Freja glow. With a thought, Brenna grabbed the embroidery piece and tucked it in the front panel of the dress, a symbol of Ayworn, of Freja's status, for all to see.

"Perfect," she declared.

A throat cleared behind the partition. "Someone want to explain why a tiny man dressed as a frog told me to grab bride gifts before whisking me from my room?"

Both sisters split into wide smiles. "Arne!"

Brenna reached around the partition and dragged him in, hugging him fiercely. "I'm so glad you made it."

"Me too," he mumbled into her hair before hugging Freja. "What exactly did I make it to?"

"Freja's wedding, obviously." Brenna drank in the sight of her brother. It had only been a few weeks but he looked older, tired, the title of crown prince settling more on his shoulders. He obviously hadn't been given time to change as his bed clothes were rumpled and his hair in disarray.

"Uh-huh," he said, eyeing Freja's dress. "Sure, okay. Whom are you marrying, dear sister?"

"King Óðr."

He blinked, the name not ringing a bell. Brenna leaned into him and stage-whispered, "That's the king of the fae."

"The fae king," he repeated weakly. "Freja's marrying the fae king."

"I was just about to help her with her make-up," Brenna said as if this were a normal day. "Are you going to help or gape like a fish?"

He gaped and Freja smiled. "No make-up. No make-up, no masks. I want everyone as they are."

Brenna's lip trembled traitorously and she sniffed. "But I wanted to paint on Einar's face."

"Just, hang on a minute," Arne said, finally catching up on the conversation. "You two were on a mission to stave off the darkness. What am I missing?"

"Nothing," Freja said, enjoying the mystified expression on their brother's face. "This is the final step."

"Marrying the fae king?" he asked in disbelief. When he got two confirming nods, he continued. "Mom and dad don't know about this."

"Nope," Brenna said, popping the 'p'. He glared at her nonchalant attitude. "She's pulling a classic Bri move. I'm so proud."

"Who's going to tell them?"

"Well," Brenna dragged out the word. "I'm banished and Freja won't be allowed to go to Ayworn for at least ten years so…"

His entire expression dropped in a deadpan, his left eye twitching. "Oh, goody."

Brenna laughed, with Freja joining soon after. Arne, never one to be left out of the joke for too long, rolled his eyes and cracked a smile. It really wasn't that funny; the idea of the three of them being separated so thoroughly. It had been just them for so long that the idea that Brenna might go months or even years without sight or word of her siblings sent chills down her spine. But they were together now and once more defying their parents, turning their parents into the butt of a joke, and everything was right once more.

As the laughter died, the sisters told of their adventures in bits and pieces, catching Arne up to how they ended up in a wedding with the fae king. He was appropriately attentive and scolding in places, but did not argue the necessity of the marriage nor talk Freja out of her decision.

"You know," he drawled as they came to a close on their adventures. "I missed the days where all I had to worry about was this one getting into fights with draugs."

He ribbed Brenna as she stuck her tongue out at him. Freja smiled at them both, smoothing out her dress. "You two need to get ready. I'm not sure when the ceremony will take place."

Freja badgered Brenna into a clean, forest green dress that held a subtle web print that shined in the light and forced Arne into a tunic with a glittering blue hem. There were no shoes to be found in the room and Delja helpfully told them most fae went without during special ceremonies. Once properly dressed, she introduced Arne to the rest of their motley crew.

Einar was unimpressed and bored, and Brenna resisted the urge to break his leg again just to get him to sit still. Sensing imminent violence, Delja smiled at her and put a hand on his shoulder. He instantly calmed.

Bergfue reentered the chamber and bowed to Freja. "If you are ready, my lady, I will escort you and your group to the ceremony."

XXIV

Et bryllup

A wedding

$\mathcal{A}$ traditional Aywornian wedding took weeks, if not months, of planning and negotiations. In truth, the negotiations would begin years prior, with the heads of houses meeting informally to feel out the arrangement. Despite the scorn and ridicule the king and queen gave out over the dozens of proposals for their daughter, they no doubt met with individuals and had a particular family in mind already.

The wedding itself would have three parts: the handfasting, the exchange, and the dance. Handfasting intertwined the colors of each house, a representative of two families joining followed by an exchange of heirlooms, swords most likely, as a symbol of protection, and then a dance to celebrate.

There were also a bunch of stuffy traditions that Brenna never took part of as an unmarried participant. Given that it those were her mother's favorite part of weddings, she was always glad she never had to participate.

Had this been a traditional wedding, with the groom of their parent's choice, Brenna would have been shoved to the side, stuck with stealing glimpses of her sister. As was common with her childhood, she would have been in the shadows.

This wedding got her praise simply for letting her be so close with her sister, by allowing her to prepare Freja and walk with her, by offering her one last chance to make memories before they walked different paths.

The second major difference was the location.

Instead of leading them back to the tavern, Bergfue brought them outside which inexplicably opened up to a large clearing, despite being in the middle of the town. Mage lights hung in the trees, casting a warm white light on the soft meadow.

Brenna caught glimpses of attending fae in the shadows, but no others entered the light. They lingered in a wide circle, just outside the meadow, hidden in the shadows of the trees. Bergfue motioned down the flower-lined path and did not follow.

King Óðr stood in the middle of the meadow, dressed in resplendent green and gold, tiny gold leaves braided into his dark hair. He was still in the form of an encicingly handsome young man, adding to the illusion that this wedding could pass as normal. Arne and Brenna walked Freja to him. Brenna gave one last tight hug and Arne offered a chaste kiss on her forehead before they both stepped back with the others.

The mage lights dimmed, allowing the bright moon and stars that shone above to bathe the clearing in a softer glow. The fae hidden in the shadows chanted and sang quietly, filling the air with notes of their language, the whisper of trees and trills of birdsong. King Óðr held his hands out to Freja.

Her hands did not tremble as she rested them on his, and she met his gaze with all the bravery and defiance belonging to Aywornian royalty.

"For the ceremony to be viable, I must use your full name," he said quietly, his voice carrying only just to their scant group, swallowed by the gentle chanting among the trees.

Freja nodded her acknowledgement. She took a deep breath and gave her name to the fae king. "I am Freja Eriksdóttir."

He whispered to the wind in the strange tongue and flowers, heather, moss all intertwined in the air to form a crown, which nestled on Freja's head. The flowers sparkled more brilliantly than jewels and, for a moment, Brenna swore she could see the fabled fae mark on her sister. Freja glowed with inner power and beauty that did not belong to a human.

He continued to speak magic into the air and heather and flowers swirled around their joined hands. The chanting crescendoed around them. Threads from the Aywornian crest pulled free and joined the handfasting. A single strand of red hair wrapped around their wrists, soon followed by a black strand.

The chanting stopped.

Magic stilled.

King Óðr switched to the common tongue. "Freja Eriksdóttir, tonight under the blessing of the full moon we join as one. Do you swear to bind yourself to me? Do you swear to join the fae? Do you swear to honor and protect your new people?"

Brenna's heart raced and she held onto Arne to keep from reaching out and pulling her sister away, to keep from stopping the wedding. She took a deep breath and held it as her sister stood tall and proud.

"I swear to bind myself to you as surely as you bind to me," Freja said. The threads around their wrists flashed at her vow. King Óðr did not blink at her inclusion, only waited for her continued vows. "I swear that the fae will become my people just as those in the kingdom I was born in. I swear to honor and protect all those who would call me queen."

Magic flashed as bright as day, then faded until the soft light of the moon was all that lit the clearing. Brenna's breathing was harsh in her ear as her eyes adjusted to the sudden darkness.

The bindings of the hand fasting were gone and Freja's hair was in a simple braid to signify her married status. The flower and heather crown turned gold in the process. King Óðr, still holding her hands, brought her hands together and winked. When she opened her hands, Freja held the last queen's heart, her last stand against the darkness. The last piece settled loosely in the middle, waiting for someone to heal it.

"Welcome Queen Freja," he whispered, "to the kingdom of the night."

Freja's answering smile was breathless and uncertain, until she looked over at Brenna. She took a deep breath and held the heart to her chest as she said, "I am Fae Queen Freja Eriksdóttir and I will not allow this darkness to remain."

Magic built once more and a song filled the air, an Aywornian lullaby of all things. One that promised peace and safety to a child in the dark. The jewel in her hands that held the past fae queen's desperation and love and hope for her world pulsed and spilled out. It washed over them like a wave on the shore.

To Brenna, it felt like Hilde carding her hands through her hair after the end of a long day. It was being surrounded by the smell of baked bread and roasting meat and honey mead as Hilde held her close. It was Freja's laugh and Arne's steady hand on her shoulder. Everything she loved, everything worth fighting for, seeping into the land and reclaiming it from the shadows.

"Well done," King Óðr said as he turned Freja to introduce his wife to her family and friends.

Brenna rushed forward and hugged her sister again, joined swiftly by Arne and then the rest of their friends until it was a tangle of limbs and tears and laughter.

A few brave fae ventured from the woods to greet their new queen.

Freja pulled back and beamed at her new people. "Customs of my people include a dance after a marriage to celebrate. Perhaps we can have some music? I would love to hear the songs of my new land."

They needed no further encouragement. The fae were, after all, chaos and fun incarnate. Instruments were produced and a lively tune filled the air, encouraging all to partake and let loose. Delja gripped Einar's hands and led him in a circle around the meadow, laughter trilling out. Arne held out a hand to Freja with a wink as the king took a step back. A fae with wings like a gossamer firefly somehow enticed and enchanted Tapio to twirl awkwardly through the flowers.

Brenna watched detached and wanting. The darkness was gone. Her sister was married. Joy and despair swirled within her, churning in her gut and adding a touch of brittleness to her smile.

A throat cleared beside her and she blinked as she looked up. King Óðr stood next to her with his hand out in clear invitation. "Since your brother has whisked away my bride, it seems fitting I lead you in this first dance."

With her heart falling like a stone in her gut, Brenna took his hand.

As a little girl, before the constant degradation from her mother wore on her, Brenna loved to dance. Before the mask became a prison, before the whispers of the court shaped her image, she would move through the fastest dances with her eyes closed and her face beaming. Dance meant she was not in a stuffy classroom learning broken histories and dull bloodlines. Dance meant laughter and freedom.

As King Óðr led her through complicated steps, she could feel that call to childhood innocence beckon her. It warred with the grief of losing her sister and rallied with the exuberance of freeing the world from shadows.

"She is not lost," her companion murmured, as if reading her thoughts. Was that another skill of the fae? "Changed, perhaps. But I swear she will not be harmed by me or mine."

"Am I not allowed to grieve the change?" she asked, trying to settle her emotions into words.

All the grief and fear she had been running from since that first day, since Freja looked at her with cow eyes as they heard of Hilde's death, crashed on her and settled uncomfortably next to the happiness. Because she was happy. She was so relieved that they succeeded, that they were all here and safe and had endless possibilities stretching out in front of them. The grief did not cancel that joy just as the joy did not smother the grief.

She was neither and both.

King Óðr twirled her around and her head spun.

"I have a proposition for you," he said as she organized her thoughts.

She tensed and stumbled through the next step. Her eyes narrowed as she regained her footing. "Is now truly the time for boons?"

He grinned. "Relax, faeling. I'm not here to bite."

"Good, because you'd meet the bite of my blade if you were." Brenna had no qualms making such a threat in the midst of his stronghold. He may be married to her sister, but she had no favorable opinion of the man.

King Óðr laughed as if she were merely a babe squabbling, spinning her to the outer edges of the meadow where shadow reigned more than light. He pulled back and before she could demand his reason, held out a folded cloth to her.

A very familiar patched and well-loved cloth.

She took a step back in shock, her heart stuttering. "What do you want?"

"A promise." His words flowed like honey mead, enticing her to dull her senses and fall into the sweet relief. But her cloak, Hilde's cloak, kept her anchored, reminded her of the countless days and nights of honing her skill, reminded her that she was not weak and she was not soft.

Brenna did not reach out for the cloak, no matter how desperately she wanted to, and she did not let her hands tremble. "A promise of what?"

"That you will not take up arms against my people in some misplaced belief that I have stolen your sister. That your legacy will not be the destruction of our people."

Part of her wanted to tell him just where he could stuff his demand. Part of her wanted to snatch the cloak, her cloak, from him and run. But a small, quiet part of her told her to stop and listen.

Because the love of a sister could be turned and corrupted, spreading out like disease until everyone all but forgot their names, but still felt their impact. Because the darkness started with one woman's vindictive desire to keep her sister close. Because a young woman who lost her home and lost her family knew ancient secrets that twisted magic.

She could see the path that led to the mania and desperation. Even now it tempted her down to the dark, to where she could be the one in power, the one in control.

Over the king's shoulder, she caught a glimpse of her family and friends, drinking in the victory and delighting in magic. Arne laughed at something Einar said as Delja braided flowers in Tapio's hair. Freja searched for her and smiled from across the meadow, carefree and lighter than Brenna ever remembered her. A picture of peace. A promise of hope.

Brenna took a deep breath and met his gaze, his eyes dark as night and twice as secretive. "In exchange for the return of Tatterhood, I swear to view my sister's people as my people.

As long as you keep your promise to protect her and cherish as is her due, then I will not seek vengeance against you and yours."

Brenna would not promise to never, for the fae were fickle and ever-changing, but as long as Freja was safe and happy, she had no reason to seek violence.

King Óðr's mouth pressed in a thin line before he bowed his head. The cloak shimmered in his hands, then settled on her shoulders.

For the first time since arriving on the island, Brenna breathed easy.

"I am aware how little weight my words have with you," King Óðr said as she relished in the feeling of home in a worn out hood, "but your sister is safe here. We protect our own and she now belongs here."

"The fae are the reason for so much strife in my life," she said, with less vitriol than she had once held. "They should have left my mother childless."

"Your mother should have followed the instructions given to her and only consumed the first flower," he retorted with a raised brow. "Or better yet, cherished the gift of two children instead of just one."

Well, there was no arguing with that. At least they could agree on one thing: Brenna's mother was a selfish, uncaring monster.

Having nothing further to discuss with her, King Óðr disappeared with a swish, only to reappear at his bride's side and enticing her into a dance. Seeing Brenna was now free, Tapio joined her, his back straight, his eyes clear.

"Here to offer me a dance?" she teased.

"You'd have to take the lead," he responded, waving his cane over his lame arm and leg.

She grinned. "I'm okay with that."

Brenna took the sling and slowly untied it so she could move his right arm to her shoulder, feeling the weight of it down to her bones. Gently, she took his cane and had it rest against a tree, then guided his other hand to her waist. She kept his gaze as she moved, silently demanding that he look at her and not focus on his feet.

Slowly, they moved and shuffled to the calmer beat now drifting through the trees. Perhaps some would claim it wasn't strictly dancing, but it worked for them. In that moment, Brenna would call it gliding, like a ship sailing through smooth waters.

"Seems like you got that ratty garment back."

She smiled. "King Óðr and I came to an agreement. I think Tatterhood has some more good to do in the world."

Humming, Tapio let his right arm fall to his side and pushed her into a spin. Her smile grew as she settled back in his arms. "I'm looking forward to it. Any chance she'll go through Faldinn? I heard that kingdom could use some help rebuilding."

"I could put in a good word for you," she teased, already knowing she would end up in Faldinn. Traveling the five kingdoms was much less enticing without someone to enjoy the journey with. And she would need a place to call home, a place she could shape and build herself.

Their dancing slowed until they simply swayed side to side, pressed close, magic in the air cloyingly sweet and intoxicating. Brenna's eyes flicked to his. He leaned in.

A throat cleared behind her.

Her mood soured as she glanced back at Arne, who was watching with one brow raised and arms crossed. Brenna huffed and whispered, "The next time we're interrupted, I really will stab someone."

Tapio chuckled and stepped back to let Arne take his place. Grabbing his cane and redoing his sling, He rejoined their friends in the middle of the meadow.

Brenna crossed her arms. "I was enjoying that dance."

"Oh, were you?" Arne teased. "Should I be speaking with Tapio about proper courting and decorum?"

"Only if you want another scar," she said sweetly, smiling and blinking up at him.

Arne huffed out a laugh. "I was just wanting to say goodbye. It's nearly dawn. I should get back before a crisis is declared."

"What? No, we still have hours before dawn." She peered through the trees and startled when she realized he was correct. Had they been dancing that long?

"When you dance with the fae, you lose time," he said with a shrug. "King Óðr was gracious to allow a way for me to return home instantly instead of by boat."

Her heart leapt to her throat as she looked to her brother. When would she see him again? She lurched forward and pulled him into a tight hug. "Don't let the terrors give you too much grief."

"Don't worry," he murmured into her hair. "I plan on shifting all the blame on you."

She pulled back with a sniff. "As if they won't already blame me."

Arne wiped her cheek, catching a stray tear. Brenna took a moment to memorize him, his wide, earnest, brown eyes, his tanned skin, his tousled hair, his lips quirked in a sad smile. "Hey, this isn't goodbye."

"Until next time," she said with a nod.

"You'll stick by these friends of yours, right? Don't make me send Idunn after you." The tease had a hint of threat. He would absolutely send Idunn and half the royal guard after her if she didn't keep him informed of her health. Worrywart.

"I'll be okay, Arne." She looked over at her friends, at Freja dancing in the fae king's arms. "We both will."

Freja thrived in the political intrigue and what better place to find intrigue than the secretive fae court? And she may be confined to the Isle, but Brenna was free to explore and sail and check in on her whenever she wished. And while Arne remained crown prince, he would be expected to visit the newly restored borders, where she could visit and catch up with him. This wasn't an ending, simply a new adventure to discover.

XXV

Ha det brap

Take care

The darkness was gone.

Everyone knew this to be true, as true as the clear skies and open borders. It was said in lieu of good morning. On good days, this simple statement carried onto the future. The darkness was gone and would never return. On bad days, the darkness was gone, so what could truly harm them? And should it return, perhaps the heroes of the five kingdoms would return to banish it once more.

Brenna wasn't entirely certain where those rumors started. If she had to guess, she would blame Einar and his loud mouth. The past six months, he traveled and chartered people across the sea with Delja, no doubt puffing his own horn and telling everyone how he saved the world. From there, it was only a hop and a skip to the blown out proportions the story now held.

Apparently they fought a kraken.

Not that she actively discouraged the stories, brought to the shores as people slowly trickled into Faldinn to poke at the ruins and remake their home. She told anyone who listened how Tapio sacrificed his arm and leg for the kingdom he now worked to rebuild. When kids gathered around her and begged for a tale, she spoke of her brave sister, who married the fae in a bid to protect the five kingdoms.

"Tatterhood! Tatterhood!"

She turned towards the call, her hood down and hair free. She rarely had the hood up these days, as the people here were used to seeing her face. Very few made comments. Those that did were kindly reminded to shove off. She was not the only one with scars and reminders of a harsher life.

Brenna knelt to the ground as a young boy skipped up to her. He was a regular that hung around her, demanding stories and demonstrations. He beamed up at her. "What do you want, kid?"

"A story!"

"You always want a story." She mussed his hair and he scrunched his nose.

He stuck his bottom lip out and widened his eyes, offering a slow blink. "Please, Tatterhood? I wanna hear about the Aywornian princess who saved the world. You promised to tell me about the horse that's a goat sometimes."

She grinned, thinking of Hrolf tucked safely in the royal stables. "Maybe later. I have to get these deliveries to the port."

"I'll do it!" He grabbed the bag from her hands and rushed off before she could protest.

She sighed. "Careful! Give it to Eevi!"

The boy was already disappearing down the lane, dodging pedestrians and construction zones.

The city itself was a strange amalgamation of old and new with rubble in between. When Tapio and Brenna first arrived, the day after Freja's wedding, the city was empty and haunted. They did not retrace their steps down the beach, but made their way to the stronghold that would serve as a castle until the kingdom could be rebuilt and the capital retaken.

It didn't take long for others to arrive, hesitantly, hopefully.

And as people arrived, as rumors spread, activity increased. They worked tirelessly to make the port city inhabitable before winter. And even with everyone's efforts, winter was rough, with everyone huddling in the makeshift castle, borrowing warmth and food.

But they made it. Spring arrived and renewed vigor with it. They had several farms going and teams working through the worst parts of town to clean and repair.

Tapio spent most of his days rambling from home to home, family to family, ensuring everyone had what they needed, encouraging his people in their efforts. Brenna dedicated her time to the rebuilding effort, occasionally joining a scouting team venturing deeper into Faldinn. Faldinn did not have the steep, forest-covered mountains of home, but its trees welcomed her just as well.

If it weren't for Tapio, Brenna could get lost in the dappled light of the woods, relishing in how bright and airy it seemed after such oppression.

But even the trees held scars from the shadows.

While she hadn't run into any draug since arriving and the strange winged creatures that tormented them on the beach were absent, gray moss clung to house corners and tree limbs. Brenna spent several weeks sectioning off areas of black tar around the town. Some houses refused to rebuild, the structures crumbling to ash regardless of how new the wood and brick used. Several alleys were cold even on the warmest days.

And despite half a year of consistent, back-breaking work, the city still contained ruins of its fall.

A throat cleared behind her and she whirled around, knife in hand, to face Ansa, a blacksmith that arrived with her family near the beginning. She held her hands up peacefully. "Sorry."

Brenna took a deep breath and put away her knife, cursing her reflexes and paranoia. "No, I'm sorry. You caught me off guard."

"You're not the only one that reaches for a blade in distress, Bri," Ansa said to comfort but Brenna brushed it away.

She did not want to think about it. "Was there something you needed?"

"A call for Tatterhood at the old mill. Probably needing some extra hands to get it started."

Work. Brenna could focus on work. She nodded and took off for the mill on the outskirts of the city. While she didn't need to go by the alias of Tatterhood here, the comfort of the name wrapped around her like a blanket, or a well-loved cloak. And instead of stopping thieves and criminals from taking advantage of the darkness, she now helped as a steady hand and runner. People were just as likely to call for 'Bri' as they were to call for 'Tatterhood'.

She stopped outside the old watermill to take in the damage. The waterwheel was leaning, mired in the mud, and the connecting rod cracked and broken. It would need to be replaced before the wheel could be reset. The building itself seemed in good shape from the outside, but she couldn't see the roof.

Stepping inside revealed a dusty room being overtaken by vine. Sunlight filtered in through the collapsing roof and she sighed at the broken crank. A lot more work than just replacing the rod then.

"Hello?" she called out, surprised by the lack of people onsite. Was there another mill nearby?

"Over here!"

She followed the call to the back of the building, where the land stretched along with the river, clear for several kilometers before the trees encroached. A patched blanket covered the spring grass with a basket of dried fruits and meats. Tapio grinned at her, his arm strapped to his chest as he leaned against a polished, carved cane, made by one of the woodworkers in the city.

Brenna raised an eyebrow as she joined him. "I was told someone needed help here."

"Yes. I desperately need your help finishing this meal," he said with utmost seriousness. He let his cane fall to the blanket and held out his hand in invitation.

Biting back a smile, she took it and flared her skirt to sit as if at a grand picnic her mother would put on, where she would be decked in jewels instead of dirt. Brenna smoothed her skirt as Tapio joined her, fingers catching on a new rip. At this rate, her dress would have more mends in it than her cloak.

"So what's the occasion?" she asked as he passed the food to her.

Tapio hummed. "I was told, with quite a bit of ire and a smidge of kindness, that I should cease my worrying and take a break."

"I'm sure you took that gracefully." She smirked as he huffed. He was just as bad as she was about helping others and not himself.

"I am king, of course I took it gracefully," he said as he took a bite. Her grin grew fond at his declaration.

Tapio had not taken the kingship gracefully. As per the traditions of his people, a trial should have been held to determine the next king. But the kingdom was in disarray and, as Brenna pointed out often and at length, he went through a trial saving his kingdom. No other game or competition could place higher merit than the sacrifice he underwent to banish the darkness. Thankfully, all those that returned to their homeland agreed and gladly accepted Tapio as their leader and king.

His willingness to serve and rebuild with his people helped sway any doubters.

A spring breeze wrapped around her, flicking her hair and smelling of wildflowers and new growth. "We'll need to start sending border patrols out soon."

"I've already got a plan," he said with a wave of his hand. "And that kind of talk is not taking a break."

"You're taking a break. I'm under no such orders." If only because the worrywarts of the city hadn't managed to pin her down yet. Tapio raised an eyebrow, knowing all too well her tendency to overwork herself and avoid the people who would stop her. The silence stretched and he continued staring her down. She shifted and grumbled, "Fine, whatever. I got a letter from Freja."

"And how's Freja?" he asked, dusting crumbs off his tunic.

"Absolutely mad." Freja took to her role as the fae queen as an eagle to the sky; she was born for it. She took great pleasure in describing everyone she managed to surprise in each letter. "And destroying any expectations the fae may have had about her. She said she made one fae noble squeak after eviscerating him."

"What did he do?"

"Imply she was merely a token on the king's arm." For a people that valued truth and sought only the deepest relationships, implying Freja was nothing but a shiny trinket the king would toss at a moment's notice was gravely insulting. Freja took great pleasure in putting the noble in his place. The amount of detail she put in her letter made Brenna feel as if she were there and part of her ached at the thought.

He chuckled, the sound rumbling in his chest, breaking through her melancholy. "Sounds fair. You should visit her."

Brenna finished off her meal instead of responding. She missed Freja. She missed Arne. The work she found here was distracting and rewarding, but her room was cold and empty. Arne promised to visit over the summer disguised as a diplomatic mission. Freja wouldn't be able to set foot on Faldinn soil for ten long years.

Nudging her shoulder with his, Tapio regained her attention. "You should visit. You miss her and that's okay. We can handle a few days without our resident hero."

"You're a hero too," she reminded him. "And I'll think about it. Maybe when Delja and Einar visit next."

Since Delja could no longer dwell on land, she and Einar stayed almost exclusively on their boat, where she could have easy access to the sea whenever she wished. They stopped by frequently, bringing supplies that may or may not be stolen. Brenna didn't ask, Einar didn't lie. And every time they left, Brenna found one of her belongings turned into a flower for at least a week.

Which ensured she had something to yell at Einar about each time they returned. Speaking of: "Remind me to educate him on why he shouldn't turn my things into plants."

"As long as you don't 'educate' him with your knives."

She pouted. "Spoilsport. Fine."

They basked in the sun, silence settling over them with ease. She closed her eyes and leaned on his shoulder, taking a deep breath as another breeze washed over them. The peace that filled her days was unusual and odd, something she never knew growing up, but she liked it. She hoped it would last.

Tapio shifted under her, his voice low to match the serene atmosphere. "I have something to show you, c'mon."

"Show me what?" she asked. There was very little to the city that she hadn't seen at this point and, surprise picnic aside, she doubted he could show her something new.

He rolled his eyes as he stood and held out his hand. "Have a little patience."

Pursing her lips, she helped him pack up the blanket and empty basket, storing it just inside the old mill. She walked with him, hand sneaking into the small gap in his arm brace. Six months of hidden dates and stolen moments in between rebuilding. Brenna could hardly believe Tapio was hers and she was his.

They walked along the outskirts of the city, where few ventured unless they had business. Tapio passed the road into town and followed an animal path through the grass.

As they passed behind the castle, he pulled her up a slight incline. Just as she was about to complain or pester, she topped the small hill and he turned her toward the forest.

Nestled in the spring grass were stone markers, dotting a pattern in the stretch of flat land. The stones started at a point then broke out in two gentle curves before converging back to one point, like the outline of a ship. About half a dozen 'ships' decorated the landscape, with another half finished.

Her eyes traced the lines, looking for meaning, before looking at Tapio. "What is this?"

He studied the field, his voice low. "You said your people honor their dead through pyres. This is how my people honor them. Each stone is a memorial. Usually, each field would belong to a family, a marker of those that came before, but this is for everyone that has come back, to honor those who couldn't."

Her breath caught as the ache in her soul made itself known. On good days, she could ignore how fiercely she missed Hilde, missed her guidance, missed her care. She swallowed over the stone in her throat. "Does it help?"

"It helped me," he said with a shrug. "I didn't realize how much I had been carrying them with me until I put them to rest."

Tapio had been lighter these days, the shadows of grief easing back as purpose and healing filled him. When Brenna thought of the man she met in the tavern, falling into drink and misery, she almost couldn't reconcile the two.

"How does it work?" she asked, her voice barely above a whisper.

"You select an appropriate stone." He waved to a pile of rubble and stones, then traced a path with his cane. "Then place it in the next available spot as you reflect on the one who passed. Some mark their stones with runes or adorn them with flowers or scented oil. Each person does it a little differently."

Brenna took a deep breath and nodded. "How do you pick the stone?"

"I, well, I pick the heaviest I can carry, but it's up to you."

Taking another breath, she pulled away and walked over to the pile. After picking through a few of the rocks, she picked a heavy, oblong stone that was nearly as large as her torso. She made sure it was secure in her grip before turning and heading for the half finished line of stones.

Halfway there, Brenna understood why Tapio would pick the heaviest. Concentrating so hard on not dropping the rock, her arms straining and her legs growing sluggish, the rock became a manifestation of her grief: heavy, oppressive, inescapable. Hilde had been her mother, the mother of her heart. Hilde had given her purpose, care, love, and in an instant she was gone. Brenna hadn't had time to process, really. She had to save Freja and then the world and then rebuilding and surviving and the ever present ache dulled to a smolder in her heart.

She stopped to take a breath, to readjust her grip, and continued.

The stone fell to the ground with a thud. She knelt by it and pushed it more upright. Her hands traced patterns on the rough surface and she pulled her knife, the first dagger Hilde put in her hands. It was almost too small for her now, her palm overtaking the slim handle.

Hilde always told her that family of the heart meant more than family of blood. She meant to draw the connection between the twins and Arne, how they were siblings regardless of parentage, but Brenna decided it meant she could make her own family, her own parents, her own siblings. She didn't share blood with Hilde, but she did share her heart.

Making the first stroke, Brenna was careful to keep the line precise and clear. One downward stroke. Two diagonal. Two on top to complete the rune. Heart. She traced over the lines several times to deepen them, to ensure the etching lasted. The sun began its descent as she sat there, pouring her grief into this simple stone. When she finished, she replaced her knife and pressed her hand over the rune.

"You are not forgotten," she whispered. The ache within her eased.

She sat back on her feet and closed her eyes, taking a moment to relish in the quiet dusk. As the light began to shift to golden, Brenna stood and walked back over to Tapio.

He offered no words, simply holding out his arm for her to take, offering his presence as a balm against the grief in her soul. She stepped up to his side and leaned in, making no effort to move forward or back, simply basking in the quiet moment for a little longer. Dusk shifted to twilight, the last of the sun's rays giving way to night. Lanterns began to dot the roads and windows as people retired for the night.

"Thank you," she murmured once she was ready, taking a deep breath and a step forward.

Tapio hummed, stepping with her. Song drifted down from the castle as they approached, beckoning them to dance and laugh with the people. "You are not alone. And I have a good feeling about what our future holds. The darkness is gone after all."

"The darkness is gone," she said with a grin. "And I think you owe me a drink or two."

"How about a dance instead?" While Tapio had a glass of ale or wine when his people asked for it, he kept the promise made on the boat, refusing to turn to drink to settle his emotions.

"I don't know. I get a lot of dance offers."

"Kingly dance offers?"

She snorted and stopped just outside the main hall of the castle, where all the workers, noble birth or not, would be piled into, eating and drinking and dancing. Brenna turned toward him, looking him in the eye, heat and light swirling in her. "What makes it a kingly dance?"

"It's with me, of course." He pulled her close, leaning until their noses touched. "I've only danced with one princess and plan on keeping it that way. At least until I make her queen."

Brenna grinned. "Deal."